CW01590190

PRAISE FOR *THE LE*

'Propulsive, confronting, compelling. A masterpiece.'

CHRIS HAMMER, AUTHOR OF *THE VALLEY*

'*The Leap* is a modern *Wake in Fright.* Confronting, tragic, brutal, compassionate and funny. A brilliant examination of the prejudice and violence that lies at the heart of this country. A novel that speaks truth about crimes past and present.'

MICHAEL BRISSENDEN, AUTHOR OF *SMOKE*

'This novel is an explosion of truth-telling about Australia's bloody past, taking us on a tumultuous outback crime adventure, sometimes hilarious and often outrageous.'

JULIE JANSON, AUTHOR OF *BENEVOLENCE*

'Paul Daley's vivid rendering of an outback town ruled by fear, alcohol and barely suppressed violence, damned by a malevolent and unspoken past, is unforgettable. It will disturb your nights.'

TONY WRIGHT, JOURNALIST

'Paul Daley shatters the great Australian silence with a penetrating story that reveals the truth and trauma of Country. From his elegant and excavating pen comes another important and revelatory work.'

NICK BRYANT, JOURNALIST AND AUTHOR OF *THE FOREVER WAR*

A *Wake in Fright* for the 21st century. Savage, hilarious and ultimately profound, *The Leap* hurtles into Australia's heart of darkness with exhilarating results.'

JAMES BRADLEY, AUTHOR OF *LANDFALL*

'This is a read-in-one-go thriller. One moment I was having cold chills, the next nervous sweats, but there was no way I was going to stop. If Graham Greene had the idea for *Wake in Fright* and dropped an unsuspecting English diplomat into an outback hellscape, it would look something like *The Leap*. But not quite. Paul Daley uses his contemporary eye to put a twist on a classic and create something new, sinister, and totally captivating.'

MALCOLM KNOX, AUTHOR OF *THE FIRST FRIEND*

'Unflinching, razor-edged and raw. Another tour de force by Paul Daley.'

JOANNA JENKINS, AUTHOR OF *THE BLUFF*

'Paul Daley continues his ongoing examination of the frontier's lasting effects, repainting *Wake in Fright*'s Bundanyabba hell-mouth with a 21st-century understanding of dispossession and racial division. Here are the drinking culture, the unconcealed bloodlust and the deluded squattocracy, all seen through the baffled eyes of a post-empire Briton. Only a writer of Daley's quality could bring empathy and nuance to the canon of Australian bush noir.'

JOCK SERONG, AUTHOR OF *CHERRYWOOD*

THE LEAP

ALSO BY PAUL DALEY

Jesustown
On Patriotism
Challenge
Canberra
Beersheba
Collingwood: A Love Story
Armageddon: Two Men on an Anzac Trail

THE LEAP

PAUL DALEY

Summit Books Australia

THE LEAP

First published in Australia in 2025 by Summit Books Australia,
an imprint of Simon & Schuster (Australia) Pty Limited
Level 4, 32 York Street, Sydney NSW 2000

Summit Books and colophon are trademarks of Simon & Schuster, LLC.

10 9 8 7 6 5 4 3 2 1

Sydney New York Amsterdam/Antwerp London Toronto New Delhi
Visit our website at www.simonandschuster.com.au

© Paul Daley 2025

All rights reserved. No part of this publication may be reproduced, stored in a retrieval system, or transmitted in any form or by any means, electronic, mechanical, photocopying, recording or otherwise, without prior permission of the publisher.

A catalogue record for this book is available from the National Library of Australia

ISBN: 9781761632525 (paperback)

Cover design: Luke Causby
Cover image: Taras Vyshnya/Adobe Stock
Typeset in Adobe Garamond Pro 12.5/17pt by Midland Typesetters, Australia
Printed and bound in Australia by Griffin Press

MIX Paper | Supporting responsible forestry FSC® C018684

The paper this book is printed on is certified against the Forest Stewardship Council® Standards. Griffin Press holds chain of custody certification SCS-COC-001185. FSC® promotes environmentally responsible, socially beneficial and economically viable management of the world's forests.

for Joe Daley

Part I

This was not the city of his memory. From the air it was another place entirely – unsettling, uninviting. When he'd last seen it from a plane he was a backpacker crammed into the middle seat, straining over Lucy to snatch a first glimpse of that fabled harbour. Its totemic bridge. The Opera House. Everything had been so radiant then, the sky and water the most vivid blue, a luminosity he'd never known. It had all been there. Waiting for him. Just as it had on the TV travel shows he'd savoured in Oxford's winter gloom. Just like in the brochures: the only place, besides Santorini, that the advertising pictures did justice to. The city had been Ben's to uncover. A new now.

But tonight, close to dusk, the view from the window of Seat 2A in Business Class was malevolent. Banks of crimson-edged dark cloud and sheets of thick black smoke obscured so much of what he'd been yearning for, although occasionally the sea would snag a bolt of eerie yellow light on its inky surface. There was a dystopian, though quite spectacular, end-of-days unearthliness about the scene. Then, as the plane banked it offered a gun-barrel view of the red glow of uncontrolled bushfires south of the city. They looked like the fleshy, gaping mouth of an active volcano. He used his phone to snap a few photographs.

Should he be worried? Ben wondered. He well knew the havoc airborne soot could pose to aircraft mechanics. Indeed, the pilot had warned that the plane might divert if there was too much ash in the air – to avoid potential engine interference.

Engine interference? Ben had a pilot's licence himself, and a good appreciation of aerophysics. Learning to fly in his forties had been a matter of doing something that he could fully control. An assertion of doing over being done to. As pilot, he would be responsible for every decision – each instrument reading, control execution, and aircraft movement – on-ground and in the air. The pre-take-off checks of fuel and rudders and hydraulics; the constant in-air gauging of wind speed versus pressure, altitude and thrust – it all assuaged his desire for control after a period of being subjected to the vagaries of circumstance. In the cockpit he alone set the course. If something were to go wrong it would be on him.

As the aircraft banked again, and bounced and shook on the updrafts, the chatter of the crew strapped in their seats was dulled by whining hydraulics. Ben pressed his face to the window as the plane arced deeply into a descending turn over the Pacific, black and shimmering now, immediately below. That glorious ocean. He'd dreamt for decades of being back in it. And so he had planned a quick dip in the Bondi surf if he got out of the airport in time, but the dusky light and the smoke and the grimy air would probably cheat him of that.

Despite the turbulence, it was a light, tiptoe landing. He smiled. The wonder of flight. He turned his phone on. Global roaming quickly connected to 4G. He chose his most dystopic shot of daunting fire and smoke, strobing yellow light and ash. He posted it on Instagram.

Ben shivered from a little dopamine spike as the likes – ♡♡♡ – dashed in. They included one from his eldest daughter Suze, preceding the comment *Ewww! Looks like Armageddon!!* He thought it unusual she was awake so early in London. They always had to drag her out of bed for school. And was she never offline, day or night?

But she was spot-on. Armageddon seemed to be right outside the aircraft.

It was dark by the time he was green-lighted through Immigration and Customs, even though the process was quick thanks to his diplomatic passport. He lugged his big red Samsonite off the conveyor and wheeled it to the taxi rank, breaking into a sweat in the sticky, malodorous night, its air a damp, dark blanket of smoke and humidity. By the clock it should still have been a midsummer dusk – that radiant, glowing hour he'd sentimentalised, when the southern light softens and melds with the cooling air of imminent evening and a gentle southerly. But the smoke and the soot had smudged out the day's remains.

Something feather-light landed in Ben's hair. With his fingers he combed out a whisper of scorched gum-leaf. He observed it on his palm. It was still warm, not too far from its escaped fire.

His new boss, the high commissioner, Sir Gordon, had offered to drive – or rather, be chauffeured – to Sydney to meet Ben and take him to Canberra, his home city for the next three years. But Ben wanted a weekend in Sydney. In Bondi, his old stomping ground, where he and Lucy had spent three of their six months in Australia during their gap year. Languorously carefree times of sunshine, sex and ocean, free of the strictures of endless study, parental expectations, and those interminably oppressive bleak British days. Months not yet encumbered by the future's onerous freight of adult responsibility: a career, marriage and kids, the mortgage, school fees and vet bills.

There'd been five of them in the group back then, all mates from Oxford. He and Lucy hadn't been especially close at university, but something about that Sydney summer – the damp heat, the constant proximity to each other's near-naked bodies on the beach and in the cafes and beer gardens, all the bronzed flesh and the pheromones in the air – had brought them newly alive and physically attuned to one another.

New Year's Day was the beginning of their ever since. Bondi Beach, packed with bathers. The sand hard to see for all the tanned bodies. Foreign accents – English, Scots, Irish, Israeli, Nordic, Canadian, German – challenging the barely dominant voices of the Australians and Kiwis. The sky that impossibly vivid, flawless, Whiteley-esque blue – clichéd yet somehow true. A gentle swell cascading into a foamy shore break, just a hint of off-shore breeze puffing the diamantés of spray oceanward from the crests. A near-still day of intense, unseasonably dry heat. Post-swim, Ben and Lucy lay on their stomachs on towels facing each other. Her skin was goosey from the cool Pacific, droplets bejewelling her thighs, firm shoulders and the hollow of her tanned back. A fine patina of salt and sand crusting her cheek. They were so close he could see the barely discernible fuzz of blond down tracing her jawline as the light snared it. Her eyes held his. He returned her smile.

Now, all these decades later, they'd soon be back together under the southern light where it began. As a family now, with three children, a dog, and the travails and joys of twenty-something years of marriage trailing them. This time, though, he wouldn't be sleeping in a thirty-dollar-a-night bunk in a back-packers'; he'd booked a room at the five-star hotel opposite the beach, where he planned to sleep the slumber of the jet-lagged dead. First thing in the morning, a Saturday, he'd throw himself into the Pacific and laze on the sand in the sun for the day, before taking a leisurely Sunday-morning flight to Canberra.

The plan was that Lucy and the kids would come just before the Australian school year began. Ben would have a few weeks – plenty of time – to get his feet under the desk at the high commission, to navigate the city and arrange the children's schools. He'd find the perfect house and set it up for their arrival. There was nothing too onerous ahead of him. Aside from his acute mindfulness of Lucy's anxiety at packing up in London, taking the kids out of school, leaving their friends and her aging parents, and travelling across the world to follow Ben yet again, it was all cake and icing in his mind.

He had reconciled himself to the professional truth that Canberra wasn't exactly Washington. But the peaks and troughs of his working life, its dark challenges and small triumphs, had given him a clear perspective on ambition and prospects. And for a mid-to-late-career diplomat like Ben, Canberra was a comfortable and sought-after posting in a sentimental corner of the old empire, associated, in the service, with lifestyle and comfort. As Counsellor assigned mainly to cultural duties, he had no need really to anticipate anything too left-field. There would be plenty of travel across the so-called wide brown land, lots of theatre opening nights, and entertaining of British dignitaries, sporting identities and soap stars and musicians when they passed through. The most pressing consular work in Australia for British diplomats usually amounted to looking in on banged-up members of the Barmy Army during the Ashes, or waiting for news on some English tourist who'd gone bushwalking underprepared.

Ben told himself that he deserved this appointment after all he'd endured – everything he'd sacrificed – for the service. The hardship posts he'd done – Thailand and Cambodia – had exacted a heavy toll.

Cambodia, from which he'd returned four years earlier, had from the very start carried some unique challenges, mostly to do with hygiene (Lucy had been hospitalised with sepsis after cutting her foot) and personal security. They had both been plagued with anxiety over the inability of their eldest to settle at boarding school back home while they'd been in Phnom Penh with the younger two. These were the sorts of things that service families routinely withstood, however – part and parcel of the job. Hiccups and challenges that you found a way around. It was the unexpected that still reverberated – the freak accident towards the end of the Cambodia posting that almost took Ben's life, and which also threatened, briefly, his sanity and career.

The past couple of years had been a period of grinding inertia back at Whitehall. So much of the work – treaty, trade and policing cooperation post the 2016 Brexit vote – he found mind-numbingly dull, but he endured it stoically, Britishly, in the hope of being rewarded with one last, cushier posting. While there was never any certainty about the events, dangerous or otherwise, that a posting could present, he knew the office would avoid placing him anywhere he might see too much too soon. Lucy would have been pleased had he been content to see out his days at Whitehall, with its generous pay and benefits, for she also feared that Ben was never much further than a few emotional stress fractures away from a potential relapse. She didn't want to take the gamble of allowing misfortune to invade their family's wellbeing again.

But in the end, after months of discussion and gentle argument, of weighing up pros and cons and what-ifs, which was the way of their always civil marital negotiation, Lucy had softened. No less nostalgic about Australia's space and warmth and good living, thanks to her own memories of that magical half-year in their twenties, she agreed, as Ben had been confident she would.

At his last appraisal, when he'd sat through numerous interviews and psychological evaluations, he'd apparently failed to overly impress. He was not, his superiors candidly told him, ever likely to make a head of mission, largely due, they said cryptically in their opaque bureaucratise, to his 'potential susceptibility to the detriments of extreme stress'. In other words, they didn't think he was tough enough after what had happened.

Still, it was also acknowledgement that he'd done the 'very hard yards' – as one superior had put it, with such characteristic Englishness as to evoke postwar queuing for rations and a hardy anticipation of unending adversity. Yes, he'd endured alright, and bloody well recovered – with the help of dozens of counselling sessions, with which he'd fully engaged, and medication he'd eventually weaned himself off. Endured courtesy of stringent personal routines that became, at times, obsessive: daily swimming, running or cycling, a strict diet, mindfulness, disciplined sleep. And of course, learning to fly during that initial recovery year – gardening leave. He had rebuilt himself to the point where he could fly.

And now here he was. About to begin what could be a dream posting. Counsellor at the high commission to Australia was as good as it might get for Benedict Fotheringham-Gaskill, MA Philosophy and Theology (Oxon). But as good as it got was pretty damn good as far as he was concerned. And not a bad way at all to go out. He would make the most of these few precious years back in Australia. They would be the reward Lucy and the kids were due. Witnessing his pain and recovery had been hard on everyone. Who knew – maybe Canberra would even become a glorious, career-advancing triumph? At worst it could be the leisurely victory lap before an early retirement on his generous Foreign Office pension in Surrey – or maybe Majorca or Brittany.

It's all in front of us, again, he thought as the cab delivered him into the Bondi night.

When the driver stopped it was all garish light – red, yellow, green and blue – from the takeaways, cafes, bars and ice-cream shops. Groups of young men and women jostled and linked arms, five-deep on the footpaths. They ate from grease-stained paper bags, glugged down booze from cans. The air, already rank with the smoke, had a noxious, sickly-sweet fug of vape emissions – cherry, bubblegum, grape and musk – along with tobacco fumes.

Campbell Parade was lined with muscle cars – double-cab urban utes and big-engined, twin-exhaust, hotted-up sedans – emitting nondescript music, doof-doofing and distorted. From the cars protruded tattooed limbs and heads wolf-whistling and yelling.

As Ben wrestled his bag from the boot, he experienced a swift wave of nausea. He surveyed the street between the cab and the hotel door as if through a veil of grime, saw a gap in the crowd and went to negotiate his way through it. A young bloke, dyed-blond mullet, shirtless, Southern Cross tattoo on his chest, crashed into him. A cigarette flew from the man's mouth onto the ground. The man stumbled and fell heavily, trailing his smoke to the footpath.

'I'm sorry,' Ben said, stopping and extending a hand to help him up. 'I didn't —'

His hand got slapped away. 'Piss off, mate, 'fore I punch your fucken lights out.'

Ben hurried across to the hotel and through the revolving door, Hogarthian realism eclipsing his idyll.

He checked in. Went to his room and shaved and showered, pulled on a clean T-shirt and boxers.

He stretched out on the plump, king-size plus bed, sinking into the luxurious white softness, and FaceTimed home. He wanted to celebrate his arrival with Lucy and the kids. But Lucy was perfunctory with him. Not terribly so, but her slight impatience immediately deflated him. Didn't he know what time it was in London? She reminded him that it was a work day for her and that she was doing more than her usual share of the juggle in his absence. She sounded frazzled as she explained how she was trying to herd the two younger kids out the door to her parents' place, where they'd go daily until school returned the following week. Fourteen-year-old Jerome, who thought he should be able to stay home alone with the eldest, Suze, sixteen, was pushing back and arguing every step of the way. Surely Ben recalled?

Jerome and Amy, meanwhile, were determined to attend school right up until they left for Australia in late January, in order to be with their friends. This had been another source of simmering tension around the move. Before he'd eventually flown on alone, Ben had suggested it would be better for them to pack up the house in Putney, go to Australia as a family, and choose and set up a place in Canberra together. That way the kids could have an Australian summer holiday before starting school in February, get to know their new city and make neighbourhood friends. Lucy had been firm but polite: Ben was to go and do his job and she would finesse the parenting. He had conceded for harmony's sake.

'Say hello to your father,' Lucy said to the kids, her morning made-up face zoning in and out of focus on the screen. He could see that they were in the hallway, the front door open to a bleak, wet, midwinter street behind them.

Amy, ten-year-old familial afterthought, smiled into the phone. 'I miss you, Daddy. We saw the Australian fires on telly. Are you sure you're safe down there?'

'Yes, baby girl,' he assured her. 'I'm really quite safe, love. I miss you too.' And he did. Her affection was always so raw and urgent, without the emotional guile of adolescence. What he'd do for a cuddle from his baby right now.

'Bye, Daddy.'

Lucy again: 'Quick, Jerome, say hi to your dad – then get your bag. We're going to be late. And yeah, take your football. Grandad might be up for a kick.'

Jerome, with a fourteen-year-old's weary surliness, said from off-screen in a deliberately monotone voice, 'Hi-bye old man.'

Lucy's face reappeared. 'Ben – maybe call later? We really have to fly, darling. I'm late already.'

'Sure. Is everything okay?'

'Yes of course, Benny. We're managing just so. But you know, when it's only the one of us . . . It's the morning, you know?'

'Yes. I know. But Luce – it's great to be back here. You'll love it. I know. It's —'

'I'm sure. But the fires do look dreadful, Ben. Listen, can we talk later? Tonight our time? Take care, darling.'

And they were gone. Vanished into 17,000 kilometres of distance.

For a moment the call rankled. How adept, he thought, Lucy had become over the years at derailing his emotional overtures by tossing the prosaic in their way. True, weekday mornings were a juggle, and he also realised, thanks to their counselling sessions, that such emotional evasion was, while intrinsic to Lucy's reserve, partly a defence mechanism – the consequence of walking on eggshells during the unpredictable worst of his post-Cambodia oscillating moods. It had become something of a learnt pattern for her even when he was calm and travelling well, and overtly inviting her in. He also understood the stress she was under ahead of the move. Solo-parenting three kids, including two sullen teenagers, was bloody hard – thankless, really – at the best of times. Still, she did seem very harried and distant.

He further knew, all too well, that it was quite normal for the trailing spouse to be anxious before a posting. Would the kids settle in and make friends? There was the disruption of having to put on hold her career as a pharmacist. Again. Finding work in the new host country was always a challenge. Repatriating was no less difficult. Former colleagues – once career juniors or equals – had invariably left her behind professionally. She'd have lost touch with friends. And this time there was concern about her elderly parents. Would Charles and Sybil be alive in three years' time? Regardless, they would, in old age, be denied their only grandchildren.

Ben was also mindful of Lucy's unspoken anxiety: would he cope with the pressure, the unknown potential challenges? Was he strong enough? Or might the job push him to the brink again?

Then there was the endless diplomatic entertaining which Lucy, as the assumed homemaker, was expected to oversee. She mostly did this with patience and good humour; an accomplished mimic, she would have Ben and the kids in stitches as she impersonated the sleazy Israeli military attaché or the liposuctioned, botoxed, toxically boring, social X-ray wife of some visiting British Tory MP at a dinner they'd attended or hosted. Publicly, of course, she was always dutifully charming and generous.

On the other hand, at least Lucy knew what she'd signed up for with this posting. She too was nostalgic about Australia. Her and Ben's shared love, their quarter-century together, was intimately tied to the place. He hoped their time here would strengthen their love still more as they moved deeper into middle age, and provide an adventure – likely a safe one – for them all.

But for now, these next few weeks were all his. He had this weekend by the beach before getting to know his new city (always a wondrous and fun experience), meeting his colleagues, figuring out the job and finding the perfect family home. Time was a matter of constant negotiation in their marriage, as for most working couples. In the midst of family and work commitments, they both frequently longed for personal space. Thinking time. Alone time. Yet so often he ran from it when it arrived. But given that Lucy had insisted on staying in London with the kids for a few more weeks, he was determined to indulge the luxury of all this me-time.

Ben closed his eyes, tried to find that state of weightlessness and thoughtlessness that preceded sleep, the way one of his cognitive behavioural therapists had taught him. He tried circular breathing: in one-two-three-four, hold, out one-two-three-four . . . But there was no way he could possibly sleep. His mind was weary but his body told him it was 8 am in London, that he ought to be returning from a run or a swim or a cycle or a session at the gym about now, ahead of a light breakfast. He contemplated hitting the hotel gym. But the sounds of the night from the street below beckoned, despite an inner voice of better judgement whispering room service and rest. He gave in, decided to head out for a while and wander Campbell Parade. Perhaps get an ice cream. Or sit somewhere on a drink and people-watch. After all, how often was he back in Bondi?

He donned an old pair of Levi's, cleaned his teeth and combed his thinning salt-and-pepper hair. He slid on his new brown R.M. Williams boots. Well, not quite actually the iconic Australian boots. But close to. They were a thoughtful gift from Charles and Sybil, who were inordinately proud of their son-in-law, for all he'd recovered from and for being rewarded finally with the Canberra posting. Lucy's parents had priced the genuine article at Harrods, baulked at the £600-plus price tag, and sought a less expensive and near-identical pair of mail-order Turkish knock-offs made from buffalo hide. Brand name M.R. Willston. They'd had Lucy covertly trace Ben's runners to get the correct fit.

Just so as to look the part, Charles and Sybil had written on a card accompanying the boots. *Everyone from the prime minister to the dustman seems to wear them down there.*

The leather of the M.R.s was unyieldingly stiff, the insoles hard and unpadded, unlike the genuine boot. But what the heck, he thought, no pain no gain. And they looked pretty much the same. Nobody would know the difference.

Down on the street the smoke seemed more acrid than when he'd arrived. People were coughing, rubbing their eyes and complaining. Still, they were four-deep outside the fish-and-chip, burger, ice-cream and kebab shops. The bars and pubs were pumping. Across the road Ben could see backpackers lounging all over the park by the beach, scoffing chicken and chips, souvlakis, gelato, and drinking tinnies of beer and pre-mixes. He was struck by how white it was. Even in Anglo-Saxon ground zero, Putney, there were more non-Anglo faces.

The crowds felt overwhelming. He was suddenly repelled by the rubbish on the footpath, the yelling, the drunkenness. The beggars outside the convenience stores. It was as if his idyll, clung to for decades, had been overrun, soiled and sullied by his own countrymen and others. Subsumed into this unseemly, sordid reality. Of course, places always seem new, relatively undiscovered, when your horizons are as narrow as Ben's had been back then. Experience had also taught him that a revisited beloved place rarely lives up to the memory of it. And anyway Bondi had, after all, been a magnet for tourists since before federation. But that mattered little to Ben, who could only think that right now his Bondi was extinct. A memorial, if subtropical, Pompeii.

At the pub, he had to queue to get in. His boots were rubbing on his heels. Nobody had told him that M.R.s were such a bastard to break in. The bouncer looked him over, nodded approval. 'In ya go, mate.'

He ordered a pint of Foster's. It was what he'd drunk during his Australian months – still did in London sometimes, where it was often on tap. *Foster's – Australian for Lager.* He remembered the TV ad from when he was a little boy. Paul Hogan standing in the drizzle outside some dreary, mouldering West End watering hole, selling an unrealisable antipodean dream to people like Ben's dad, who really preferred room-temperature Boddingtons.

The barman laughed. 'Foster's! Maaaate. It hasn't been on tap round here for twenty years. Where've you been? We send that cat's piss straight to England.'

He thanked the barman and ordered a boutique lager.

Nearby, a bunch of twenty-something hens in short skirts and low-cut blouses were drinking red stuff from schooners through glass straws shaped like penises. The bride had a blue veil topped with a pair of devil's horns. Wobbly pegs. A pack of Irish blokes, their ankle-length chinos and white cotton shirts skin-tight over frames honed on construction sites, sniffed about predatorily.

He caught a little of the hens' conversation.

'He had the hugest cock I'd ever seen and I just said, "Stop waving that thing at me or I'm gonna need fanny surgery."'

Ben's eyes were stinging and red from the smoky air. He sculled his beer. It hardly touched the sides. It was icy and refreshing. The alcohol gave him an instant frontal cortex buzz, warm and accommodating. He wrestled his way to the bar for another. He would allow himself two. He tended to carefully monitor his intake. A bald guy with blond dreads and a dagger tattooed on his forearm tried to sell him drugs: GBH, coke, smack . . . bud? No thanks.

The scent of the morass of steamy humanity juggling drinks and balancing on uncertain legs was a fusion of body odour, perfume and after-shave, stale cigarette smoke and booze. Ben had long been a social smoker and relished the airborne smell, though he hated it on his clothes and hair. Especially when he drank in pubs. Lucy called him a secret smoker, alluding to the fact that he would occasionally buy a pack or cadge a few during a night on the tiles with the boys, then try to cover the smell with mouthwash and mints. He could go for months without a smoke. So she didn't – and he didn't – see it as a problem. In any event, Lucy was hardly one to throw stones, given her partiality to a vape when she was out with friends.

He took his beer and stood by the window. Surveyed the street. It was getting busier and noisier. Two men, maybe in their fifties – shorts, rugby guernseys, tasselled loafers, no socks – had another fellow suspended between them, one of his arms around each of their necks. His feet dragged limply behind him as they walked. They stopped abruptly on the other side of the open window, where the man in the middle convulsed and threw up on the footpath.

'Gaz, you arsehole – it's all over my shoes. Time to chuck you in a taxi, pack you off home to the missus.'

Suddenly several bodies collided into Ben. He dropped his beer. The glass exploded as the beer fizzed and frothed across the polished concrete floor. He let out a groan and stumbled, but kept his feet and stepped quickly aside. The bouncer had the Irishman who'd been hassling the bride pinned around the shoulders from behind. One of the other Irish lads, meanwhile, had crash-tackled the bouncer and was on his back, one arm around his throat. With his free hand he was punching the bouncer in the head. A tangle of twisted bodies fell to the ground on top of the shattered glass as more security men tore at the pile of people, trying to break up the fight.

Ben bolted for the door of the pub, every flight sensor in his body and brain urging him out. He walked back to the hotel, his heart racing, breath short and uneven, hands trembling. He knew he was quite safe, largely inconspicuous amid the hectic hubbub of the street, yet panic was beginning to take hold of him, slowly tightening its grip on his arms and chest. This spectre clutching him was as familiar as it was frightening, though it had been a couple of years since their last serious encounter. What he needed most right now was to call home. If he spoke to Lucy and the family, everything would be fine. Recalibrated. Calm and measured. He looked at his watch. Lucy and the kids wouldn't be anywhere near home yet. That call would have to wait.

He stepped up his pace as he neared the hotel, his strides meeting the rhythm of his consciously regulated deep inhalations and exhalations, learnt and assiduously practised to combat anxiety and its malicious twin, panic.

Sighing with relief, he sat on the bed and slid the boots off. There were raw blisters on both heels and one of his big toes. At the minibar he unscrewed both miniatures of Johnnie Walker, poured them and topped the glass with cola.

His hand still shook with adrenaline as he put the drink to his mouth. He gulped it down like medicine. His heart slowed. His breathing regulated. He checked the time in London again: midday. Still hours too early to call. He turned on the TV. Ether News – the national, private-subscription service he'd read about in his cultural briefing notes. What the notes had tactfully, diplomatically avoided saying was that 'Night-time Ether', including the current show, was manned by a loony cabal of sensationalist right-wing nut jobs for whom the most rampant, bovine populism was an aspirational KPI and who regarded no conspiracy as too outrageous to broadcast.

The coverage was wall-to-wall fires on the south coast. Reporters in protective gear doing live crosses from smoke-filled beaches where entire summer populations of tourist towns were seeking safety. In the studio the agitated anchors carried on about all the fires, every single one, being either deliberately lit or the result of 'native fire-stick back-burning'. So-called global warming and extreme continental temperatures had nothing at all to do with it. Ben just couldn't remain engaged with this insanity. His eyes lost focus and he fell into a fitful jet-lagged sleep propped on the bed. The bellicose sounds of Ether filtered in and out of his consciousness, invading his dreams.

He and Lucy were out the back of Bondi beyond the break, the deep azure water hugging them as they trod water, arms wrapped around each other, eye to eye, nose to nose. The shark siren sounded. But they didn't panic. Both knew they would be fine, safe as long as they stayed in each other's arms. Still holding one another, they gingerly paddled towards the shore. The shark suddenly surfaced in front of them, fleshy jaws yawning open, ready to swallow them whole like Jonah's whale. This was no typical shark, it was a Disney version – blue-skinned, red-gummed, its neat, pointed teeth glinting in the sun. Ben raised his fists and the great fish cowered and danced a retreat across the water and all the way up the golden beach.

He woke startled. Head pounding. He had a desperate thirst, a slight headache, and his heart was racing again. And he was famished.

He dressed quickly, splashed some water on his face and took two paracetamol tablets. He went downstairs, ready to attack the day. Through the windows of the breakfast room there was even more smoke outside than the night before. The air was an ugly beige miasma.

He ate ravenously. Bacon. Sausage. Cheese omelette. Two slices of toast and a Danish. Two coffees. He considered calling home again. But it was now quite late in Putney. Lucy would probably be asleep after the usual Friday night routine: homemade pizzas, then an episode or two of *Outlander* or something with a bottle of wine. She and Ben were often in bed, exhausted, by 9.30 on a Friday. Jet lag and booze had stolen the opportunity to speak to her now. Last night's drinking had been somewhat excessive by his recent standards.

Breakfast helped, though. Next, the ocean – the glorious Pacific would clear his head. With boyish anticipation he raced upstairs and put his swimmers on under his shorts. He donned his flip-flops and a fresh T-shirt, grabbed a towel, then went back downstairs and crossed the parade to the beach.

But it had been closed by the surf lifesavers. The near-deserted beach was covered in a patina of dark ash, the air was acrid. He walked across the sand, trailing a set of stark footprints in the darkened crust. At the shoreline he stood and looked down at his toes in the shallows. He could barely see them through the syrupy black effluvia of ash and half burnt leaf matter. It was as if the small swell had been slowed by the thick muck it carried – it resembled some sort of grey jelly. For months after securing the Australian posting Ben had fantasised about swimming in the Pacific again, in its clean, briny, refreshing perfection. He'd pictured the symmetry of neat lines of swells that rose as they hit the sand bars and peeled off as they broke, white foam frothing against the blue, the back spray sparkling in the sunlight.

But there'd be no swimming at Bondi today. Or any time soon, by the looks of it.

He bent down and peered at the small dead marine creatures – fish, crabs, a tiny seahorse – that lolled in the murky filth about his naked feet. The air held a waft of putrefaction. Some sort of rotting flesh. A fish perhaps. Ben's sensing of this vague odour coincided with the delivery onto the shore of a child's flip-flop. It was corroded, as though it had been in the water since long before the fires, and with the rank smell it triggered a flashback.

The lagoons filled with fetid bodies after the impossibly big rush of water. The stench. The corpulent rats. Ben trawling through makeshift morgues in sweltering hospital corridors, in shipping containers and ice-cream vans swarming with blood-drunk mosquitos, trying to compare photographs of smiling, vanished loved ones with the bloated, decaying bodies of British tourists amid all the other corpses. It remained his great haunting. Immovable. The smell. The squelch of accidentally stepped-upon rotten human tissue. The memory never dwelt too far from his shadow.

He retreated from the beach. Went back to the hotel pool. It was way too warm, too heavily chlorinated, and was in no way a match for his dreams of the Pacific. He floated on his back, eyes open. The sun strained to show itself through air that resembled a London pea-souper of his childhood. Ennui began to saddle him now, like a dead weight on his bare stomach and chest. He felt alone and empty. Unmoored. He wished desperately for home, with all its imperfections and demands, all the familiar safety it afforded.

Back in his room he was restless but weary. He thought of sleeping. He considered going down to the bar for a beer. He really did feel like a cold beer. But it was still early. He made a cup of tea instead.

The airline rang. Due to the smoke, his flight to Canberra next morning had been postponed until Monday, possibly late afternoon. But he was due to start at the high commission Monday morning, he said. How about another flight today?

No. Nothing til Monday.

He glanced at his watch. It was barely midday.

Monday. No way, he thought. No way. I can't stay here another day. But it wasn't just because of work. He was beset with an urgent desire to escape Sydney. It had all been such a bloody let-down. A deception, even. It had discombobulated him terribly. The fires had taken that travel-brochure-blue water refracted through the signature blinding sunshine, for so long frozen in his memory. They had stolen the sky, that pristine Arcadian light. Boxed it up in black and grey. And all those bloody bogans on the street and in the bars had completed the sham.

He decided he'd drive to Canberra right away. He found a hire car company nearby and arranged to collect the vehicle in an hour.

It was a trip of three hours or so, and was resonant of navigating a Midlands fog. Drivers had their hazard lights on. Most sat well below the speed limit, keeping their distance. Nobody overtook. There was no point, in the slow trail of cars, lights flashing a collective garish yellow, snaking through the murk of western Sydney and into the Southern Highlands. At two in the afternoon it looked more like dusk.

He eventually turned on the car radio. Amid a fizz of static it was just picking up the ABC station in Canberra. The newsreader, in his nasally accent, announced that it was news time. Then came the trumpets of the ABC's signature music signifying the bulletin, the 'Majestic Fanfare'. He remembered it from his last visit, and though it had been altered since then he still thought it pretentious and overly British. But then modern Australia was, sentimentally at least, still quite attached to Mother England.

While Ben loved so much about Australia, he also found it slightly perplexing, in the way, perhaps, that young nations can seem to the very old. He couldn't for the life of him understand why a country that had defined itself through anti-authoritarianism, individualism, and a claim to some unique type of naturist mateship, had voted against becoming a republic some twenty years earlier and hadn't reconsidered the question since. Ben modestly prided himself on being in some ways quite an unlikely member of the United Kingdom's diplomatic corps. He was privately an anti-monarchist and in favour of Scottish, Welsh and Northern Irish independence. His republicanism came from Irish Catholic ancestry on his mother's side: the Gaskills of County Antrim, dog breeders and militants who'd come to London via Liverpool, where they'd stopped for a generation.

So it was ironic that he had effectively become one of Britain's instruments of continuing global influence. He would tell friends that this had happened almost by accident. A degree in theology and languages, while intellectually engaging, had seemed to equip him for little professionally beyond teaching. But he was averse to that idea. He'd grown up watching his mother wearily marking papers late into the evening at the kitchen table, her dedication to public education financially unrewarded and under-appreciated. He'd always liked to write. Poems and short stories mostly, and he'd thought that one day he might write for the newspapers and, eventually, maybe even a novel – perhaps inspired by those six months in Australia. After his gap year, he applied for several journalism traineeships, picturing himself as a foreign correspondent in South-East Asia or perhaps somewhere in Africa. But he'd never made it beyond the final interviews.

In the end, about to leave university and planning a future – marriage, home, kids, dog – with Lucy, the foreign service, while not where he'd ever envisaged himself, potentially ticked a lot of boxes. There was travel and the opportunity to live abroad. To use his aptitude for languages. The younger, more idealistic Ben rationalised that it need not be forever. Who knew – it might eventually enable a segue into journalism? And the insight it would bring into the machinations of civil service might align to an extent with his Labour values, and make possible an eventual second career as a backroom political operative, something that had also appealed to him as a student.

But the longer he stayed in the service, the easier it was to do so. There was the money, which – together with Lucy's earnings – facilitated their SW London lifestyle. And then, at a certain point, not least after Cambodia and his recovery, came an inertia, along with the possibility of a cushier posting and, ultimately, the generous pension.

On the radio, the leading news item was of course about the bushfires. Blazes so extreme, so awful, some on the news were dubbing them 'The Black Summer Fires'. The country was burning uncontrollably. Holiday-makers and residents were trapped in blazing townships all the way from the Victorian border to the central coast of New South Wales. People were being incinerated. Wildlife destroyed. Hundreds of homes turned to cinders. A convoy of cars was crawling up the mountainous inland, from the seaside hamlets around Batemans Bay to Canberra, due to the closure of the Princes Highway. Toxic levels of smoke were in the air. The authorities were telling everyone to abandon their summer plans. To go home. Stay there. Inside. With their pets. Forget your coastal holiday this year.

There was a brief item about the arguments for and against the proposed recognition in the Australian Constitution for First Nations peoples. Ben recalled seeing something or other about it – a dot point or two – in his briefing notes.

Next came sport, of course. Always sport. Sport happened in Australia no matter what. Neither flood nor bushfire nor cyclone would ever halt it entirely. Australia was leading in the cricket test against New Zealand. There were injury concerns ahead of the Canberra Raiders pre-season training.

The final item was so brief as to be an afterthought: an Australian flight attendant had been found dead outside the apartment building where she stayed during layovers in Riyadh, Saudi Arabia. She had fallen from a window. Australian consular officials were engaged. Local police were investigating.

Ben didn't envy the Australians in the Saudi mission who'd have to deal with the dead woman and her family. He'd certainly done more than his share of such work, not least in Bangkok and Phnom Penh. It was always heartbreaking, and thankless, dealing with the grieving family of a young person who'd gone to travel the world and died misadventurously. Negotiating with local authorities – cops, the coroner, Customs – to get the body released and shipped home was inevitably a nightmarish tangle of red tape. But hopefully such hard yards were behind him now.

Ben stopped at a roadhouse to fill the car and take a piss. When he paid for the fuel he bought a sausage roll. He also bought a packet of Dunhill Reds and a lighter. What the fuck, he thought – the whole place was filled with smoke anyway and he was all alone. Smoking had always been synonymous with freedom and travel anyway, so why not? His mind flitted to him and Lucy buying a carton of duty-free and a bottle of single-malt when they landed in Rome on their honeymoon. They'd driven to their hotel in San Gimignano and arrived at midnight. Perched on the windowsill, chain-smoking and drinking Scotch, they revelled in one another, and in the moonlight reflecting off the rained-upon cobblestoned piazza and the Duomo.

He stood by the car and scoffed the sausage roll. He lit a cigarette. The smell was as delightfully forbidden as the warm sensation in his throat and lungs and the poisonous head-rush of nicotine. How he'd loved smoking as a young fellow. So much that he'd long vowed that if he lived til eighty he'd become an enthusiastic smoker once more. He finished the smoke before driving on.

At the first of a series of roundabouts on Canberra's northern outskirts, he slowed the car. He could see little of the city itself as the highway segued into a wide avenue, and on either side and on the median strip, the grass was parched. The dead lawns out front of low-rise blocks of flats and offices were littered with green e-scooters. The branches and leaves of tall eucalypts drooped wearily. On the opposite side of the road, a stream of soot-blackened holiday-makers' cars, surfboards and storage pods on their roofs, bicycles on racks at rear, streamed towards Sydney, having escaped up the mountain from burning coastal hamlets.

He was surprised that the main avenue into the national capital's city centre should be edged with such unseemly, run-down housing blocks, similar to the sink estates he'd seen on the outskirts of so many British cities. They were of red brick and dilapidated, with small windows, miserly and pointless balconies, and exposed stairwells. He wondered: Are residents given a suicide helpline number when they move in? A large black and white dog sat in a kids' blow-up pool in front of one block. Broken toys – a wheelless scooter, a plastic slide lying on its side, the rusted metal frame of a swing set – punctuated the expanse of dust and dead lawn.

Downtown Minsk post-nuke strike, thought Ben.

In contrast to the busyness of the highway, the cars on his side of the road were so conspicuously absent that he wondered if every local really was inside due to the air quality. Perhaps it was always like this in January during school holidays?

The sat nav guided him across a lake devoid of watercraft. Sheets of smoke hung close to its surface, disturbed only by the foaming jet from a high fountain. To his left, the old government offices and the original Parliament House – white and ornate as a 1920s wedding cake – stood conspicuously in the desiccated gardens, monuments to a forgotten and never much celebrated federation. To the right, amid wilting rose gardens, was a deserted croquet court and the Hyatt Hotel, its front door attended by a doorman in knickerbockers, white shirt and peaked cap. A little further on he came to his new workplace, the high commission, behind which loomed the Chinese embassy with its dragons and turrets in all their red and gold ostentation.

The road forked around a steep rise into which the newer Parliament House was embedded, only the feet of its towering metallic flagpole visible through the toxic air. Here too the grass was singed brown.

He stopped in the underground carpark of his hotel, a low, round structure diagonally opposite a synagogue and surrounded by official-looking buildings. He wheeled his suitcase to the reception desk, checked in and went to his room, a pleasant enough suite with a view of Canberra Avenue. He felt flat, but not as melancholy as he'd been in Bondi. He was glad to be rid of Sydney.

He looked out the window at the six-lane road lined by functional buildings. There was only a smattering of traffic and he still hadn't seen a pedestrian. Going for a wander in his new city was an option he quickly passed up. There was the noxious air to consider. And his weariness.

He uncapped a beer from the minibar. He sat in an armchair by the window. His headache soothed almost immediately. Thank god for beer in a hot climate.

The TV was set to the ABC's 24-hour news channel. The 'Majestic Fanfare' again. Fires everywhere. Some government politicians were blaming arsonists. The prime minister – a running to fat, obdurate-looking chap who resembled nothing more closely than a Clapham used car salesman with a sleazy grin – was dismissing the idea that climate change was contributing to the fires. Then came file footage of the man holidaying in Hawaii a few weeks back, when the fires had started. Thumbs up for the tourist pic. That shit-eating grin again. Other footage showed him getting heckled when he visited a fire-stricken community. 'I don't hold a hose, mate,' he was heard to say.

Then a shot of him awkwardly trying to shake some traumatised, reluctant – clearly hostile – firefighter's hand.

What a rolled-gold tosser, Ben thought. Read the fucking room why don't you, boy-o. Christ, this huckster would give Boris Johnson hope.

A subsequent item reported a record number of shark sightings. Something to do with rising water temperature. Deadly snakes, meanwhile, were everywhere, slithering into towns to escape the fires. Ben laughed out loud at this, an Englishman's full antipodean nightmare. Sharks and snakes, holy Jesus!

And then there was another item about the dead flight attendant in Riyadh, with more details this time. She was 38-year-old Charlene Sloper, originally from the Central West Downs, who had worked for a number of airlines including Qantas and British Airways. More recently she had been with the Middle Eastern airline Airabia, working mostly out of Dubai and Riyadh. Her death was reported as an 'apparently tragic accident, with no evident suspicious circumstances'.

There was a headshot of Charlene. Blond hair tousled around her shoulders, immaculately pencilled dark eyebrows over big Icelandic-blue eyes. Full lips and sculpted cheeks. The reporter described her as a former model and aspiring actor. Ben could imagine her on screen. She was certainly striking. Though he also saw a girlish softness and thought there was an innocence about her. Sad. The world was so terribly cruel to the gentle and the kind.

Saturday night. He wondered again if he should venture out, find a restaurant or a bar. But he couldn't be arsed going anywhere in the filthy, smoky heat. There were cabs, of course. But where to go? Given the dearth of people about and the smoke, he imagined many places would be shut anyway. He could go downstairs to the hotel dining room for dinner, but the prospect of dealing with people – anyone, bar or table staff, other diners – gave him hives. He cracked another beer and ordered a room-service steak sandwich with chips.

Later, he took his laptop out to the balcony. He smoked (vowing with each ciggie to quit when the pack was finished) and drank tea. He checked his private Insta account. Dozens of followers had liked his aerial shot from the aircraft window of the distant fires: ♡♡♡♡♡♡♡♡♡. There were loads of comments. *The time of your lives. Adventure of a lifetime. Green with envy* 😭*!!!* One was from an old school-gate, fellow-parent-cum-footy-mate: *Keep your wits about you Benji – between the death adders, the sharks and all those friggin copycat Ivan Milats . . .*

Just that afternoon, driving through smoke that was like a Birnam Wood mist, Ben had seen the signpost to Belanglo State Forest. The 'backpacker killer', Ivan Milat. In October he'd read in *The Times* an obituary of Milat, who'd recently died in a prison hospital, still refusing to disclose the burial sites of other likely victims. Ben knew Milat's crimes all too well. The man had been arrested while Ben was in Australia those decades ago, and his murders were tabloid fodder in England and across Europe, where his victims came from. Back then it had put paid to Ben and Lucy's plans to hitchhike once they'd left Sydney for the regions. The crimes had chilled them. The fabled Aussie bush and its lonely highways were a haven for human monsters.

'Ben, darling, what time is it there? You look utterly exhausted.'

'Late Saturday night, Luce – well, late for me. Eleven hours difference, remember.'

'Saturday night in Bondi – and it looks like you're alone in the hotel! Whenever did you stay home on a Saturday night when you had the chance not to?'

'Bondi was terrible. A shit show. I couldn't stand it. So I bailed this afternoon and drove down to Canberra. Through the smoke.'

He told her how much Bondi had changed for the worse since they'd lived there. How it was full of pissed fighting lads and slutty hens on the ran-tan, drug dealers and aggro idiots.

'And what's more, you know that memory we have of the water – the blue, the turquoise ocean, the yellow sand? Well, it's gone, Luce, nothing more than a figment. It was disgusting, black and dirty. Heartbreaking.'

'Did you take a picture? You know how you said you'd take a photograph and send it? For old times.'

'Luce, you're not hearing me. It was *disgusting.* Unrecognisable. An absolute nightmare. I couldn't wait to leave. I had to get out or I was gonna go crazy.'

At this she frowned with concern. 'Darling?'

He knew the tone. Not too interfering. But a look that reflected her concern.

'Nah. Heavens, sweetheart, I don't mean fucking old-fashioned crazy. I just mean mad. Pissed off. Disappointed. I'm really okay, if that's what you're wondering.'

He knew she would be.

'Oh, Benny . . . It's just that, you know why I've been concerned about this whole thing. Tell me you're all good.'

'I'm actually great. Everything's fine. I've got a cruisy week ahead. Tomorrow I'll have a look around town. Check in to work Monday. Meet the mission. Find us a house. What's not to like?'

There was small talk. The dog. God, how the dog would love Australia! Better watch the ticks and snakes, though. The various tradesmen who weren't turning up to get the Putney place rental-ready. Her folks.

And then she looked at her watch. 'I've got to go, love. Saturday morning, you know. Amy – ballet. Jerome – football. Talk again later.'

Love you. Love you.

He went to the bed. Fell asleep in his clothes again.

He'd not planned on spending a lone Sunday in Canberra before starting work. But having woken early and again eaten a huge breakfast, he was in good spirits, buoyed by the conversation with Lucy and a reasonable night's rest.

The air outside was still acrid. It wouldn't do to go walking far. He stopped at the concierge station in the lobby with its array of pamphlets. 'Top 10 National Cultural Institutions.' The Australian War Memorial was '#No 1 as voted by Tripadvisor'. This baited his curiosity. Why would such a museum be so damn popular in a country this young, a nation whose military history involved little more than trailing empires into their foreign wars? He decided he'd see.

The sat nav guided Ben's car along broad roads, once again near empty, bordered by full-canopied though distressed blue gums, plane and oak trees, and over the lake on Kings Avenue

Bridge (he wondered: Which king?). There followed a series of roundabouts leading to Anzac Parade, at the top of which piously perched the memorial, capped with a vast green copper dome.

Ben compared the outside of it with London's Imperial War Museum. That building was far less architecturally distinctive, more prosaic and austere, befitting a nation accustomed over so many centuries to the human cost of war. The Australian memorial, standing alone at the foot of a small mountain in the bush, invited reverence. The Anzac tradition, Ben knew, was akin to a secular religion here. Anzac Day was cheek by jowl with Australia Day (which, he knew, more and more people apparently now called Invasion Day) when it came to public celebrations.

As he entered the memorial's near-deserted atrium on that first Sunday morning, he was confronted by one of the landing craft used in that cherished moment of Australian tragedy, the Gallipoli invasion of 1915. Ben was cynical as to what else he might encounter, convinced already that the place would probably only further arouse his anti-war sentiments. His paternal grandfather and several uncles had served in the military and returned variously incapacitated, their children – including his father – inheriting the legacy of their trauma. Ben disliked stories and mawkish movies about soldierly heroics, never more so than after seeing so many dead people in his work. He also had an aversion to guns.

Yet he was surprised by his emotional responses as he surveyed the dioramas of the seminal Australian actions in the Great War – Gallipoli, Fromelles, Bullecourt, Beersheba, Jerusalem and Damascus. Then came the World War Two galleries and the experiences of Australian soldiers in the Pacific, the terrible privations of those who became prisoners of the Japanese in the labour camps of Singapore and Burma. He inferred a political and nationalistic tenor in the displays. He was attuned to something that was implied here about national character. It was a not too subtle narrative about how some instinctive all-for-one symbiosis between officers and men had fostered collective endurance and survival in those dreadful camps. That fabled Aussie egalitarianism. Perhaps it was true after all. If so, what was its genesis? The bush, perhaps. Even though these Australians were soldiers of the empire, their experiences seemed to Ben to be somewhat at odds with Britain's, whose privileged officer class was quite aloof from the cannon fodder, who were more likely to be proletarian soldiers.

On his way back to the car he braved the malodorous air to wander briefly amid the exhibits outside. Simpson and his donkey in bronze; everyone knew that story. An explosives-detection dog and his handler in Afghanistan. A metallic effigy of the revered general, Monash. He stopped before a wall of dark concrete and reflective glass. A flame flickered in its pebbled foreground. It was labelled 'For Our Country', a monument dedicated to Aboriginal and Torres Strait Islander service personnel.

He began to cough. He needed water. He took a handkerchief from his pocket, unfolded it, placed it over his mouth and nose and hurried back to the car. His feet, in these bloody M.R.s, were killing him.

On Monday he woke early, feeling optimistic and upbeat.

This job was out of the box. A one-off opportunity to live a fantasy for a while. Which Brit didn't want to escape their miserable isles for a few years of Australian light and space? These bushfires would pass. The skies would clear. He and Lucy and the kids would holiday in Sydney (perhaps Manly instead of Bondi) and Melbourne, at Uluru and in the Daintree. And yes, they would all eventually get to frolic in the Pacific. They would put the stresses of London behind them. Who knew, the Foreign Office might even extend his appointment, once the kids were advancing at school. They sometimes did that. Lucy would surely get part-time work.

He shaved for the first time in three days, showered, and put on his new grey suit (Savile Row) and the white shirt he'd ironed the previous evening. He thought he'd get to the high commission early, perhaps grab a light breakfast on the way. Sir Gordon had told him he'd be there from 7.30 sharp to greet him. Maps said it was barely a kilometre away – a fifteen-minute walk. He decided to brave the smoke, which appeared to have dissipated somewhat overnight.

He told the app to take him to a cafe on the way.

Soon he was tramping across a sienna paddock of long grass wedged between a square glass monstrosity housing a law firm and the startlingly bland Department of Foreign Affairs and Trade. The R.G. Casey Building. Sharp seeds were piercing his socks through the elastic of his M.R.s and the cuffs of his new suit trousers. His boots aggravated the broken blisters on his feet. He cursed himself for wearing them instead of his dress shoes. But he was in Australia and so he'd persist. Endure the pain and discomfort, like all those fellows in the dioramas at the war memorial.

The temperature was already in the high twenties. He was sweating. He removed his jacket and slung it over the arm he was carrying his briefcase with. At the footpath on the other side of the paddock he kept following the directions. Brisbane Avenue. National Circuit. Then a cafe just near a big government department. *Closed until 20 January. Happy NY* read the sign.

What the hell was this place?

The app led him to Queen Victoria Terrace, across the near-deserted Commonwealth Avenue, and on to the gates of the high commission. He looked at his watch: 7.35.

He ran a hand through his hair. It was slick with sooty sweat. He took a white handkerchief from his pocket and wiped his face. The handkerchief was blackened. He bent down, pulled the prickles from his socks and trousers. Rubbed the toe of each boot on the opposite calf and blew his nose. This was supposed to be a city, a capital city, he thought. A national-fucking-capital city. It hardly seemed like a village, let alone a bloody town.

The high commission's security fence was tall, spiked metal bars suspended between concrete pillars, but he found the building itself quite underwhelming. Plain white concrete render with a face of two rows of four-paned dark windows hiding behind roof-high, carefully manicured conifers. It was almost un-British in its resolute absence of imperial conspicuousness. The only giveaway was a modest sign at the front gate and the large Union Jack that sagged breathlessly atop the flagpole on the flat roof. He pressed the buzzer on the intercom; the gate opened immediately, no question asked. Before he could ring the bell at the front door it swung open swiftly.

A very thin bald man in an impeccable black suit, white shirt and black tie stood before Ben. His shoes were highly polished. This heightened Ben's awareness of his own dusty boots. The man looked Ben over.

'Welcome, Mr Fotheringham-Gaskill. I see you found us. Follow me. I'll take you immediately to his excellency. Oh, I'm Mr Mallory.'

Mallory neither offered his hand nor any warmth. But he did immediately exude an ostentation that the building itself had failed to.

The marble entrance foyer was modest and Marie Kondo-bare, with just a modern settee in dark fabric and a low black coffee table. There was, naturally, a large portrait of a much younger Queen Elizabeth. And there were flags: British, Australian, Aboriginal, and Torres Strait Islander. Ben followed Mallory as he turned into a hall, padding silently along behind on a blood-coloured runner of thick carpet set atop dark polished parquetry. His feet sank into the carpet pleasantly, briefly relieving his blisters. The walls were hung with photographs of the famous. Mostly men. Disraeli. Churchill. Thatcher. Major. Blair. Former high commissioners. Boris-fucking-Johnson.

Mallory knocked once on a white door with a brass handle, which he turned before any summons came from inside.

The high commissioner sat behind an expansive teak desk. He was staring at a computer screen and made no move whatsoever to rise.

'Your Excellency, Benedict Fotheringham-Gaskill.'

The delay before Sir Gordon acknowledged him was only a split second or two. But it was gesturally freighted with the studied, entitled diffidence that ruling-class men, schooled in it at Harrow, Eton and the like, spend a lifetime employing to remind others who is who in the societal zoo. Ben knew the type backwards. Ben, the clever scholarship boy from Barking, the son of an off-licence grocer and a comprehensive English teacher, who'd had to wait tables and pull beers to support himself while at Oxford. Such men – they were nearly always men – carried on like entitled *Brideshead Revisted* extras. Due to his double-barrelled name, Ben was often mistaken for one of them, but only initially. His mother, despite being born in Liverpool, had always identified as an Ulster 'cultural' Catholic. She wasn't devout. But neither had she entirely shaken her political/religious influences. So she would attend Mass at Christmas and on some feast days, and eventually sent her children to Catholic schools. When she married Ben's father she insisted on their children having both surnames, in proud acknowledgement of their Northern Irish Catholic/English Protestant ancestry. Ben had long ago grown weary of explaining his hyphenated name; he always introduced himself as Ben Gaskill.

Ben knew Sir Gordon Woodhead only by reputation; the two had not met. Sir Gordon had been David Cameron's Secretary of State for Levelling Up, Housing and Communities. A supposed progressive conservative, if such a beast could ever be possible, he was banished to the backbench in a pointless power play to shore up Cameron's job a few years back. Rewarded, finally, for his discretion in going quietly by Theresa May, with a plum posting to the old colony. He had a sharp tongue. A Wodehousean wit. Machiavellian charm. Or so it was written in *The Spectator*, which seemed to adore him. He was the kind of Englishman who told people what it was that they thought rather than inquiring it of them.

Now the high commissioner stood quickly. He was dressed as if for a tropical posting, in a loose-fitting, expensively cut suit – cream linen and silk blend at a guess – and a sky-blue shirt offset with a kind of clubby tie with a motif of racing yachts. Sir Gordon was rather short, with the expansive girth of comfortable Belgravian life, and a proud bouffant of slightly absurd orangutan-coloured hair. He removed his reading glasses, the better to look Ben up and down. His hand, when he shook, was limp and soft, the knuckles sprouted with wiry red hair to match his head's.

'Benedict – you must think me dreadfully rude. Do come in. Sit down. Tea? You must have tea. And I can see you could use some water. Yes, water and tea, please, Mr Mallory.'

'Thank you.'

'I'm sorry, Ben. I was a little distracted by this terrible business with the Australian air hostess – the stewardess?'

'Sir?' Ben had quite forgotten.

'You know, the one who died in Riyadh a few days ago? It seems the Saudi officials may think her death rather more suspicious than . . . self-harm. They're interviewing a range of foreign nationals who stay in the same apartment building. A couple of Irish, apparently. But no Brits, thankfully. So not our problem.'

'Sir.'

'Charlene! That's the dead girl's name. Poor girl. Charlene! So very Australian, that name. I've never known of a British Charlene, have you? No. Not even an American one. But everyone in Australia just adores a Charlene. Something to do with a TV show, or so I'm told.'

'*Neighbours*.'

'Quite. Well, this Charlene – Ms Charlene Sloper – is not from the suburbs. Hails from some godforsaken place out in the middle of bloody nowhere – known as the Central West Downs. A town called The Leap. Odd name for a village. Wherever do they find such names here, I wonder. But I digress.'

Sir Gordon exhaled heavily as he resumed his seat behind the desk. Two large windows facing the street pitched big squares of light onto the polished wood floor. There were bookshelves with metres of what looked, from the spines, to be antiquarian volumes. Ben noted some early House of Commons Hansards and a few predictable classics – Dickens, Hardy, Conrad. The high commissioner had a hard copy of Robert Hughes' *The Fatal Shore* before him on the desk, its pages aflutter with protruding sticky notes, annotated. Must be working on a speech, thought Ben. On the walls were a couple of landscapes – one a very English horse-and-hounds affair depicting a fox hunt beside a bucolic stream, the other of the Thames at dusk. Houses of Parliament. Big Ben. Radiant streaks of tangerine sunlight reflecting off the mighty river. It resembled a Turner. There was also an early photograph of the high commission, standing out monumentally, along with the old Parliament House and a couple of other public-service buildings of white render, on the dusty, rabbit-riven Limestone Plains. And, inevitably, another photograph of the Queen.

Ben thought the room and its occupant had an air of indolence and languor.

Small talk. How did Ben like Australia? 'Trust you had a wonderful time in Sydney – one of the great cities of course, should've made it the capital. Oh, did I just say that?' Canberra, according to Sir Gordon, was comfortable in a quaint kind of way. Deathly quiet, though. 'Little fine dining to speak of. Wait til you're in Sydney and Melbourne for that. You must live on the south side, Ben – Yarralumla. Griffith. O'Malley at a stretch – there's fabulous bang for your buck there. Grand houses, five or six bedrooms for the same rent as a Chelsea bedsit. Many diplomatic families opt for it. But Ben, do avoid the north side – it can be rather . . .' He paused, searching for the word.

'Sir Gordon?' Ben prompted.

'Oh, I don't know – *republican*. Alternative, if you like. Sandals and yoga. Tofu. Chooks and fruit trees in the backyard.'

'I see, sir.'

'Yes. Anyway Ben, it's all terribly affordable – especially given the state of the poor old Aussie peso – two and a half to the British pound, I'd remind you. And of course, our relocation people will sort some housing options for you.'

In fact, if Ben was amenable he could look at houses that very afternoon; one of the locally engaged administrative staff would see to that. Ben told Sir Gordon he was thrilled at the idea. He wanted to find a new home and settle in, get it ready for the family's arrival as soon as possible.

The high commissioner then named Ben's family: Lucy, Amy, Jerome and Suze. He'd done his homework. But how hard could it be after all? And really, what else did he have to do?

'They will be coming, I gather, Benedict, in time for the new school year?'

'Indeed, Sir Gordon.'

'I think you'll find this is an excellent place to raise youngsters. Wonderful schools. Open space. Clean air – most of the time. We have found, however, that this posting can be quite taxing on spouses. The capital can be quite a lonely and isolating place. It would be rather indiscreet of me to tell you that several marriages of my people have fallen into disrepair recently. Very sad, to be honest.'

'Yes, Sir Gordon.'

'But I'm certain you'll all do remarkably here. As I say, it's a very family-oriented posting. You must excuse my amateur tilt at marriage counselling. I know you'll all settle in just stupendously, shan't you, Benedict?'

Mallory brought the silver service and poured the tea. He placed a glass of iced water in front of Ben on the high commissioner's desk. Ben drained the glass, slaking his thirst in several deep gulps. Sir Gordon seemed to regard this with a vague distaste.

There was more small talk about administrative matters. Security. Meeting the other staff. Welcome drinks at the Hyatt on Friday evening. The mission's chargé d'affaires would arrange everything for Ben, but if he had any questions or any problems, Sir Gordon's door was always – always, Benedict – open. Despite his initial misgivings about the man, and his butler, Ben thought it all well oiled, civilised and reassuring, after his discombobulating weekend.

'Benedict – or you'd prefer Ben, I'm quite sure.'

'Yes sir, Ben. Thanks.'

'Well, Ben, though I do think you'll find Canberra – Australia – a satisfying posting, it's not – how not to be impolite here, Ben? – it's not the most exciting of postings. Of course there is natural disaster aplenty, as evidenced by these damned fires. And we're just as likely to get floods at the same time in another part of the continent. But it's not like being in Europe or the Middle East where wars can ignite from cinders in a moment. But given your duties will be largely cultural, I think you'll find there's plenty to engage with. And let's face it, Ben, one does rather get to the stage in one's career, and life, where excitement is not always a priority. If you know what I mean?'

With this, Sir Gordon raised an unkempt simian eyebrow. Ben did wonder quite what he meant.

Sir Gordon continued, 'And Ben, correct me if I'm wrong but I assume you've quite had your fill of excitement.'

'Indeed, sir.'

'So, Ben, in order to help acquaint you with Australian culture I've taken the liberty of putting your name forward as the representative of Her Majesty's government this evening at a reception at the national gallery. It's just down the way there. Drinks and canapés at six. Most agreeable. It's in honour of some new acquisition. A celebrated work of Indigenous art, I'm told.'

'Delighted, Sir Gordon.' And this was true. Ben was very happy to go.

'Good-oh, Ben. That's the chap. I'll have my driver take you. Now do finish your tea – I know you'll be raring to get your feet under the desk.'

*

Ben's office was a smaller, darker version of the high commissioner's, the light from the window blocked by a pencil pine. The walls and shelves were empty. He sat down behind the desk – functional and modular, with none of the antiquity of his excellency's. From his briefcase he took a small framed photograph, him and Lucy with the three kids between them. Everyone in their togs, he and Lucy and Suze in shades, all standing, arms linked, on an outcrop of smooth rock that vanished into turquoise sea. Their summer holiday in Vernazza two years ago. They looked as they'd been – happy and relaxed. Tanned and fit from swimming and walking, despite the pasta and pizza.

There was a box of his new business cards on the desk. There it was in gold-leaf Times New Roman on the cards: his name and title. It was also noted that he was working on the unceded lands of the Ngunnawal and Ngambri peoples.

Ben smiled. On to the next adventure, he thought, reclining in the desk chair and plonking his M.R.s on the desk, while studying his elegant new business card.

There was a single knock. Before Ben could respond, a man he instantly judged fussy had entered. He was Sir Gordon's physical opposite, svelte, about Ben's age and, like him, slightly above average height. He wore a tight grey flannel suit that accentuated his chiselled, laboured-for leanness, a white shirt and a navy tie emblazoned with some sort of military-style crest.

He smiled superficially as Ben scrambled to get his boots off the desk, stand and offer his hand.

'Good morning, Benedict. I'm King – Roderick King. Chargé d'affaires.'

Ben registered King as a compact, neat, efficient, slightly effeminate ex-Royal Navy type. He had a pink complexion that looked like it had been scrubbed raw with a nailbrush that morning. Thick, side-parted hair of a chocolate labrador brown, so distinctive that Ben decided it just had to be dyed. Or a rug.

King's voice was educated Yorkshire. He smiled with a faux warmth to add emphasis after each sentence or two, baring large, even pinker gums and small, pebbly teeth. This he may well have intended as a gesture of congeniality, but it was easily taken as a particular brand of Are-you-paying-attention-idiot-or-am-I-moving-too-fast-for-you-here? condescension.

He instructed Ben to feel free to address him as Roderick or King. 'But I am never to be called Rod! Remember that, please, and we shall get along just famously.'

'Got it, Roderick,' said Ben. 'And I'd prefer Ben to Benedict, please.'

King was flawlessly civil-service punctilious. His brusque manner no doubt thinly cloaked an impatience with most people who happened into his orbit. Ben was familiar with his ilk from his decades in the Foreign Office. He was the type of man who sat in men's clubs and told the wait staff, without 'please' or 'thanks', that he'd 'take' a double Haig with water. Ben distrusted him intuitively.

King went through a list of proforma dos and don'ts. All of them went without saying but he said them regardless. Do make friends with the locally engaged staff, they keep the mission turning over. Do accept every invitation to cultural and sports events and do be on hand to assist A-list thespians and sporting identities, especially the England cricket team, when they come to play the PM's XI.

'And now for the big don'ts,' he went on. 'Don't ever speak – even at public events – with anyone from the Chinese or Russian embassies. Without casting any judgement on your character, Ben, don't ever engage prostitutes. Don't ever get drunk in public, and do always apply the three-drinks rule. Do not be reckless with your corporate card.'

He spoke to Ben as if he were an errant schoolboy.

There followed a couple of hours with 'the IT chap', as King described him, setting up Ben's laptop, sorting passwords and log-ins, running through online protocols, and procedures for the storage of classified documents, including where to securely dispose of shredded papers so that the Chinese or Russians or whoever else couldn't jigsaw them back together.

There was a new mobile phone with an Australian number. He needed to sign a receipt for it. Ben patted his pockets for the pen he couldn't find. The IT man produced his own retractable pen.

'Here you go,' he said, clicking the pen a couple of times as he handed it over. *Click, clack.*

Ben startled, then pulled himself together. 'Sorry,' he said. 'Where do I sign?' His computer and phone sorted, Ben attended a morning tea ostensibly in his honour, though the high commissioner and King were absent (impromptu meetings!). Many staff were still apparently on summer holiday and wouldn't return until after Australia Day, which, Ben was reminded, was when the nation really cranked itself, yawning and sun-kissed, back into work mode. Those who turned up for the pear and ginger cake, raspberry friands, sandwiches, blinis and tea were English and junior. They were studiously courteous but reserved, and seemed not terribly interested in Ben. Having missed breakfast, he was happy to grab a few smoked salmon blinis and some cake while making small talk, mostly about the fires and the smoke.

The exception was an Australian woman, Aimee, whom he judged to be in her late thirties. She arrived late and enthusiastically introduced herself as the person who'd show Ben some houses that afternoon. Unlike the other staff, she was less formally attired, in a sleeveless cotton dress with unstockinged legs. She had found eight prospective houses, she told him, and they'd leave after lunch if that suited. One o'clock? She'd drive.

Ben spent the rest of the morning acquainting himself with the rather labyrinthine hallways, communal staff areas, and related buildings of the high commission. He waited for Aimee, as agreed, at one, and he was slightly peeved that she turned up ten minutes late. She was full of apologies: her eldest had forgotten his swimming gear, and holiday day care was taking them to the indoor pool this arvo.

'Sorry about the state of the car,' Aimee said as she turned onto a freeway that girdled Parliament House. 'Bloody kids, you know.'

He did know. A slight aroma of pet dog, a kid's lunchbox and sports bag on the backseat, a half-filled water bottle and empty crisp packet and coins, discount petrol dockets in the console – the familiarity of the car tugged at him.

'No worries,' he said, instinctively reclaiming the phrase from a quarter of a century past. 'Kids, dogs – life. You learn not to be fussy about a messy car.'

'I hear you,' Aimee said, turning off the freeway. She pointed out the hospital where all her kids were born.

'That's where you'll go if a brown snake or a redback bites you.' She smiled mischievously.

'Haha – but you see, I'm an Englishman unafraid of the storied wildlife. I've lived here before.' He told her about the gap year.

'That makes sense. I thought there was something a little more . . . at ease about you. The cork not in quite so tight, I hope you don't mind me saying.'

'Not at all.'

Ben wondered how Aimee managed in the oppressively courtly environment of the high commission. He learned that she had four kids under ten, her husband was a tradie, and her aging mother had just moved in with her deaf golden retriever. Her warmth and easily shared family details evoked in him an immediate imagining of her home: a house on a quarter-acre block with an above-ground pool, a porch strewn with bikes and scooters, a ute in the driveway. The kind of house he wanted, replete with a menagerie of pets; their own and neighbourhood kids playing tippity-run cricket on the lawn; a garage crammed with surfboards, kayaks and boogie boards, golf clubs, balls of every football code and camping gear.

'So,' she said, 'I'm already unsure if these places we're about to look at in O'Malley are right for you. You'll be surrounded by other diplomats. The houses are big enough for an indoor game of Rugby Sevens but you'll still feel claustrophobic. Plus, there's hardly any footpaths and you'll have to drive to the shops for milk and bread.'

Both the first two houses were indeed cavernous, mausoleum-like. Every room was far too big. The kids, accustomed to close living in the Putney terrace, would become too distant here, he thought, retreating to their capacious bedrooms, each with ensuite – the four of them shared one bathroom in Putney – thus too easily avoiding family commune. Besides, the streets were too neat, their trees still saplings. O'Malley felt like a toy suburb. The deal breaker was no pets. No. These places would not do.

They got back in the car, and in the space of just a few kilometres he noticed five or six dead kangaroos on the edge of the road, guts squished out, mutilated by car tyres. This he found unaccountably disturbing: wasn't the roo celebrated on the nation's coat of arms?

Signposts: *Cooma 115*; *Narrabundah*; *Woden*; *Swinger Hill*.

Swinger Hill?

Shops. Why the need to signpost shops? Shops just were, in his experience. You walked round the corner and there was the high street with its shops. It was the same in the Sydney of his memory.

They drove onto another freeway that bisected a steep, forested hill and he told Aimee he wanted to be able to walk to a village.

'Easier said,' she laughed. 'This place was planned so you could walk in open space to the heights or to nowhere at all – not to a village. But let's see what we can do.'

The next two houses were in Yarralumla, and were the opposite of the O'Malley places. Each was dark and poky, south-facing. He couldn't imagine his family living there. The agent, sensing the high commission housing allowance, said he had another, in nearby Red Hill, that he hadn't intended to show them. It had 'great bones', he said. Amazing light. It was a 'little lived-in' – a much-loved home belonging to a family who'd, ironically, gone to London for a few years.

And a dog would be just fine.

The house, all acutes of glass, steel and concrete from the outside, was situated due north on a very steep block, and appeared to belong more in the Hamptons than the bush capital. It looked out over a canopy of European and native trees. Ben knew it was the one as soon he followed the agent inside.

The place was radiant with light, even with the smoke and ash; it shimmered on the white walls, scuffed as they were by family and pet life, and on the cathedral ceilings. The master bedroom also overlooked the trees. He imagined lying in bed with Lucy on a winter Saturday morning, the acrid smoke replaced by then with an icy Canberra mist that would slowly dissipate by late morning into pristine sunshine. He'd heard about such brilliant

Canberra mornings. There were three more bedrooms, a second bathroom, a serviceable kitchen, a dining room that would seat twelve or fourteen – perfect for diplomatic dinner parties. There was plenty of room in the garden for the dog and a trampoline for Amy. The lounge room, again with north-facing windows, had a vast open fireplace. The house was beyond comfortable without being ostentatious.

He stood there listening. He could hear no traffic. Nothing but birdsong. Magpies warbling, cockatoos screeching. A neighbouring dog yapped. The distant thrum of an aircraft engine, but nothing like the roar of jets over their house under the Heathrow flightpath. None of Putney's grimy raucousness, honking buses, pubs with vomit and dog shit on the footpath out front. This house was a haven.

Yes. Ben felt that this could be their home. They could be happy here together. Lucy, he was sure, would adore it.

He nodded approvingly to Aimee. She said sotto voce, so the agent couldn't hear, 'Don't seem too bloody keen. We want the non-dipo rental price.'

A two-year lease was signed that afternoon. He emailed Lucy a link to the house. He couldn't wait to talk to her about it.

He was in the afterglow of finding the perfect new home when he attended the drinks function at the national gallery. His name tag – the full, hyphenated, double-barrelled number – identified him as from the British High Commission.

The jacketless men wore dark chinos and open-necked shirts. The ubiquitous boots. The women too had a casual, dressed-for-the-climate elegance. There was lots of sun-kissed skin. Ben felt stuffy in his Savile Row number but glad for the M.R.s, even with his blisters. He'd dusted them off since the morning. He removed his tie, pocketed it.

The mood in the room was buoyant. He grabbed a glass of fizz from a black-tie waiter. A couple of gallery officials sought him out, welcomed him. One of them, a dark-skinned woman with dyed-blue hair, was a curator of Indigenous Australian collections and acquisitions. She introduced herself as Barbara Jardine – Barb – and explained that the work they were celebrating tonight, a seven-panel set of oil and acrylic paintings documenting climactic and topographical change in the Western Desert over the past two hundred years, had set a record price for an Indigenous purchase. She cited a figure in the multiple millions.

'So,' he said, 'I imagine there's one exceedingly wealthy artist in the room tonight.'

'Unfortunately not,' she said. The artist, an old woman, had died, acclaimed but impoverished, some years ago. 'We got it from a dealer in Alice. Paid poker with him until he couldn't resist the offer. He blinked. We could've gone further. You've no idea how deep some of the patrons around this room will dig for a worthy cause.'

'That's reassuring,' he said.

'Also known as white guilt.' Barb laughed. 'Cheers.' They clinked glasses. Made small talk. He told her, because he had to share the news with someone, about the house he'd just secured for his family.

'Red Hill! Nice. Posh, but not too posh. I grew up there. Went to the local primary. No Blackfellas there any more, though, not since they knocked down all the commission flats and gave the land to the white-shoe brigade.'

She asked him if he'd seen much of the city.

'Only today, really, looking at rentals. Yesterday I went to the war memorial. I expected to loathe it. But not a bad show as it happened.'

'Hmm,' she said coolly.

Grasping for some common terrain, Ben said, 'It was gratifying to see the mention of Black diggers around about. And that beautiful sculpture in the grounds honouring Aboriginal service people.'

'You're right, it's beautiful enough. But it only tells part of the story.'

He wasn't too sure what she meant. But he sensed he was treading on contentious turf. Someone pinged a glass. Time for the official proceedings.

Barb handed him her card, lowered her voice and told him to call soon; she'd take him on a tour of the gallery's extensive Aboriginal and Torres Strait Islander collection. Definitely, he said. For sure.

'But tonight,' she said, 'if you only see one other thing here, make sure it's the burial poles out front. Now, excuse me. I have to go do my bit.'

The room fell silent as a man began playing the didgeridoo. Its guttural, haunting sound evoked something ghostly to Ben. He wondered if it might be that of a wailing spirit traversing a plain of saltbush at dusk or something. He checked himself: perhaps this was too much of a cliché, a white man's narrow imagination inspired by something flowery he'd read, or maybe fertilised by the Australian movies he'd seen years ago. *Walkabout*. *The Chant of Jimmie Blacksmith*. *Jedda*. *Rabbit-Proof Fence*. Regardless, the music was transporting. Unsettling. Ancient. It reminded him of that old fellow with the painted body down at Circular Quay half a lifetime ago.

Next, a very old Aboriginal lady gave a welcome to her country. The director of the gallery acknowledged the Indigenous custodians of the land of Canberra. Then Barb made a short speech. She started with the bushfires and the acrid air outside.

'They are the consequence of global warming and climate change on these shores, that began with land-clearing and uncontrolled, post-invasion burning.' There was gentle applause, mumbles of agreement. Barb thanked the gallery's benefactors. 'Your understanding of the importance of showing the nation the profound impact on Country and Indigenous habitat of geomorphic heating is appreciated,' she said. The artist, she went on, had deserved the celebration in life that she was now being afforded posthumously. 'It's a sadly typical experience in Indigenous Australian art.'

The applause at the end of her speech was deafening.

The director introduced the federal arts minister, a tall, beefy man like a rugby player gone to seed. Slightly florid, wearing a too-tight suit, no tie, but a green and white pocket handkerchief in his breast pocket. He bowed his head before acknowledging the custodians and the old woman who'd welcomed them all to her lands. He paid homage to the curatorial staff and the director for their persistence in acquiring such an important work.

'Art,' he told the room, 'is the key to the door of Australian reconciliation between First Peoples and us permanent visitors. And it is through art, such as this remarkable acquisition we celebrate tonight, that we can begin to see the continent through the eyes of its first custodians, so that we may stroll with them in friendship and become more mindful, more respectful, of their ancient learnings and wisdom. In that is paved the path of true reconciliation.'

The minister continued to bang on about his government's commitment to the arts and Indigenous people as the room grew restless. There was eye-rolling, and murmurs of disquiet and impatience. Tepid, barely polite applause.

People mingled afterwards. Ben took another drink. Number two. It slid down a treat. Together with the persistent jet lag, it made him rather mellow. A little sedated. He was always pretty good socially, confident and at ease, diplomatically proficient at small talk without being cocky. A trick of the trade. But he knew – perhaps because of all the solitude of late, the filthy smoke, that gnawing sense of agitation and ennui he'd had since the disappointments of Sydney – that he risked loquaciousness with another drink. In any event, he had his personal reasons for self-imposed moderation. He was also busting for a smoke and he did want to look at those burial poles Barb had mentioned, which he'd glimpsed from the corner of his eye on the way into the function.

He wandered out to the foyer. The installation, he learned, comprised two hundred traditional hollow-log coffins commemorating the countless tens of thousands of Indigenous people killed in the Australian frontier wars. They were painted with all manner of motifs – birds, fish, crocodiles, yams and flowers, serpents and lizards – in an array of vivid colour.

He was surprised when Barb touched his elbow.

'Quite some speech,' Ben said.

'Mine or the minister's?'

'Well, both, I suppose. For different reasons.'

'Thanks. Interesting word, "reconciliation", don't you think? Politicians love to bandy it about. It means reunifying. But you can't have that without an original conciliation. And that's never happened.'

'Right. Of course.' He'd never really considered that.

'Anyway,' she said, gesturing to the burial poles, 'you won't read that on the sign there, but this is the proper monument to our mob killed defending Country. This is our only true war memorial in this city.'

Barb had to go. They said goodbye and he promised to call her at some point. Ben spent another few minutes admiring the poles before walking the short distance back to his hotel, smoking as he went. Might as well enjoy rotting his lungs since the shitty air would do so anyway, he thought.

His good mood after finding the house had been enhanced by the gallery event. If tonight was any indication, his work would be enlightening, the cultural interface engaging and the society warm. He decided to ignore Sir Gordon's pessimism about fine dining and failing marriages; he was sure they would all settle in here nicely.

Back in his hotel room he called Lucy. She didn't answer.

His new phone pinged.

> Benny can't talk love. At the vet with Nancy – doggy runs & vomit. 🤮 💩 Doubtless something she gobbled on the high street. Speak a little later darling.

Next morning Sir Gordon summoned Ben as soon as he reached the office.

'I imagine you're settling in nicely, Benedict – Ben. And I trust last evening at the gallery was pleasant. Yes. Good.' He didn't wait for an answer, but Ben already knew his boss was a teller, not an asker.

'Alright then, Ben, good-oh. It's not too soon to get down to some work. It's a tad consular in nature, I'm afraid. Seems we may have a little strife to deal with. The stewardess, Ben – the Australian air hostess we spoke about yesterday, dead in Riyadh. Well, the two women questioned by the Saudi police were initially said to be Irish. But in fact, as it happens they are from Northern Ireland. Ulsterwomen. Two Belfast lassies. Catholics. Not much good has ever come out of West Belfast, to my mind.'

Ben felt the heat of anger rise in his cheeks. Tory politicians of Sir Gordon Woodhead's era were, despite Good Friday, despite power-sharing in Ulster, invariably fiercely pro-loyalist. And anti-Catholic.

'But I digress,' the high commissioner went on. 'They've been arrested, it seems. They are British nationals, as you'd now be aware. This is all pre-emptive, mind you, but should this escalate, it would very much help our embassy in Riyadh if they had a full brief on the dead woman. I'll ensure you get the cabling from Saudi and Whitehall on our two. And a contact over there in R.G. Casey, who may be of some assistance. There'll be an intelligence briefing soon. Roderick will help you out with both.'

'Thank you, Sir Gordon.' Ben swallowed his contempt.

'And Ben, I'll be absent for the rest of the week, until Friday when I'll return for your welcome drinks. I'm driving up to the Sydney residence this afternoon with Lady Laura. But always on the phone of course. Let's talk again in a day or two. Ours should be out of custody by then and winging it home to Ulster with any luck. Hopefully it's less than a storm in a teacup.'

'Yes sir. Of course.'

Ben made himself a coffee in the staff kitchen and took it into his darkened office. He'd barely had time to sit behind his desk when there came a knock on the door. Roderick King appeared almost simultaneously without invitation.

'Morning, Ben,' he said, gliding across with an outstretched hand offering him a manila folder.

'Morning, Roderick. Thanks.'

A label on the front said *SIS – Secret: NoForn*. Ben had seen many such files during his postings and varied desk duties. Special Intelligence Service. No Foreign Eyes.

'The Charlene Sloper incident,' King said. 'We don't have much, I'm afraid. Though it seems she was something of the life of the party. Once a model and actress. Quite the looker too, as you might expect of a stewardess. A very good sort indeed, one might say.'

Inside the folder were two documents. One was an article from the *MailOnline* about Sloper's death, which described it simply as a fall. Ben read on for a moment while King, who had stealthily made his way around the desk, looked over his shoulder. The article made no mention of suspects or arrests by the Saudi police, recounting only that Ms Sloper had been on layover after a flight from London Heathrow to Riyadh, and had died on the footpath below the apartment building where she regularly stayed with other expatriates from a range of countries.

A picture of Charlene accompanied the article. It showed her from the waist up, on a recent beach holiday, according to the caption. The photo looked to be Insta-composed. She wore a brief red bikini top over an ample bosom. She was tanned, with her hair in a long blond ponytail that was slung forward over one shoulder. Her broad smile revealed teeth that were clinically straight, chemically whitened. Her eyes were wide, very blue (coloured contacts, perhaps?) and warm. She was undeniably beautiful, but in a vanilla-ish kind of way. She might've made it as a model, Ben supposed, though she lacked a certain X factor. An actor? He doubted it. There was nothing intriguing or mysterious about her. Though she did fit the perfect male stereotype of a female flight attendant.

The second document was a single page, also marked secret. It offered scant details on the two arrested British subjects, beside a small colour headshot of each:

Betty Kilfoyle: dob – 7/01/1980, Belfast, N. Ireland;
resident, Londonderry, N. Ireland. Catholic. Healthcare worker.

Veronica ('Vronnie') Adair: dob – 11/11/1981, Belmullet, N. Ireland; resident, Belfast, N. Ireland. Catholic. Healthcare worker.

Unimpressed with this offering – a single, publicly sourced media report and basic British immigration details – Ben said, 'Yes, I see you're right. Not much to speak of at all.'

King, defensive, bristling, said, 'Well, it is the New Year's break. The Foreign Office is on skeleton staff. As you know. Though I expect we'll have more information presently.'

'Thank you, Roderick. Meanwhile, we might as well wish Betty Kilfoyle all happy returns.'

'I'm sorry?'

'It's her birthday. She turns forty today – see?' Ben indicated on the document.

'Quite,' King said. 'I'm sure they'll be bringing her a cake at sharia plod HQ in downtown Riyadh. The strife and mischief some of ours get up to when travelling, I don't know.' He tut-tutted censoriously.

'But we don't remotely know what's happened here yet, do we?'

'We can surmise. Airline stewards. Hostesses. And nurses. We all know what they get up to, don't we?'

'Do we?'

'Come on, Ben – you're a man of the world.'

'Look, regarding Ms Sloper's death, I'll reserve judgement for now.'

'Indeed. How thoroughly professional of you, Ben!'

'You are right about one thing though, Roderick. Ms Sloper does appear to be a very good sort.'

Ben was trying to build rapport with this cold, punctilious man, who he'd have to work alongside – or under – for the next few years.

'Was, Ben. Was a good sort. I imagine they're still washing her off the pavement. Ten storeys! Good heavens above. Now,' he went on, 'I believe Sir Gordon has advised you to make contact over at DFAT. The Aussie department is invariably so very helpful. Always managing up. I'll give you an email introduction to the fellow we deal with over there. Barry McKenzie.'

'Really – he's called Barry McKenzie?' Every English person had seen that film.

'Well, actually, no, his name is Craig. But we call him Barry. Our little joke – a nod to the film.'

'Um, sure. Okay then. Please let me know when you have any more details about Ms Adair and Ms Kilfoyle. I imagine consular in Riyadh are in contact with them?'

'You'll know the very moment I do.'

Ben looked again at the small photos of the two Ulsterwomen. They were chalk and cheese compared with Charlene Sloper. He decided they were resilient types. Hard women.

Kilfoyle had wiry, reddish-brown hair that stood straight up from her skull like a Cossack's fur hat. She was thin-lipped, fair-skinned and freckled, hazel-eyed. Adair's head was tilted slightly to one side. A corner of her mouth was curled into the beginning of a forced smile. She had a protruding top lip. Waves of dark, thick hair. Raven eyes.

But what could a photograph really impart about a person?

Ben emailed Craig McKenzie. It was the first email he'd sent from his high commission computer. His pre-programmed email signature made clear, like his new business cards, that he was working on unceded Aboriginal land.

Almost immediately came a response: *Sure mate. Wander on over in an hour or two. Gonna have lunch down the trough. Wanna join?*

Ben: *Sounds irresistible.*

McKenzie sent his mobile number, told Ben to text when he arrived.

A slight breeze had shifted some of the smoke. It was still hellishly hot. Ben's blistered feet, while better than yesterday, still hurt to walk. His eyes, nose and throat itched. It was just after midday and he was starving. He had missed breakfast again because he'd lost track of time running on the treadmill in the hotel gym. He smoked as he walked to the R.G. Casey Building and texted McKenzie when he got there.

Down in five.

'Benedict.'

He turned around. McKenzie was walking towards him with his hand extended.

'I knew it must be you. Only a bloody Englishman would wear a suit jacket and tie on a day like this.' They shook hands.

'I'm ravenous, mate. Let's go eat. Inside with the air-con, eh.'

McKenzie signed Ben into the building. In the cafeteria they lined up with others, pushed their trays along to the service staff, and took their meals to a corner table by a window. Outside, magpies sought shade under heat-stressed eucalypts, beaks open. They looked to be panting and in urgent need of water.

They chatted informally while they ate. McKenzie was friendly and open, a surfer from Sydney's northern beaches.

Landlocked now in the capital. At first he hated the joint, he told Ben. It had no centre, just isolated suburbs seemingly devoid of people. He'd been lonely. But he'd been back and forth now after two postings and had grown to love the place. The bush. Great lifestyle. Two hours from the coast and the snow. Smart, educated population. Outward-looking. International. Usually great weather – not this filthy shit. Hot and dry in summer, cool and clear in winter. Huge houses, cheap as chips compared to Sydney.

'Give it some time, mate. Let's have a drink one arvo, eh? I'll introduce you round.'

They moved on to Charlene Sloper. What did McKenzie know?

'Waiting on a post-mortem. But a horrible mess, poor girl. Got the pics from the Saudi cops upstairs. Send 'em to you if you want. Not something you want to see while you're eating, though,' McKenzie said, shovelling in a forkful of chicken schnitzel. 'The Saudis think it's open and shut. They reckon she was pushed by your two ladies. But who really knows? There was a stack of booze in the apartment. Evidence of coke, other drugs. Rooting of course. There'd been some sort of party. I mean, hosties and nurses together, right?'

Ben shrugged and said, 'I'm waiting on a read from our own consular people. Last I heard they hadn't seen our two yet.'

'I'll tell you this for free,' McKenzie said, 'maybe prepare for the worst. The Saudis are telling us they're likely to charge them. But that doesn't mean they've got any proof that would stand up in a court here. You know, they pride themselves on the safety of their country. And if those ladies are charged and convicted by the judge then they'll be subject to sharia punishment. Death by stoning or beheading. Likely in public, too. Swift and summary so-called justice, convincing evidence or not.'

'What can you tell me about Ms Sloper?'

'Only that she's from a place out back of butt-fuck west called The Leap. Think three-fifths of the way to the middle of fucking nowhere. Pioneering grazing family. Once hallowed farming country gone to shit. Rabbit plagues and feral pigs. Never-ending drought. Full of Flat Earth Party-voting, climate change-denying, wife-battering, God-bothering, gun-nut, ground-zero, racist, fundamentalist fuckers. Pardon my French. Apart from that it's a terrific place. She did well to get out of there. Ran a mile as soon as she finished school, apparently. Started modelling. Swimsuits. That sort of thing.'

'What about the acting thing?'

'Had a few small parts in soaps. This is in her twenties. Gave up on the dream and became a hostie. With the flying kangaroo first, then a few other airlines. Finally Airabia. But not full-time. Still, she somehow managed to live between London and Dubai. And she'd this crash-pad in Riyadh when she did that route.'

'Not full-time?'

'No. And naturally I wondered what else she did for a crust, so I did some digging.'

'Yeah? And what'd you find?'

'I believe the polite term is glamour modelling.'

'Oh, like Page Three Girl stuff?'

'Bit more than that. There are websites that specialise in this sort of thing. Pay per view. People pay to view pics and vids of people getting their gear off. And doing all sorts of stuff. Our Ms Sloper had started doing that. She was doing okay by all accounts too. Well subscribed. But nothing too lurid. Certainly nothing that'd make you jump out a window with shame. Or inspire someone to chuck you out.'

Ben said, 'It's a bit sad and desperate, isn't it. The beautiful girl with all that promise, reduced to doing that. And then to end up dead on the street.'

'Don't get me wrong,' said McKenzie, 'I'm not being judgy, mate. People can do whatever they like. I'm not perfect. Who is?'

'Not at all. And her choices don't make her a criminal. Her poor bloody family having to deal with all this, though. They must be beside themselves.'

'Yeah. We're in contact with the family. Father's the contact point. Cecil Sloper. A farmer. Signs are he might be a somewhat thorny customer. But, you know – grief and everything. Oh, and there's a brother, Kenneth. The mother's long dead.'

Back at his desk after lunch, Ben began adding to the file on Charlene Sloper. McKenzie sent him the photos of the death scene, which was just as he'd described it to Ben, a horrible, distressing mess. The woman was unrecognisable.

The landline rang. It was King telling him to turn on his television.

'The story is taking off, Ben. Dead girl's father is about to be interviewed. I'll be round to yours presently.'

Cecil Sloper came onto the screen, standing in front of a barn with an obsolete horse-drawn harvester. He was a beefy man of perhaps seventy, in canvas overalls and a flannelette shirt. Beside him stood a middle-aged man dressed almost identically, who Ben took to be his son. Kenneth was even taller than the old man; neither possessed Charlene's arresting good looks. The rim of Cecil's battered hat shaded his eyes, so that his face was only clear from the bridge of his nose down. Even on the screen he had a beetroot complexion that looked hypertension-induced.

A reporter stood a few metres in front of Sloper and his son, killing time with inanities about the story. He called the countryside where he stood 'bucolic'. Cecil Sloper, he said, was 'a foundational pillar of the community – a pioneering scion'. The dead woman Charlene – *Charlie* – was one of the district's 'most cherished daughters'.

King walked into the office just as the TV image shifted from the reporter onto a man in an ill-fitting seersucker suit walking out of the barn. He was very skinny, almost cadaverous, all bony features and limbs, and he limped badly, dragging his left leg. His trousers were hoisted well above where his waist would have been if he'd had one, and he wore a trilby over unnaturally boot-polish-black hair.

Ben winced. 'Looks like the undertaker of Swindon,' he said.

King surprised him by guffawing. Ben had thought him incapable. 'Or the pox doctor's assistant from Slough,' King said, and they laughed together.

The reporter eased back into camera range and said hurriedly, 'I believe this is the lawyer representing the family of the dead woman.'

The undertaker of Swindon or the pox doctor's assistant from Slough, introduced himself as, 'Mr Howard Worcestershire – pronounced Wooster, please, LLB, solicitor at law and representative of the Sloper family in matters legal and financial.'

Worcestershire continued, 'Mr Cecil Sloper wishes to make a short statement about the untimely death of his precious and much-loved daughter, Charlene. He and his son, Kenneth, will not be taking questions. Henceforth, I'd ask you to respect their privacy as they most distressingly grieve their daughter and sister, and direct all further inquiries through me.'

The father spoke calmly, in a slow, nasally drawl perhaps an octave too high for a man so physically imposing.

'Three days ago me and my boy Kenneth discovered that the light of our life had been doused, snuffed out in a wanton act of violence. Our light, our hope, our love – Charlene – was viciously thrown from the window of her apartment. There is no doubt that she was murdered and that the two women under arrest in Saudia Arabia are responsible for her death. No doubt. They will be charged and punished accordingly. Here in this country we also respect God's way and his administration of justice. We look forward to the day when our Charlene's death is avenged, and we will respect that process. Thank you.'

Christ, thought Ben. McKenzie hadn't been exaggerating about Cecil Sloper.

King said, 'A damn fine thing these Slopers believe in procedural justice for our two nationals. The stupid man has already convicted them. The Saudis will be watching closely everything the family says, of course, when it comes to the so-called trial of these women.'

'I'm waiting for something from the embassy in Riyadh,' Ben said. 'They were supposed to be meeting with the Saudi cops this afternoon. Hoping also to see Ms Adair and Ms Kilfoyle. They're going to push for them to be placed under house arrest – get them out of the cells at least, until the trial.'

'Good-oh. Yes, Ben. They are keeping me in the loop, too, of course. The high commissioner also wants to be kept in touch at every step. We'll brief him tomorrow.'

'Sure.'

'This, I safely predict, is going to become something of a spectacle. A dance. A game. Diplomatically speaking, I mean. A game in which the losers stand to get beheaded.'

'Or stoned to death.'

'Quite. Barbarians that they are.'

By the end of that week, Ben's mood had sunk once again. The media interest in Charlene Sloper's death had intensified, both in Australia and back home, and he was starting to feel an irrational, creeping responsibility for the two Ulsterwomen. This on top of his residual, hard-to-shake jet lag and unaccustomed aloneness had sapped him of energy and drive.

Too much about the Charlene Sloper case, and the high commission's heavy engagement in its management, was tripping all sorts of anxieties in him. If he was at home he'd busy himself with domestic and family life. But right now the contorted sense of guilt that was starting to possess him was only made worse by all this alone time. It had barely been a week. But he longed for the comforting ballast of family.

He found himself wide awake at 3 am most mornings, plagued with unspecific terrors and thoughts of worthlessness and, worse, culpability, that he'd battled intermittently since Thailand. Compounded tenfold by Cambodia. By four most afternoons he was nodding off at his desk. Caffeine helped.

Ben was out of the building by six most evenings. Nobody at the high commission tended to work very long hours, perhaps following the example of Sir Gordon. Ben had got into a pattern of walking the short distance to the hotel. Before heading up to his room, he'd park himself on the big patio overlooking the burr-filled, sun-yellowed field and the R.G. Casey building, and have a beer or two. He was still smoking, quite heavily now for a reformed social smoker. The bushfire fumes had partly dissipated. The city was no longer blanketed in thick smog, and smoke from the distant fires now hung higher in the atmosphere, thinner and wispier. But there'd still been no rain. It was dry as chips.

He hadn't managed to talk to Lucy about the house until late on Wednesday evening, and he'd been determined to keep things light and optimistic, to shroud his neediness. He said he wondered if it would have been best had he waited in London for a couple more weeks so they could all travel together to Australia. He said perhaps he'd been too hasty, because they could've all stayed in a serviced apartment for a few weeks when they arrived in Canberra, while the kids started school, and then taken their time to find the right permanent place.

He meant it. He longed to be back there with them.

'Don't be silly, Benny. It's all fine. We'll all be there soon enough and it'll be good,' Lucy said in the practical, reassuring tone he knew well and relied upon.

She laughed, then, saying there'd been a bill for six hundred quid to have Nancy's stomach pumped. 'The vet thought she might've eaten a rat bait – or maybe the whole rat. The kids were hysterical. We all thought she was going to die. God help us if something happens to that dog, Ben. Just hope she'll be fine next week when I've got to put her into quarantine.'

When he asked what she thought of the Red Hill house she sounded vague. 'Oh, um, it looks nice. It's perhaps a little austere with all that glass and concrete. A bit exposed, maybe? I think I was rather imagining a quaint renovated terrace, like all those lovely rows in Sydney. This one looks, I don't know, untethered.' He knew she was kidding. But only just. She added, 'It's not your fault, love. Things always look different on the web. I'm sure it'll work just fine.'

Canberra wasn't anything like Sydney, he told her. Then: 'You okay, Luce? I'm hearing that you're stressed out. I get it. You're dealing with a lot of shit.'

'Literally – with Nancy!'

They both laughed and she continued, 'Benny – yeah, I'm fine. It's just a lot, you know. I don't want to complain but the kids are antsy. Suze is flat-out saying she just doesn't want to come. She'd prefer to board back here in London. Amy and Jerome are worried about the fires. They can see on TV that the whole country is basically burning. It's a bit frightening for them.'

God, he thought, the bloody British media and Australian bushfires. Bushfires and bloody crocodile and shark attacks! And serial killers who murdered Brits, of course. They never seemed to care about much else that happened in Australia. Ben didn't want to argue with her. The fires did look horrendous on TV. And it was true that many had died and lost their homes. But Canberra was safe. The smoke would clear. He thought it best to end the call lest it exacerbate any further dormant tensions that couldn't be solved from a different hemisphere.

'I hear you, Lucy. It looks scarier than it is. But it will clear, darling. It's even clearing as we speak. And you know this always happens before a posting. It's incredibly stressful. Just remember – Australia. The light. The space. Remember? Bondi . . . the ocean.'

'That was all a long time ago, Ben. But it's still fixed in my mind, love. It's still precious to me.'

They said they loved each other and ended the call.

Ben went onto his balcony and smoked a cigarette. Donkey-lit a second. He was disappointed, more with himself than with Lucy's comments about the house. He wanted her to think the place was more than just fine. He felt he'd let her and the kids down. He'd been elated when he'd found that house and the lease was signed. Now he felt uncertain. Like it might be a terrible mistake.

The following evening, he was back sitting on the hotel patio, reading a book about his new city. 'An accidental miracle', the writer called the planned capital. Chicago architect Walter Burley Griffin and his wife Marion had pushed on with their elaborate, beautiful, dreamlike design for the capital of a new nation of 'bold democrats', when the contemptuous local planners tried to scuttle it in favour of a more prosaic model. The locals won in the end, forcing the Americans out, so that only the geometric whispers of the fairytale city they had drawn were ever built.

Only one more day and it would be the weekend. Just two more nights now in the hotel. On Saturday morning he would have the keys to the house. By now his mood had swung again and he couldn't wait to move out of the hotel, to set himself up with a decent bed, a sofa and some rudimentary kitchen stuff. He'd be in there Saturday evening. He was desperate for a feeling of homeliness. He wanted to re-moor. Cook himself a meal. And then finish setting the place up for his family.

His phone pinged with an SMS. Sir Gordon.

May we speak, Ben?

Of course sir.

The high commissioner called immediately.

'Ben, I've just had word confirming that the Saudis have now charged both of our nationals with the murder of Ms Sloper. Our people in Riyadh are yet to meet with Adair and Kilfoyle, but they've been promised a consular check in due course. The police are going to parade them before the local and international media tonight our time.'

Ben wondered why he wasn't being kept more tightly in the loop of such communication. Sir Gordon was quite clearly micro-managing the Australian side of things. He felt the anger rising in him.

Swallowing his annoyance, he said, 'As anticipated, I guess, Sir Gordon.'

'Yes. Our ambassador in Riyadh couldn't get near the police, but he managed a briefing of sorts from the Saudi foreign office. The autopsy on Ms Sloper revealed a very high level of blood alcohol. Also the presence of OxyContin and GHB.'

'I see. Medical painkillers that are also used as party drugs.'

'Not the sort of thing you and I go in for,' Sir Gordon said. 'But, you know, if you're in a partying type of set, foreign nationals getting together behind closed doors in a country with sharia law, it's the sort of thing one might indulge in. Consular says there'd been a party at the apartment earlier in the evening that Ms Sloper died. Both Saudis and foreign nationals present, including Kilfoyle and Adair.'

Ben was familiar, from a distance at least, with that sort of expatriate partying. Emissaries from many Western countries, not least in Saudi Arabia's diplomatic compounds, were notorious for the type of what-goes-on-tour-stays-on-tour drinking and drug-taking, and the *rooting* McKenzie had referenced. Booze and drugs routinely came in through the diplomatic bags, in such great quantities at times that foreign missions had illicitly supplied the wealthy Saudi elites willing to break sharia law with a fine bourbon or Barossa red. One fabled Australian diplomat, it was said, had set himself up for life after the foreign service with real estate investments afforded through the illegal sale of booze he'd imported to Saudi Arabia under diplomatic cover.

Sir Gordon said that the police report and the post-mortem were at best inconclusive. Someone might have actually seen Ms Sloper pushed out of the window. Or not. She may have jumped. Or she may simply have fallen. There were, however, some signs consistent with strangulation.

'Although – who knows what other asphyxia-related activity might've caused that?' Sir Gordon said, chortling. Ben could envisage him raising one orangutan eyebrow and tapping his nose knowingly as he spoke. 'Ms Charlene Sloper was no angel.'

'Then it seems we really can't rely on the integrity of the police work or their post-mortem.'

'Too true. Their police, the judge, their government will want a quick clearance, no matter what. Though on the post-mortem, Ben, I must concede that the Saudis have proven rather adept at cutting people up recently.'

His excellency chuckled some more at himself. It took Ben a moment to recognise the attempt at black humour – a reference to the murder, dissection and disposal of the body of a journalist in Istanbul's Saudi embassy a few months back.

Ben feigned laughter. 'Quite, Sir Gordon,' he said.

'There is something else, apparently. So the Saudis claim.'

'Sir?'

'They insist that one of the Ulsterwomen – Ms Adair, I believe – had Ms Sloper's ATM card on her when arrested. Both women had been recorded on CCTV making multiple withdrawals after Ms Sloper's death. Using her card.'

'That is grim news, sir. Though it doesn't mean they killed her of course.'

'Well, if it's true. But again, who can really know? Regardless, what we do know is that the judicial process, such as it is, will move swiftly. Under sharia law, murder is a *qesas* crime. It is routinely punished by retribution. If you take a human life, yours will be taken by the state. But there is a strange conditionality to it. The judges will sometimes urge the victim's family to accept *diyyeh*, a payment of money in order to spare the life of the accused. Blood money. A number of foreign nationals accused of capital offences in Saudi have been spared and even freed upon payment of *diyyeh*.'

Ben was wondering what all this was leading to when Sir Gordon said, 'The foreign secretary just called me. He wants us to act pre-emptively. He wants us to explain to Ms Sloper's family the benefits of behaving compassionately towards these two women.'

'Ah, so you want me to accompany you to see Mr Sloper?'

'No, Ben, Lady Laura and I've much to do in Sydney. Mr King and the support staff will make the necessary arrangements for you to leave tomorrow.'

This Ben received as a vicious stomach punch. He flinched as he felt the air suddenly stall in his lungs. An icy wave of paralysis bear-hugged him. He struggled for breath. Began to sweat. These panic attack symptoms were too familiar. But he felt powerless now to fight them. I need to move into the new house, he thought. Get ready for Lucy and the kids. I can't possibly travel now. And these women – why are they suddenly my responsibility?

'And Ben,' added the high commissioner, 'the welcome drinks we'd planned for you tomorrow evening – we'll reschedule them for when things settle down. Once you get on top of this little drama.'

Ben remained sitting on the patio, book in his lap, seething at Sir Gordon for putting him in this position. The Tory prick! Fuck him. I've been here barely a week, feet hardly under the desk, and the silly old twat throws this at me. He should be taking responsibility, rather than micromanaging and then suddenly peeling off when it gets too hard and sitting on his fat arse by the harbour. So much for not much consular work in the new gig.

Meanwhile, an inner voice was whispering to him that he couldn't be relied on, that he would inevitably fail at this quest too. He had an urgent need to talk to Lucy, but she would be at work. Calling her there was unfair. In any case, she'd enough on her plate right now.

He struggled to rechannel his negative thoughts. But he couldn't help looping back to his last call to her. Was there something wrong in Putney? Apart from the ordeal of packing up and leaving? And Lucy's underlying weariness about the stop-start nature of her life as a trailing diplomatic spouse while wrangling her own career? She tried not to let it show too much. But she really did mind. He knew that. And the more she tried not to show it, the heavier his guilt, and the feeling that he was an inconvenience, a source of pain – a burden and a let-down.

He went up to his room and ordered a burger with chips and a bottle of white wine from room service. Usually a stickler for fitness and diet, he was suddenly conscious of his inertia, the crappy food, ciggies and booze. The new, uncomfortable snugness of the belt around his waist.

He turned on the ABC. Just in time for the 'Majestic Fanfare' before the news bulletin. Charlene Sloper was the lead story.

'The family of an Australian flight attendant who was allegedly murdered after an illicit drug- and alcohol-fuelled party in Saudi Arabia insist that the two British women charged with her murder and robbery must face the full brunt of the local sharia law.' The story cut to vision of Cecil Sloper, again standing in front of the ancient harvester in his barn with his son and his lawyer. This time he wasn't wearing a hat, and Ben saw that his eyes were narrow, an almost-albino pale blue. His comb-over was flapping like some hirsute flag in the bluster.

The camera panned away for a moment to a whirly-whirly of dust and grass seed, and the wrecks of an old Bedford van and EH Holden, grown through with weeds. They had been abandoned alongside a decrepit manual plough, as ancient as the harvester, its wooden handles weathered away.

Then Cecil Sloper was talking to the camera with the deranged zeal of a hate-filled street preacher. 'Have no pity,' he said, 'let life be given for life, an eye for an eye, tooth for tooth, hand for hand, foot for foot. Deuteronomy 19:21.'

Oh holy fuck, Ben said to himself. He poured more wine.

His phone rang. Sir Gordon again. Ben took a deep breath to steel himself.

'I take it you've caught up with the latest from Mr Sloper?'

'I'm watching now.'

'Good-oh. I think we've got our work cut out, Ben. Do let me know how you get on when it comes to securing a meeting with him.'

'Yes sir. Though I've no idea how I'm to inveigle my way into his life.'

'Softly, softly, Ben. I'd suggest you try the lawyer. He looks like he might be easily flattered. Or cajoled. Or tempted. Spend some time with him. Have a drink with him, Ben, the man evidently likes a drink.'

He wasn't sure what to say to that.

'Go well, Ben,' Sir Gordon added. 'And do take good care.'

Part II

Ben waits to take off in one of the smallest commercial planes he's ever been in, a twin-engine, open cockpit with eight seats either side of the aisle. He is the only passenger and sits in the front right seat. From there he can see the instruments as the pilot goes through the pre-flight checks and fills in the requisite paperwork. A left-hander, the pilot uses a pen that Ben recalls the savant kids at school favouring, a Bic disposable ballpoint with four different inks – blue, black, red, green – and a separate button for each. He smiles, recalling how the kids at school called them 'nerd pens'.

The plane taxis. The aircraft is new and the pilot old, which hopefully means experienced. Still, Ben is on edge as they climb up through sheets of gossamer smoke and dust, bumping and jiggling on the turbulence created by updrafts. Below, the plains of the capital surrounding all those imported trees are a sun-burnished yellow and tan, punctuated by the shimmering black lake and the city's curious geometry. The weird hexagons and roundabouts. Now he can see what he's been reading about: the ghostly visage of the Griffins' only partially realised plan, scuttled by an Anglophile conservatism fused with antipodean, postcolonial bureaucratic complacency. They had poisoned forever the Griffins' memory of Australia; it was a little-England haven for philistinism. It was a similar story, Ben is aware, when the Danish architect of the Sydney Opera House fled Australia, dispirited and never to return, his aesthetic vision crushed by those same mediocre elements.

The plane follows the main highway, the Hume, towards Sydney for a few minutes then banks and turns sharply inland. Small towns eventually give way to a vast scorched landscape, little patchwork squares in various hues of tan, hazel, charcoal and coffee. The sandy remnants of waterways, now dry, snake their way over the land. Empty dams, crows' eyes in the desolation, stare upwards. All of this he views through a thin mantilla of smoke and dust.

Inevitably his thoughts slide to Lucy and the kids. Maybe it would be best after all if Suze did stay in England and boarded to finish school. What sixteen-year-old wants to move so far away from their friends? The others would surely settle into the Red Hill house once they discovered its elegance and charm. The dog would love it. That huge yard. Lucy and the kids would cope with their terror of snakes. Ben is at once fuming and sad that he isn't using the weekend, as planned, to set it up for them.

The pilot touches down briefly in a town with a shallow brown river trickling through it. He is on the tarmac long enough to off-load some cartons and several stacks of newspapers. Back in the plane, he hands Ben two bottles of water and a packet of pretzels. Ben necks one of the waters, trousers the pretzels. The pilot takes out his nerd pen once more to jot something down. Clicks it.

His Thai driver, Sonny, steers the car gingerly through the chaos. Trees snapped in half like toothpicks. Building material in piles – planks and roof tiles and broken sheets of plaster. House contents – computers, sodden books. Then boats of all sizes. Jet skis. Splintered and buckled by a terrifying force, they have all married to form huge piles of rubbish along the side of what's left of the road, after the bulldozers came through to clear. Every few metres a blackened and swollen hand or a leg, or somebody's head, is visible in the rubble.

Dogs snuffle through this bedlam. Now and then a gunshot; cops and soldiers shooting the now ownerless, marauding dogs and injured, distressed farm animals. No cats. They've all managed to flee the wave.

The air-conditioning in the Range Rover is pumping, not only because it's sweltering out there, with humidity pushing 98 per cent, but because the cold blast of air, along with the smear of mentholated jelly on their top lips, counters the rank aroma of decaying human flesh.

Then they are outside the car. Wearing industrial masks as they tread around the detritus of the surge: prams, bicycles, toys, clothing, shoes, splintered palm trees, pool furniture, umbrellas, cars, motor scooters. Flip-flops, hundreds of them, a disarmingly pretty confetti in pink, yellow, red, blue, white, green. A rubber bouquet for the carnage.

Ben and Sonny are here for the guesthouse where a tour group from Scotland and Wales was staying. The concrete walls and ornately tiled peaked roof are oddly intact, even the gargoyle dragons at each end. Few places have kept their roofs. Perhaps the wave didn't surge to that height so far inland. This gives Ben some hope for the possibility of survivors. It diminishes when he sees three or four of the dead floating face down in the fetid swimming pool.

Inside, they both retch at the stench. Even through the masks. The building is a cavern. Every floor and room and everything in it has been sucked out of the place by the force of the retreating surge. That stench – there must be bodies in here.

But Ben sees none as he walks about, hand over his mask, fighting the impulse to gag. Maybe they escaped, he thinks. But why such a stench?

And then comes the *click, clack*.

He jolts upright, his heart going crazy, and for a split second he has the terrifying sensation that he's free-falling from the sky. But the tiny plane is descending over the parched Central West Downs, towards The Leap.

'Won't be long now,' the pilot calls back to him. 'More's the pity.'

The engine pitch lowers as the plane noses into a gradual descent. They fly over a moonscape of bone-coloured rock that soon gives way to a lake of salt, as vast as it is white, and smooth as vanilla cake frosting. The banks of the lake gradually transition into pink and then red earth punctuated with patches of greenery. Suddenly the crimson finishes and it is all grey rock formations – dramatic cliffs and escarpments, with trees and shrubs and grasses reaching out of the crevices. There are darkened crevices creasing the cliffs. They'd be waterfalls if ever it should rain again. At the base of the cliffs is the beginnings of a waterway which he knows, courtesy of the map he looked at online the night before, is the Babylon River, named by the Bible-fearing first white settlers in the early 1800s. But the Babylon in drought is reduced to a wide meandering creek. The slowly descending plane traces the river. He can see the broad, muddy banks and the gnarly trees – river red gums? – that cling to higher ground. Out to his right are three windmills, grey blades stationary in the shimmering heat haze. There's a small cluster of buildings – a large metal barn, a hay shed, and what looks to be old stables circling a grander white farmhouse. A small airstrip. Miles of white wooden fences. Sheep jostle about the troughs under shade trees.

The plane banks sharply left then angles into a wide turn to the right, giving a view of the town and a glimpse of tarmac at the aerodrome a couple of kilometres beyond. The Leap, he sees, is pretty much a blink-and-you'll-miss-it place. Bigger than a village but not really qualifying as a town, by English standards.

On the inland side, away from the river, scrub and stone country extend to the horizon, and in the middle of the scrub is a large patch of green, conspicuously verdant, hemmed by low white pickets. At one end there's a scoreboard and Victorian grandstand, corrugated roof stained with rust. And in the middle of this lush green disc is the sandy strip of the cricket pitch.

From the air at least, the place looks civilised enough. Not at all in keeping with his envisioned ramshackle outback hamlet of dirt roads, humpies and tin shed houses. Decades back, he and Lucy had 'gone outback' on a guided camping trip from Alice Springs. He remembers well the landscape and vegetation, the spartan buildings on the huge pastoral properties, and the more hand-to-mouth, two-person settlements. This looks quite different.

The pilot lands uneventfully, stops next to the terminal – more a hangar with glass windows – and cuts the engine. A man in hi-vis wheels the stairs to the plane's door. He unlatches a hatch on the undercarriage and retrieves Ben's suitcase.

Outside, the air is still and bone-dry, the sort of air you don't sweat in while you're moving. Only when you stop still. The light is an eerie off-yellow, a combination of smoke and dust; the noonday sun is a weak, burnished, moonlike orb, though its heat feels no less intense for that.

Ben's boots no longer rub quite so badly as he crosses the tarmac with the pilot. His daily walks to and from the high commission have almost worn them in. This persistence, until the burst blisters hardened and began to crust into scar tissue, felt something like a penance. For what? The anxiety he was causing his family, perhaps. Or that flickering internal sense of worthlessness, the angry urge to prove himself otherwise that has plagued him since Thailand and Cambodia? Or just plain old residual Catholic guilt? He had that in spades, of course. Couldn't shake it. The old parish priest of his childhood, Father Clutcher, would've said to 'offer it up to Jesus, my son, offer it all up to Jesus'. The message was reinforced in the confessional in his senior years at his private Catholic school, when weekly confession was still mandatory: 'All pain has a reason, son. The Lord does not make us suffer needlessly.'

'Welcome to The Leap,' says the pilot. 'Better you than me, mate.'

'What do you mean?'

'Oh, just a bit of a strange place. Your Leapers tend to do things in their own unique way. Pray a lot. Drink a lot. Fight a lot. Keep to themselves.'

'You're not staying over then, I gather?'

'No fear. I avoid hanging around whenever possible.'

Inside the terminal the pilot indicates a small door marked 'Private'.

'I'm in there for a cuppa and a snooze, mate. Then I'm refuelling and heading to Adelaide. Good luck, eh,' he says.

They shake hands.

The car rental desk is closed. A sign says to call a landline phone number 'in case of desk in-attendance'. Ben turns his phone on. No signal. He takes note of the number and looks around for a public telephone. There are two rows of empty, well-worn, red vinyl seats, vending machines for Coke and snacks, and yes, in the corner, a blue payphone. He goes over. A note is taped to the keypad: *Out of Order.*

Damn!

He goes out to the front of the terminal. He's the only person about. He can't see a taxi rank or a bus stop. In front of him is an expansive rise of red earth dotted with spinifex and ghost gums. In the middle are what look to be the bleached bones, complete with horns, of a cow or a bull, the symmetrical arcs of its rib cage resonant of the frame of a Norse longship he'd seen as a child in some British museum or other.

The silence is enveloping. No breeze to whistle through the outstretched arms of the ghost gums or rustle the inert spinifex. No vehicles. No animals. Any sensible living creature, except him, would surely be seeking refuge from the midday sun.

Ben lights a cigarette, sucks in the smoke. He drinks a mouthful from the bottle the pilot gave him. Now he's sweating profusely, as he looks this way and that, wondering what to do, feeling slightly disabled by indecision and enervation.

A crow breaks the silence, its cawing like that of murder reverberating. Once. Twice. Ben shudders.

He's considering going back into the terminal to ask for the pilot's help when a spiral of dust begins to coil skywards from the unmade road where it breaches the hill. A car – recognisably white beneath the veneer of red dust – meanders down towards him. It turns onto the aerodrome access road and stops in front of him.

The passenger side window opens. A voice from within, its owner hidden in shadow, says, 'Right there, mate?'

'Not sure, to be honest. I'm just wondering how far it is to town. I can't seem to find a taxi.'

The driver laughs dismissively. 'There's only one actual taxi in town, mate. That's Raoul Moir's people mover. Raoul's Maxi Taxis. But he's off the road at the moment. Hit a pig when he took a fare from the pub the other night. Didn't help that he was pissed as a fart. Still, not all his fault – pigs are a big bloody menace, and a fair bit of sport, round here. I'll tell yer that for nothin'.'

'No worries. So do you mind telling me – how far into town?'

'Only 'bout six kays.'

'Right . . . I should get walking then, I suppose.'

'Don't be bloody silly. Whitefella like you'll be shrivelled on the vine inside two kays. I'll drive you. Chuck yer shit in the back.'

The back seat has a roll of fencing wire and a sledgehammer on it. Ben puts his suitcase on top as the driver gets out and comes round to the passenger side.

Extending a hand he says, 'Nelson Tyson. Pleased to meet you.'

'Ben Gaskill. And I appreciate this.' He takes a last draw on his cigarette and stubs out the remainder.

Nelson wears faded blue jeans, stained with splotches of oil and dust and frayed at the cuffs, along with a sleeveless blue and black flannelette shirt. Green thongs.

Nelson pushes his hat back from his forehead. 'Tell you what, I'd kill for a smoke.'

'No worries. In fact, here – have the pack. I'm giving up.'

'You sure?'

'Yeah,' says Ben. 'Take them.'

'No shit, that's generous. Ciggies are like forty bucks a pack these days, I mostly only bludge, really.'

'My pleasure.' Ben lights the cigarette for him and hands Nelson the lighter. 'Have this too. I won't need it.'

Nelson takes a drag and smiles warmly at Ben as the smoke curls from the corner of his mouth. 'Thanks again, though honestly I'm not sure The Leap is the kind of place I'd wanna be trying to quit the fags cold-turkey.'

'I don't doubt you're right. Nelson, you say? After the lord of the British admiralty?' Ben realises it's a lame joke as soon as it's out of his mouth, but Nelson laughs anyway.

'Not likely I'd be named after any lord, mate. Mum named me after Mandela.'

'Ah. Apologies.'

'No sweat. Hope you don't mind me saying, but you sound like you're not from anywhere round here. I'm guessing Adelaide. You've got that kind of Adelaide thing going on. *Cadence*. That's it, kinda fancy. Bit camp, maybe, you know? I mean, no offence – I'm not homophobic or anything. A few of my mates are gay. I'll tell you, though, The Leap is maybe as tough a place for a gay person as it is for a Blackfella. Or a lot of women. That's for sure.'

He gives Ben a harder looking-over. 'Or maybe you're from Melbourne, at a pinch. Definitely went to a posh school, judging by your voice, I'd say.'

Ben laughs. He likes the way the fellow speaks his mind. He's candid without being at all rude. 'Actually, I'm from London.'

'That's even further away. Had an Englander live here in The Leap for a bit, few years back. A sort of writer type. Bit of a sad, solemn bloke, really. Nigel. Nigel from Norwich. Sometimes Norwich Nigel. Or just Nor-Nigel. People eventually just called him Norwich. From a posh university in England. Anyway, it didn't go so well for him here. Moved into a little shack out there, just east of The Babylon. To be alone, he reckoned. Just him and his creative thoughts. To write. Tried to grow some vegies. Pigs ate 'em. Went a bit freakin mad with it all, you know. Sort of hit the piss even harder and drank himself to death when his book didn't end up going so right. Poor bastard.'

'Bloody hell.' This instantly evokes for Ben a forlorn image of some effete and dishevelled and semi-infirm and dissolute over-educated young Englishman, a hybrid of Lord Sebastian Flyte and Bruce Chatwin, say, having fled from family censoriousness so as to discover his writerly self through an outback pilgrimage, only to be driven insane by the blowflies and the stifling silence and the breezeless heat and the crushing solitariness and the dust and his unwritable story, his one recourse an ultimately fatal waltz with the gin bottle.

That shan't be me, he thinks. I'll be out of here way too soon for that.

'Yeah, I drove him in from the plane that first day he come in here, too. Nice fella. Never saw him too much after that. Picked him up and drove him about occasionally. Mostly to and from the pub. I felt for him. Just the loneliness. It can be very lonely round and about, even more so for the women. And people round here, especially the white folk, are pretty set in some odd ways. Anyway, let's go, mate.'

As he drives off, Nelson says, 'You better tell me where we're going.'

Ben reaches into his satchel, retrieves his bookings. 'The Buena Vista Hotel.'

Nelson sighs heavily. 'Hmmm. Bit of an odd joint. Very . . . never mind. But okay rooms, with private bathrooms. Not much of a vista but.'

'It'll be fine, I'm sure. It's just for a few nights. Nelson, tell me – what is it that you actually do here?'

'Bit of everything. Work on an old farm, belongs to family friends, out east of the river. So this morning I was planting trees. Regenerating, you know. But I make a bit of cash running people around. Sort of like an unofficial Uber in this old beast or my other one – the Valiant. Which is why I run out to the airport just now, see? I saw the plane coming in and I knew that idiot Raoul's off the road. I also manage the local band. Long Walk Home. They're pretty good. I'm the singer. We're playing tomorrow night at The Crown. That's a better pub than where you're staying. Friendlier. And where you should really stay. You should come along to the gig, though. I'm also a qualified stone-mason, by the way. And through that I sometimes get work with the undertaker.'

'A jack-of-all-trades.'

'You could say. What about you?'

'I'm a diplomat. I represent the United Kingdom in Australia.'

'So why are you all the way out here, then? I mean, nothing much has interested you British out here since you took our land. Come to check in, have you?'

Nelson says this with an inflective edge. But he quickly turns and winks at Ben with deliberate ambiguity.

'Um, no. It about other business. It's complicated. But it involves two British women who're in jail overseas and —'

'Yeah, I know. The Charlene Sloper thing. It's been all over the news. It's the same reason as all them TV people came in the other day.'

'Yes. I'm sure it is.'

'Well, there'd likely be no other reason they'd ever come here. The Ether TV people got the last hire car, by the way. Most of the news people are staying at The Hello Motel. Lucky for you, I suppose. All those TV types asking questions. Nobody's talking to them much. None of the locals would do. They don't like outsiders. Not that there's not plenty more you can say about old man Sloper.'

'Like what? Tell me, please – I'm here to see him, hopefully. Well, that's my plan.'

Nelson is quiet as he slows the car and they enter the long, wide, sealed main street, Gallipoli Way. It is lined with shops and dwellings roofed in corrugated iron. Cars, mostly battered farm utes and bigger, more modern twin cabs, are parked at easy intervals and there are people and dogs. A man on a chestnut gelding clops along the opposite side of the road. Every third or fourth shop (homewares and appliances, bank, optometrist, bedroom furniture and carpets) seems to be shuttered – boarded up. A small crowd of men spill out of the betting shop, their backs to the street. They yell and gesture towards a TV inside. Three workers in hi-vis stand around a small pothole on the side of the road. One leisurely prods at the hole with a spade. The other two lean on their shovels and observe him as they smoke.

Nelson says, 'Cec Sloper is from what some round here call a foundation family. He thinks he owns the place and that everyone should answer to him. There's nothing in this world, including his god, that he doesn't try to control. No mirror or shop window with his reflection in that he's ever walked past without stopping to admire first.'

The Buena Vista is midway down the street. It is a long, two-storey building with deep verandahs on both levels. There are bars on all the downstairs windows.

Ben takes out his wallet, offering to pay Nelson with a card.

'This one's on me. Thanks for the smokes, mate. Call me if you need me to get you somewhere – any time.' He hands over a piece of thickly lined paper. It looks to Ben like part of a page from an exercise book. There are two phone numbers on it.

'If the mobile doesn't work, use the landline,' Nelson says. 'Mobile coverage out here's mostly useless as tits on a bull. And come see the band tomorrow night. I'll put you on the door.'

'I will.'

'Bet you don't.'

Ben retrieves his suitcase from the back seat, shuts the car door and waves Nelson off. He stays standing outside the Buena Vista for a moment, taken by the cacophony inside. There is raucous laughter. Someone imitating a dog barking. And then comes a chant – 'He's a piker, he's true-blue, he's a piker through and through – scull-scull-scull-scull' – ahead of a collective masculine cheer and the sound of smashing glass.

The air is still and hot, as smoke-laden as Canberra's had been in his first few days there. It catches in his throat and stings his eyes. Ben starts coughing.

As the raucous bar-room noise dissipates, the voice of an Ether goon blares from the TV: 'These namby-pamby do-good woke leftists who blame the fires on climate change are the same whingers who adore the wind turbines and say kill coal-power . . .' This Ether lot really do inhabit a parallel universe, he thinks. They'd be dangerous were they not so imbecilically comic. Who could possibly take them seriously?

He straightens his shoulders and walks through the door saying LOUNGE/RECEPTION.

The foyer light, a dim uric yellow, glimmers from the grimy, once-grand chandelier, only half of whose globes function. The reception desk is unattended. Ben taps the bell. Nobody comes. He waits a moment and taps again, harder, a little impatiently. He can still hear Ether, and on another TV, the races. Doomben. Race five, trifecta: 'Nasty Streak ahead of Pot Luck and Chancer's Call.'

A man appears suddenly through a flyscreen curtain of multi-coloured strips of rubber the width of liquorice straps. He's a hulking, unbecoming-looking bloke in shorts that sit low on his waist and over which his stomach flubbers, an impossibly pendulous beanbag of saggy flesh.

'Do for ya, mate?' he says, placing both hands on the counter. His unnaturally toffee-coloured hair (it reminds Ben of the vinyl sofa in the waiting room of the vet's at Putney) stands in tufts on a head disproportionately small on such an elephantine frame.

'I have a booking.'

'Name?' says the receptionist, licking his finger and thumbing through a large brown diary, its grubbied pages covered in scrawl, Post-its and stapled-in notes.

'Ben Gaskill.'

'Got some ID? Driver's licence, passport?'

He opens the passport and holds it at arm's length when Ben hands it across. Focusing on Ben's details, he gives a strange chuckle: *hic, hic, hic.*

'Ben Gaskill, eh? Says here your name's Benedict Fotheringham-Gaskill. So which is it?'

'Ben Gaskill will do. I tend not to use both family names.'

The receptionist shakes his head. 'Rightio then, Benedict. We have you in a deluxe king with private bathroom for five nights. Which means you're out Wednesday. Check-out's 10 am. Sharp.'

'Got it.'

'And a very good thing you're here til Wednesday too.'

'How so?'

'Tuesday nights at The Buena, Benedict. Tits Out Tuesday. That's when we bring in the lady barmaids – from outta town, if you know what I mean. You don't want to miss it. It's a favourite among men passing through The Leap, such as yourself. Not that we get so many now the saleyards have shut. Frackers and miners and shooters mostly. They go in for it big time.'

'Really?' Ben looks about furtively, wondering what the hell kind of place this is – hotel or bordello?

'Yes really. Actually. Anyways, continental breakfast included – from 6.30 am in the lounge. So, without the cooked, that's one-sixty a night times five equals . . . eight hundred bucks on the knocker. How're you paying?'

Ben hands over his new corporate card. The receptionist rolls his eyes.

'Internet's down at the moment. Always patchy round here. Bloody NBN. Never was hooked up proper. But you can pay later today or tomorrow. I doubt you'll do a runner, eh Benedict. And if you do we'll be sure and hunt you down.'

'I see.'

'You bet. Room's straight up the stairs, turn left, and halfway down the hallway. Nice vista of our Gallipoli Way. Sing out if you need anything. And come join us in the bar for a coldie soon as you're settled. It's definitely that time of day.'

It is not quite midday.

He hands Ben a brass key attached to a copper tag. 'Official passport, eh! What brings you to The Leap, business or pleasure?'

'Business.'

'That so? Well, enjoy your stay, eh. You'll like The Leap, I give you my word. Friendly type of a place, so long as you stick to your own business. Us Leapers don't tend to like outsiders sticking their noses in where they don't belong.'

Ben is relieved to escape upstairs. In his suite, large and airy with walls and ceiling in waiting-room bandaid beige, an overhead fan sends the diaphanous curtains billowing about the floor-to-ceiling windows that give onto the verandah.

He unpacks his things, puts his toiletries on the bathroom basin. When he goes to piss, he sees the vague remnants of someone else's shit still in the bowl. He flushes, repulsed, takes his piss and lies on the bed.

What in hell's name is he doing here? Has Sir Gordon sent him as some kind of test? To see if he has what it takes to convince a crazed God-botherer to spare the lives of two people in a Saudi jail who none of them will ever meet? Or is the high commissioner acting on a directive from London to dispatch Ben? Is this little jaunt part of some ongoing professional appraisal to determine if he really is of continued value to the service, given his past trauma?

Surely not? They'd awarded him the posting, hadn't they? Rewarded him for his sacrifice and dedication. His recovery and endurance.

As always when anxious, he has the urge to call Lucy and the kids. If he can just speak to them everything will be okay. But it's the middle of the night in London. He recalls his last conversation with Lucy yet again. Her uncertainty. Suze not wanting to come. Surely Lucy wouldn't just change her mind and decide not to come with the kids?

I'm being irrational, he tries to assure himself – part of the mantra he's learnt to fix on when entering this state. It's what happens when I'm stressed and feeling bad about myself, I project my uncertainty onto others. It will be okay. They will come. Even Suze. And we will all be together again. That's the most important thing.

He had quickly understood from his therapy sessions how reliant his emotional and psychological equilibrium is on being close to Lucy and the kids in times of anxiety. In Thailand, the wave had happened just a few months after Suze was born, when she and Lucy were back in London. Again, Lucy, and their by then three kids, had all been back in England while he finished the last month of his Cambodia posting alone, when that father of the lost wife and kids . . . Well, he won't let himself indulge those thoughts right now.

No. He will be disciplined. He will muddle through in this hideous shithole for five days, then return to civilisation and set up home for his family. He'll stay up late tonight and call Lucy. Meanwhile, the best way to get out of this place, he tells himself, is to get to work pronto. Find out where the Slopers live and meet with Cecil, convince him that his daughter's alleged killers should be spared.

Early that morning, before getting on the plane, he'd called the office of Sloper's solicitor, Howard Worcestershire, foreshadowing his arrival in The Leap and requesting a facilitated meeting with Sloper. The solicitor, according to his secretary, had been 'indisposed' and would call Ben back. He hadn't. As Worcestershire's office is almost next door to the hotel, Ben considers going directly there, then decides to ring – again – first. English courtesy.

His phone signal is oscillating between one bar and none, so he reaches for the landline on the bedside table. It's a rotary dial, sitting on a cream doily of the sort that had been all over his grandmother's house when he was a kid. A second doily adorns the table on the window side of the bed, reverentially cushioning a Gideon Bible. Odd, Ben thinks, that the bible is showcased on the bedside table. In his experience, hotels, motels and B&Bs usually secreted them in a drawer.

He calls the lawyer's number and the same distinctive female voice he'd heard earlier answers.

'Good afternoon, Worcestershire and associates. Dorinda speaking. How may I help you?'

Her voice is high-pitched, and singsong, inflecting upward on the 'you'. Ben wonders if she's a girl doing work experience.

He explains again who he is and what he wants. Dorinda sighs heavily and curtly apologises – her boss is currently working at his other office and is indisposed. Could she pass on a message to him? Ask him to call Ben back?

A little impatiently, he says, 'You'll recall I rang earlier today and left a message. You said then that you'd get him to call back. But he hasn't.'

'I said I'd ask him to call, not get him to call. I can't make him do anything, see.'

'Okay. Please *ask* him yet again to call.' Ben leaves his number once more.

He would wait, now, for the lawyer's call. He considers acquainting himself with the town, and quickly reconsiders. He doesn't want to be too conspicuous given all the media interest. Best he gets a meeting with Mr Sloper first. No, he'll wait until the cool of dusk to take a discreet stroll.

He goes out to the verandah and leans on the railings. He's aching for a cigarette. He goes back into his room to look for one of the half-packs he'd thrown into his bag. He seemed to have half-packs everywhere – a symptom of quitting several times in the past week only to find himself desperate for a cigarette and racing off to buy a new pack.

Smoking on the verandah, he looks up and down the street, and can count three pubs within two blocks of the Buena Vista. Across the road and to the left is the Red Panda Chinese, between the TAB and the stock and station agent. Then there are a couple of empty shuttered shops, the bakery ('Award Winning Pies'), and the news- and lotto-agent next door to a taxidermist and Tranquility Funerals. Australian flags hang on poles jutting horizontally from several shopfronts across the road. To the right are more vacant shops, a bore driller and tank supplier, and Brophy and Sons Gunsmiths (BEST RANGE OF BACON MAKERS IN CENTRAL WEST DOWNS).

From below comes the droning thrum of a water pump. And a hollow, metallic clunk – by the sound of it, a beer keg being hauled up from the cellar. A dog barks in the distance. Another responds.

A couple of cars drive slowly down Gallipoli Way. A twin-cab ute with a *Trump 2016* bumper sticker and another reading *The Leap – Jewel of Central West Downs*. There are few pedestrians. It's too hot. Though he can see there are people in the Chinese and the bakery. And of course he can hear them in the bar below. He decides to head back down and check it out.

In the bathroom he splashes water on his face, looks closely at his image in the mirror. There are bags under his eyes. Uncharacteristically, he neglected to shave this morning. He's ignored the chief maxim of the Foreign Office: when in the field, no matter how dire things are, shave daily – unless you've a beard. A slovenly diplomat sticks out like a sore thumb. He's dressed down so as to be less conspicuous, in faded jeans but still in his almost comfortable boots. He's foregone the tie and jacket, and left his business shirt untucked so that it hangs casually over the waist of his jeans. He's rolled the sleeves up above his elbows.

A sign in reception reads BAR in shadowed gold and black lettering inside the caricature of a hand with an index finger. He goes through the door it points to and immediately the men – it's all men – look up from their drinks. Conversation ceases. The only sounds now come from the blaring TVs, which he imagines are perpetually tuned to the races and to Ether. The latter is still railing against woke purveyors of climate change and those weaklings 'afraid' of coal.

Ben stands still and nods a general greeting to the bar. Nobody reciprocates. They remain staring for a moment then turn away and resume their conversations.

On the walls hang framed retro posters for celebrated beers. Tooheys Flag Ale: a brown longneck backdropped with the

Union Jack. The Resch's Dinner Ale ad features a lifesaver headed into the waves at Bondi, the iconic cliffs behind him with their architecturally banal, red-brick and blond-stucco apartments. At his feet, vivid yellow sand, bronzed bathers, and the frothing blue-green Pacific.

He heads to the bar, at one end of which are the taxidermied heads of two pigs with hideous twisted tusks. Elsewhere on the walls: a deer with eight-point antlers, a kangaroo and – is that actually a wombat? Surely not. Who, ever, would shoot such a loveable creature?

The receptionist is tending the bar. 'Do for ya, Benedict?' he asks, polishing dry a tray of beer glasses.

'A Reschs,' Ben says. 'Thank you.'

'No worries. But best say *please* first.'

He's taken aback. Is this some sort of joke? Surely the bloke's messing with him.

'Please,' Ben says. 'And thank you.'

The receptionist nods. He pours the beer. 'That's better. Happy to oblige. Now get that into yer.'

Ben takes his card from his wallet. The receptionist shakes his head dismissively.

'Internet's still down. Cash'd be good. But if not I'll open a tab. Don't suppose you're going anywhere. Not until next Wednesday anyhows.'

Behind him on the bar a framed portrait of a rangy-looking old man in a broad-brimmed hat peers down.

'Who's that?' he asks nodding at the photograph.

'That's the Bard, mate.'

'That's not the Bard.'

'He's our bard alright. Banjo Paterson.'

'Oh yes. Sure.' Ben remembered the name.

'He wrote about us,' said the receptionist. 'The bush. Our world. Blokes and horses, swaggies. The bloody layabout Aborigines, just as it was back then too. Worse now.'

A portrait of the Queen, circa 1960, hangs beside the Bard.

Ben takes his beer to a corner table. Ten or so fellows in hi-vis and overalls, hands and faces caked with grime and red dust, have joined two tables together. They're drinking schooners of Old and bantering loudly about some complete and utter cunt of a foreman at the fracking operation where they're working. The talk gets more and more ribald.

'Give it a year after you put that ring on her finger, mate. That's when the migraines start. Get as many fucks in as you can during that first year. Mark my words.'

They all smoke. This must be the last pub in Australia where you can smoke indoors, Ben thinks. At another table three men in grimy jeans and singlets huddle and talk in low voices; Ben can't make out about what. They are wiry and sun-bronzed, and look as if they could win a survivalist contest. One of them is slotting large cartridges into a rifle magazine. There's a broad-brimmed hat, crown down, on the table before him. The two others wear shooting enthusiast's snapbacks: EATS SHOOTS & LEAVES reads one. And SHOOT HAPPENS.

Hunters.

At other tables, and at the bar, men are poring over the form guide, ears cocked to the race call.

Nobody visibly takes any notice of Ben. Yet he feels eyes in the backs of heads boring into him. The moronic Ether commentator drones on.

Then his show finishes and top-of-the-hour news headlines come on. The bar falls silent as everyone watches. The races are muted for now.

The first item is about Adair and Kilfoyle. The Saudi Court is expected to hand down its decision today. Justice is swift in Riyadh. There is murmuring around the bar. Heads nod in accord. Then the story cuts to Cecil Sloper. This time he stands on the verandah of the homestead, his awkward son towering behind him. He seems to regard his father with anticipation – or is it fear Ben detects?

Cecil Sloper begins speaking in a theatrical tone. 'It is time to avenge; I will repay. In due time their foot will slip; their day of disaster is near and their doom rushes upon them. Deuteronomy 32:35.'

From behind the bar the receptionist bellows, 'You tell 'em, Cec – those murdering bitches.'

The hunters cheer. The old boys studying the form guide look up and applaud. The frackers clap. Concur: 'Hear, fucken' hear!'

'Sssh,' the receptionist says. 'He's still talking.'

'. . . and when the court returns the only verdict it can possibly hand down, the law of that country, delivered in the name of its God, will smite my daughter's killers down with stones or blade. And I will be there to watch justice prevail, as only it can. As it must.'

More applause.

The story ends as it segues back to images of Adair and Kilfoyle and, finally, Cecil Sloper.

'Fucken murderers,' one fracker says.

'Too right. Eye for an eye for what they done to your girl, Cec,' the receptionist says.

Ben takes a long draw on his beer. The bitter brew turns in his guts, reminding him that he hasn't yet eaten today. The alcohol has gone straight to his head. It feels good. The tension in his body, the anxiety in his head, is abating, despite the intimidating and hyper-masculine mood in the bar. He is starting to feel comfortable, even amused – engaged, at least, in the way a social anthropologist might be. He finishes and returns to the bar for another.

'So Benedict, what do you make of The Leap so far?' the receptionist asks as he flicks the tap on and off to get the head just right.

'Well, I haven't really had much of a chance to form a judgement. But people about here do certainly seem to be forthright with their opinions.'

'You mean about the Arabian stuff – and them two what murdered Cecil Sloper's precious girl? People just want justice when one of theirs is taken like that. That's all.'

'I understand that. But it's good to keep an open mind, yes? Let's just see what the court says.'

'Open mind, eh?' The receptionist shrugs. 'Whose side are you on then, Benedict?'

'The side of true justice. I believe crime should be appropriately judged before being punished. But the death penalty – surely it's always barbaric. It's not a deterrent.'

'I tell you what's barbaric – throttling a young woman and then chucking her out a ten-storey window. That's what's barbaric. Fancy treating a woman like that. We don't treat women like that around The Leap.'

Ben wouldn't know. He hasn't seen any.

'Indeed. It's hard to argue with that. Look, can I buy you a drink?' he asks, thinking there's no point needlessly making an enemy of the landlord. 'And by the way, what's your name?'

The receptionist smiles, showing a gappy mouthful of crooked grey and black teeth. 'It's Blunt. Bevan Blunt. And that's very kind of you to offer. It's not like me to drink on the job. But I will take a schooner of what you're having, now that you're insisting. I'll put them both on your tab. The net's still down, see?'

He fills his glass and holds it up to Ben. 'Here's lookin' up your mother's jumper then.'

'Cheers, mate,' Ben says. They clink, and Blunt moves on to pour a beer for someone else.

In his corner seat Ben lights up. His phone pings, the connection is back. It's a message from Sir Gordon telling him the British mission in Riyadh has cabled that the Saudi court is expected to convict Adair and Kilfoyle presently. How is Ben's progress with Mr Sloper? This is a matter of some urgency now.

Ben ignores the message.

An incoming call from a mobile phone number he doesn't recognise lights up his screen.

'Ben Gaskill.'

'Good afternoon – it's Howard Worcestershire, solicitor. Returning your call, now I'm back in the office.'

At this very moment the lawyer enters the bar with the phone to his ear, his crook leg trailing behind. The same weird suit and ridiculous trilby that Ben saw on TV. All scrawny skin and bone. Rodent-like.

He has a woman with him. Mid- to late thirties. Slightly too-short skirt. Heels. Blurry green-blue tatt of Little Bo-Peep on her shoulder. She reminds Ben of the women out on the tear, tottering about the West End late of a Friday night.

The other men in the bar turn and ogle shamelessly. Ridiculously at odds yet again, it strikes Ben, with all the purported uber-chivalry about the place.

She takes a seat at a table in the corner opposite Ben, fixes her lime-green skirt which has ridden up slightly. The lawyer approaches the bar, holds up two fingers.

'Hey, Saucy – rum and milk?' Blunt anticipates. 'Prosecco for Dorinda?' Worcestershire gives a thumbs-up with his free hand, the other still pressing the phone to his ear.

This all unfolds before Ben is able to strategise how to wrangle such awkwardness. 'Mr Worcestershire, sir, I'm actually in the bar of the Buena Vista Hotel that —'

'Then I'll see you in a moment, mate, won't I? The pub is my other office, I'll have you know.' He looks about the bar, immediately spots Ben and points at him.

Must be his clean business shirt, thinks Ben; nobody else is wearing one. The lawyer seems immune to any shame at being caught so blithely lying. He beckons Ben to join him and Dorinda at their table.

Worcestershire introduces himself and shakes Ben's hand vigorously. He introduces Dorinda – 'Dorrie' – as his niece and article clerk.

She offers her hand, palm upwards, to shake. As she does he notices the acrylic nails of crimson upon which little yellow moons are painted. As he withdraws his own hand her index finger and its talon-like nail trails gently over his palm. He can't tell for sure if it's an accidental gesture. He thinks probably so. Yet it's slightly disarming.

'Very pleased to meet you,' she says, surveying him. The edge of a prune-coloured bruise shows on Dorinda's upper arm, creeping from under her sleeve.

'Dorrie's finally found her vocation under my close mentorship,' Worcestershire says proprietorially. He quickly drains his rum and milk. 'Bit of a dry argument here, wouldn't you say, Ben?'

'Sorry?' Ben is distracted by the scabrous nature of the skin on the man's face. He scratches at an especially nasty patch below one ear.

'It's a dry bloody argument is what I'm saying. What are you having?'

'Oh, sorry, no, let me – please.'

'Well, if you insist.'

The drinks are added to Ben's tab, and when he returns to the table, the lawyer says, 'So, Ben, what do you think of The Leap? Had a look round?'

'Not yet. I've only been here a few hours and really, I just want to get straight to work, which is the reason I'm here. And for the nature of my call to you, Mr Worcestershire.'

'Call me Howard, please. Or Saucy. My friends call me Saucy, don't they, Dorrie? And The Leap is the sort of place that doesn't stand too much on ceremony, so to speak, I think you'll find. Yes, we're a friendly, informal lot, us Leapers. Hospitable.'

Friendly and informal? It's not exactly Ben's impression. Self-satisfied, narrow-minded, bigoted, cloistered and suspicious, more like it, he thinks, and he recalls McKenzie's description of them a few days back in Canberra: 'Flat Earth Party-voting, climate-change-denying, wife-battering, God-bothering, gun-nut, ground-zero, racist, fundamentalist fuckers.' He drains his own drink wearily, wondering how long it's going to take this yokel bloody solicitor to engage with what Ben actually wants from him. Could be a long arvo indeed. In which case he really ought to stay a bit tidy.

'Another round,' the lawyer declares. It is not a question.

As Saucy hobbles to the bar, Dorinda lights an Alpine. She blows smoke in Ben's direction with a determined, direct gaze. The woman makes him feel uncomfortable.

'Planning to stay long in The Leap or what, Ben?' she asks.

'Just a few days.'

'A few days can be an eternity here. I can't wait to leave, personally.'

'To a law firm in the city, perhaps, after your uncle has finished the mentoring?'

'Unlikely. He's not actually my uncle. As such. More like an old friend of my dad's. He's . . . supported me. But I don't owe him anything, if you know what I mean. And I'm not an article clerk. I just did Year Twelve legal studies is all.'

'I see.'

An awkward silence descends as Ben wonders at the nature of her relationship with the solicitor. She breaks it by asking, 'When you leave here, when your work's done, where will you go?'

'Back to Canberra. Why do you ask?'

'Do you think you could maybe take me with you? I know that I could be useful. It would be worth your while. I'd make sure it was.'

Ben can't quite believe what he's hearing. He doesn't know how to respond. Whether in the negative to her proposition, which could only serve to make things worse. Or to inquire seriously about her welfare. Or to ignore her, given all the markers she's signalling of madness and sadness or drunkenness. He's embarrassed. As she shifts forward in her chair, the better to gauge his response, Ben notices an identical bruise on her right shoulder partly obscuring the Little Bo-Peep tatt.

'Look, Dorinda, I'm sorry but, you know, I'm married, quite happily and . . .' he manages, awkwardly.

'Secret whispers, I see,' comes Saucy's nasally voice behind them. 'Already! This isn't bloody *Pretty Woman*, Dorinda. Life's not like that. I keep telling her, Ben. Pay no attention to her little fantasies. She asks every new man she meets the same question.'

'Not true,' she says.

'Enough, Dorrie,' Saucy rebukes, his voice raised.

Ben, already light-headed from three schooners on an empty stomach, takes a deep pull on his beer and changes the conversation.

'So Howard – Saucy – as you know, I represent her Majesty's Government of the United Kingdom and —'

'Of course, yeah, I know all that. Let's not beat around the bloody bush here, eh Ben? Life is short. And time is money, money's time. Around here we say what we mean and we mean what we say. So, you are here because you want me to convince my client, Mr Sloper, that he should show mercy to your two citizens who killed his daughter. That's it, isn't it?'

'Well, it's a little more complicated than that. The two women who've been charged are indeed suspects, but to date they have been convicted of nothing. And please bear in mind that they've been arrested in the jurisdiction of an authoritarian regime that oppresses women and minorities, and whose police and justice system is notoriously corrupt and opaque. I'm simply here to ask that you help facilitate a meeting between myself and Mr Sloper, so we can discuss the matter.'

In reply, Saucy polishes off his drink and limps back to the bar. Ben, gobsmacked at the rate at which the man can put it away, takes the opportunity to go to the Men's. With his forehead on the cool tiles above the trough, he pisses like a camel. He feels half drunk. But the drink also brings a perverse clarity to his thoughts. Actually, he thinks he might feel just absolutely excellent right now. He tells himself he is a good guy – clever and resourceful. Dependable. Loveable. He knows it's a pretty fine line, though. A bit like playing darts. You always play better with a couple of pints on board, but too many and your game rapidly goes to complete shit.

Back at the table, Saucy says, 'Ben, you know, I've been thinking about this a bit. There's something you must understand about old Cec Sloper. His family is six generations here now. Pioneers. They cleared that land. Quarried the rock. Built the house. Bred the cattle and sheep. Defended it from our bloody dark-skinned brethren who carried on like they'd a right to it all. The town grew up around that family. Now, Cec has done things the way his people have done, for as good as forever. He's not afraid of being unpopular anywhere else.'

'I understand.'

'But do you? Let me tell you, that girl Charlene was the apple of his eye. Intelligent, almost dux of the school. Beautiful. Talented. A model. An actress. He was so proud of her. Isn't that right, Dorrie? Dorinda went to school with her, didn't you, love?'

Dorinda says, 'She was okay, I suppose.' She shrugs. 'Bit up herself I reckon. She *always* wanted to be famous but.'

'Anyway, the point I'm making,' Saucy says, 'is that the more pressure Cec comes under, the less likely he is to change his mind. Especially while he's grieving. And right now, with those journalists camped at his gate and the editorials in those bloody virtuous lefty city papers, and some of them TV and radio people – though not on the Ether mind, they're all with him – saying he must, just *must*, express mercy, he's less likely than ever. Nobody tells Cecil Sloper he *must* do anything.'

'That's helpful to know. But can you please nevertheless arrange for me to see him?'

'I'll do my best. Be patient, Ben. Now, let's have another drink. My shout.'

'I think I've had enough.'

'Nonsense. As I've told you, we're a hospitable lot here in The Leap. A man could take most egregious umbrage if another man only drank with him because it seemed he wanted something. So have another bloody drink, why don't you.'

He gives in. Saucy hands Dorinda a fifty and she heads to the bar, leaving her phone on the table. A pink case bejewelled with fake gems.

Saucy picks it up and punches in the pass-code. Scrolling down the screen, he raises a disapproving eyebrow. Shakes his head.

Then he picks up his own phone and taps away busily, his lips moving in sync with the words.

'Just sent Cec a message,' he says. 'Let's see what he comes back with.'

By five o'clock Ben figures he and the lawyer have each shouted six times at least. But who can remember? Ben, despite wanting to restrict his consumption, is quite beyond recalling or caring. But if the way to Cecil Sloper is paved by drinking and smoking with his solicitor, well, then, that is what Ben must do for the empire.

During the course of the afternoon he's learnt that Dorinda has a relative in England who she visited as a teenager. She'd spent a rainy fortnight at Butlin's, Blackpool. The weather was poxy, the food awful. The men were handsy. Not like in The Leap where it was always sunny and dry, except for right now with all the filthy smoke and dust. She couldn't wait to get home from England. But now she'd be quite happy to be back there again. Or just about anywhere else, to be honest. Unfortunately, she no longer has a passport. It expired. And Saucy has assured her she'll never need another.

From Saucy he heard more about The Leap's 'rich pioneering history', with the pastoralists, like the Sloper family, and then the miners. 'There's still deep veins of gold out there, and fellas mining for it. Though the gas – you know, the fracking – is the big money-maker nowadays.'

The Slopers, like all the pioneers, had started using land that nobody else ever wanted, claimed Saucy. 'There were no crops, no fences, no stock, no houses, no nothing when they arrived. The land was no bloody use to anyone at all, see? They offered to share it, to live amicably, like, with the Aborigines who came wandering in from nowhere, threatening them with spears, and wouldn't have a bloody bar of it. So the pioneers had no choice but to protect their land and their cattle and sheep.'

This allowed Saucy an inevitable segue onto what he called 'the contemporaneous Aborigine problem'. None of them wanted to do the hard work on the farms or with the fracking, he maintained, they were all just waiting for a handout. 'And even now them young uppity blacks still won't let bygones be bygones with all their talk of bloody land rights and deaths in the jails and history and so forth.

'What,' he went on, 'do they think they'd be better off if the Chinese settled here? Or the German Kraut Nazis? The frog French? No end of complaining. British colonisation's the best thing's ever happened to them. The British brought civilisation to The Leap through families like the Slopers. And remember, there was hardly anyone here in the first place anyway. It was scarcely populated. All over the country, colonisation's given 'em running water, electricity, corrugated iron. KFC. Maccas. That lot'd all still be living in caves and spearing one another in the arse if it weren't for solid, hardworking Anglo-Saxon stock like us. Thank God for you British, Ben. That's all I can say. Thank God.'

With that, Saucy stands and faces the bar. He salutes the Queen and Banjo Paterson and the taxidermic animal heads.

This degree of colonial Anglophilia was something Ben had not heard even amid the Chesterfields and double-malts of the Whitehall men's clubs. It was bonkers. He hadn't known quite what to say. He was shit-faced. Goat-arsed. He knew the prudent thing would be to take his leave and retire to his room. Or better, go and eat something. Yet he felt he couldn't leave Saucy. Not until there was a reply to that text message. He didn't want to jeopardise the small possibility of a meeting with Sloper.

Now, as evening falls, the bar fills. Labourers, miners, rouseabouts. The shooters are still here, rowdy now and drunk, yelling at the television, which has been changed from Ether News to a football show. More hi-vis frackers have joined the original table, and they particpate in the banter about Damo, the one who's soon to marry. Damo appears to be showing off a nude photograph of his lucky fiancée on his phone.

The place is raucous and smoky with tobacco. Saucy and Dorinda keep drinking but Ben pleads for a Coke.

A sudden hush envelops the bar when a heavily muscled man in black overalls appears. He sets a portable disc player down on the floor and presses PLAY. Mötley Crüe's 'Girls, Girls, Girls' blasts from the tinny speaker. The muscled man begins tapping his foot and snapping his fingers, and a woman in a sheer purple bikini dances into the bar and runs to him. He curls his arm around her waist, before she grinds and gyrates her way to the frackers. Her accomplice puts an empty chair in front of them and she beckons for Damo, the putative groom, to sit. He shrugs sheepishly, as though he has no option, and accedes. She stands over him, one long, sinuous leg either side of the chair, thrusting her groin into his face. She turns, grinds her buttocks onto his lap and reaches behind to undo her bikini top. She spins back round, rubs her breasts mechanically in his face, before grabbing both of his hands and urging him to cup them. She is completely expressionless as she does all this.

'Girls, Girls, Girls' continues to blast away. Most of the men in the bar are clapping to the beat.

The stripper guides her customer's hand to the string on one side of her bikini bottoms, tied with a bow. He releases the string. Naked, she grinds her pudendum into his face. Two of Damo's mates film everything on their phones.

The woman stops perfectly still for a moment, as if to steady herself. Then she sinks to her knees, unzips the man's trousers and busily fellates him. A few moments later she sheathes him with a condom and sits riding him, face to face. Damo ends, shuddering, in an instant, just as the song finishes. She's timed it all faultlessly. A bravura performance. She looks relieved and very bored, and goes to give him a proforma, soulless peck on the cheek, but he roughly pushes her away. She shrugs, and swiftly un-straddles. Her minder hands her a bathrobe, which she puts on, then goes to the bar for a complimentary Cruiser.

Repellent as he found it, Ben had been unable to avoid watching. He focuses his blurry vision now on Dorinda. She too looks bored, apparently unsurprised at the spectacle.

'The poor fiancée,' she says. 'I wonder if she's got any idea what a dud bash she's marrying.'

Ben lights another cigarette. Saucy has paid no attention at all to the stripper's show. He is concentrating on his phone.

'The Saudi court's come back with guilty,' he says. 'Pronounced the death penalty for your two lassies.'

Ben's phone vibrates. He assumes it's Sir Gordon telling him the same. So he ignores it.

The bar clock says 8 pm. He's been in Australia exactly a week. It feels like a month.

Waking up is a trauma of disorientation.

It is the morning, right? he wonders. It's hard to tell, thanks to the smoke outside. Ben is lying on his back on the bed, still in his jeans and shirt, bootless but with socks. The room stinks. Of BO. Of cigarette smoke. Of masticated alcohol. Something else rank too. Maybe even dead.

Most alarmingly, a saucer by the bed has two butts in it, one his brand, one Alpine. He groans out loud.

His phone is beside him on the bed: 8.28 am. He has no idea when or how he returned to his room. For all he knows, he could have been asleep – or unconscious – for nine hours or for three.

He runs through some basics. Benedict Simon Fotheringham-Gaskill. Forty-nine years of age. My home is in Putney. SW-15.

Married to Lucy. Two kids. No, no – three. One labradoodle. Nancy.

When he raises his head splinters of pain course through his temples. He feels acute pressure behind his eyeballs, as if they might pop out or explode or something. He looks about the room for further evidence. No. No idea. He forces himself to prop on his elbows.

Shattered beads of memory ricochet around his consciousness like coffee beans in a grinder. The more they spin, the more elusive and fragmented the memories become. The shards will not coalesce.

This place! This godforsaken, dreadful place. The netherworld of madness. What's its name? The Gap? Mind The Gap! No. The Jump? The Bound? Similar. That's it, Leap. The Leap.

That woman – in that foreign land – had leapt. Jumped out that window. She was full of those drugs that make you bounce about.

He slowly recalls some details of the night. There had been a move to another watering hole – some sort of wine bar in an alley – with Saucy and Dorinda. It was all soft red lighting, heavy curtains and dense furniture. Did he simply imagine that two uniformed policemen had been sitting at the bar, chatting to the barkeep, who'd been wearing a hair net?

There had been martinis. Several. Then gin, he's pretty sure. Straight.

All those faces. Stubble on dirty cheeks. Grubby, rough hands. Raucous laughter. The most ribald language. Fucks and cunts all over the place. Dorinda sitting close to him on a lounge, clutching his arm, head on his shoulder at one point, Saucy scowling in disapproval or approval, it was impossible to read, as Ben chugged more drinks and sucked on cigarettes and, despite being sodden with booze, continued to feel embarrassed.

He can feel again her breath in his ear, whispering, 'Take me with you, Ben. Take me when you leave. You won't regret it. Promise.' Or so he believes.

'You don't need me. You don't need a man to leave. Just go. Be gone,' he'd said. Or thinks he might've done. 'Take control, Dorinda.'

'He won't let me.'

Then there was an accountant. No. Not an accountant. Like an accountant but called himself the pharmacist. Yes, just like Lucy! Saucy called him that too. The pharmacist. He was impossibly tall. Wore a grubby white suit.

'Here, this'll pep you up.' Two little blue pills in Ben's hand. 'Swallow them. Or stick 'em up the back passage if you're game.' Laughter. Up the back passage! And so, filthy jokes about back passages.

Ben did swallow one pill, he recalls. Jack Daniels and Coke chaser. Magic. Ben felt like he could go all night. Drink the English Channel dry.

Then a meal at the Red Panda with Saucy, Dorinda, the pharmacist. Someone else? Another pig shooter about town, though Ben didn't think he'd been in the pub earlier. Some man named Edgy. Blue singlet. Stubble. Waving a gun about. Really? He might've imagined that, too. Cops were in there also. All guffawing. Wine. More wine. More wine – 'Garcon.' Prawn toast. Lemon chicken. Honey prawns. Ben by then way too wired to eat, even though he'd been famished.

And then a late phone call for Saucy. Cecil Sloper would see Ben the next day. Today! Christ, when? He can't even recall if a time had been set.

Now he remembers Dorinda helping him to his room and onto the bed, then removing his M.R.s, one snagging on a crustily blistered heel. She'd sat on the edge of the bed to smoke a cigarette and butted it in the ashtray on the bedside table. She'd leaned in close, saying, 'Good night, you sweet, silly man.' She'd kissed him on the cheek. His last welcome recollection: her leaving straight afterwards.

Amid the noises from downstairs as the hotel rouses and the ubiquitous warble of magpies outside, a sudden mnemonic electronic sound invades his senses. So '90s. It takes him a moment to realise it's the landline.

He picks it up. But his voice won't come. 'Yrrrs,' he rasps, his throat burnt with alcohol and nicotine. He thinks he might be sick.

'Saucy here. Mr Sloper, my client – he'll see you at midday, son. Text you directions presently. Be there on time. He abhors tardiness.'

Saucy sounds surprisingly composed given the massive night that he, too, has just had on the tiles. How the hell, Ben wonders, does he do it? Maybe it's conditioning. Something like Olympic training for drinkers. The Buena Vista certainly seems like the venue in which to train amongst the elite for that marathon. Somewhere in a bruised and battered corner of his memory he recalls how last night Blunt, or one of the cops or maybe the pharmacist, boastfully described Saucy as 'probably the most piss-fit bloke in the whole of The Leap'.

Ben sits up properly now. His guts roll. Can he stand? He manages to. He drinks some water, which does nothing to ease his parched mouth and burning throat. His most pressing problem is how to get to Sloper's farm.

He tries ringing Saucy back. Straight through to voicemail. He goes to the pocket of the suit trousers he'd worn yesterday. It was only yesterday, wasn't it, that he'd arrived? It feels like forever.

There is the packet of pretzels from the plane. And a scrunched-up piece of paper with Nelson's numbers.

'Nelson,' he manages to croak out. 'It's Ben Gaskill. The British guy you met yesterday.' He explains that he must go to the Sloper farm. Could Nelson please take him? He needs to be there at midday. He would pay handsomely.

Nelson readily agrees. 'But only as far as the gate,' he adds. 'We don't much like to go onto that property. And don't have cause to. Certainly not anywhere near the homestead where Sloper is.'

He's so relieved that Nelson can drive him, he doesn't think to ask why not.

His hands shake as he shaves. He is extra careful not to nick himself. He slowly undresses and showers. Every movement releases a new surge of pain. In his forehead. In his limbs. In his eyes and throat. In his stomach. He takes paracetamol and dry-retches as he fights to keep the capsules down. He lies on the bed and closes his eyes. But the bed spins, much as it had when he was drunk for the first time as a teenager. This is the hangover from hell. The worst ever. An eleven out of ten. Still, he must go to work. The only thing that matters right now is getting access to Cecil Sloper and convincing him of his wrongheadedness in supporting the execution of Kilfoyle and Adair. Ben simply must not fail in this. He cannot let anyone else down.

He's caught in a medley of splintered thoughts and feelings about the accused women. He tells himself he's in no way emotionally invested in their salvation. It's not personal for him. As it quite simply can't be. His investment in the outcome is purely practical. Professional. It is all about doing his job well.

Convincing Charlene Sloper's family to show clemency could, after all, only stand to enhance his career – his reputation for reliability. For resilience.

That well-schooled inner voice tells him he is useful. That he has a single purpose right now: saving lives. There's been so much death on his watch. So much help he'd not been able to give. In Thailand. All those photographs entrusted to him of loved ones who were lost forever, washed away, or unidentifiable. He dreams of them still. The photographs of the vanished. Those ever-wondering, never-knowing, anguished families.

But not just there. Cambodia. Twelve years later, at the end of his posting. Lucy and the kids had already repatriated while he served out the final month. The friendly English couple, Kelvin and Mardie Clarke, from the school quiz-night team, who had made a side trip to Cambodia after a few weeks in Vietnam. A catch-up for a meal and a few drinks in Phnom Penh. They'd a couple of days to spare, wanted to get out of the city. Any suggestions, Ben?

Yes. Take the kids down to Kampot. The most beautiful old French colonial town. Delightful guesthouses. The best sunset experience ever. Take the barbecue cruise on Kampong Bay River, he'd advised. Bokor Mountain at dusk is like nothing you've ever seen. It'll stay with the children for a lifetime. Let me book it for you with Vampire Cruises. Special diplomatic discount!

Ben missed picking up the call even though the phone had woken him soon after 11 pm. Outside the near-empty tenth-floor flat where he and the family had lived for the past three years, the rain was pelting horizontally. The monsoon was early by a couple of weeks. You couldn't entirely predict it these days, the climate was changing so rapidly.

He called back. The news – as it tended to be when a call came through so late – was dreadful. A tour boat. Overcrowded.

Half of them were swimming when the rain began to hammer down at sunset. Those sitting on the roof by the barbecue and beer kegs clambered in a rush for the ladder. The boat listed sharply then rolled onto the swimmers scrambling to get back on board. The current swept the boat downstream. The fatal roll kept dozens trapped inside, while others in the water or who'd not managed to get downstairs were snagged by the railings and the metal benches and tables on the deck. Sixty-something missing. Eighteen British. No bodies recovered yet. Get down there pronto, Ben. Get a list of the dead. You must identify them.

The driver kept his face to the windscreen as they careened down the highway, aquaplaning across huge puddles, recklessly overtaking and flashing headlights, Ben making calls all the way. Slow, treacherous going. The capsized vessel, he learnt, was called *The Dragon*. The twinge of sickening guilt as he thought, Thank God – it can't be the Clarkes. Wrong tour company.

It was late morning when they finally arrived. Downstream the boat had snagged on rocks and fallen trees; rescue workers were starting to recover the dead. Ambulances and vans waited ten-deep. Bloated, battered bodies, most of them naked due to the current. Impossible to distinguish men from women, boys from girls. Water, like fire, strips identity, anonymises with such sinister efficiency.

But he had been misinformed. The lettering on the capsized bow read: VAMPIRE.

The manifest. 'Do we have the manifest of who boarded the vessel?' he demanded of the rescue team. Yes. He saw the Clarkes listed: Kelvin, Mardie and the kids. Fuck – what hope for any of them? He photographed the manifest.

Ben was advised to go back to Kampot and wait by the hospital. A makeshift morgue was being set up when he got there. He sent the manifest to the embassy; they would chase up dental records and next of kin. The crowd was mostly locals when the bodies started arriving. A number of Cambodian nationals had been onboard too. Cops were holding them back. Parents and partners wailing and screaming.

He hears Kelvin Clarke before he sees him. Ben is relieved. Maybe Mardie and the two kids are nearby, also safe. Alive. But Kelvin is emitting a bestial howl of anguish, a sound so unhuman, so primal, Ben wants to scream himself.

Ben rushes to him. Tells the police to let him come – his family were clearly onboard.

Suddenly Kelvin is calm. He had chronic food poisoning, he tells Ben. Bombed himself on painkillers and Imodium and didn't take the cruise while the others went. He stayed in the hotel. Slept right through the storm. He grabs Ben's arm and drags him towards the tent with the dead. He races from body to body, some on stretchers, others on sheets of plastic and beach towels. He hastily pulls back towels and random pieces of clothing covering the faces of the dead. Most are terribly disfigured.

'Tell me they're alive! Are they in here?' he demands.

'Kelvin, I just don't know. I'm sorry, I —'

'Are they dead? Fucking tell me now!'

'Kelvin, I can't, I'm sorry. It's just too early to say. I'm so sorry.'

'What in hell use are you then? You useless fucking prick, Gaskill.'

And he pushes Ben hard in the chest with both hands. It knocks the wind out of him. He stumbles.

'Useless. *And* responsible. It's all your fault they took that cruise. You recommended it.'

It had taken that long recovery time – of rehab, psychotherapy and group therapy, and so many other forms of counselling involving dozens of different professionals – for Ben's rational brain to accept that, no, he was not in fact responsible. Regardless, the memories of Cambodia were still fused, treacherously tangled up with those of the tsunami's aftermath and the way he had felt incapable of helping anyone, dead or alive. Uselessness and culpability. They were flipsides of his same psychologically dented coin. And his mind still, sometimes, could not bear their combined weight.

And so, it was just a short step to where he is right now, today, when he lapses into thinking that he is not only incapable of saving the imprisoned women, but that he will be the one responsible if they are executed. He will be solely to blame.

He sits naked on the bed with this reality. It chills him. He starts shivering. Gets up and turns the fan off.

From today, he tells himself, I will go on the straight and narrow. Stay sober. Be discreet. Keep away from the treacherous watering holes and dodgy characters of The Leap. I will do my job. I will be of use. A useful saviour.

He dresses, dons his boots and goes downstairs, thinking that perhaps breakfast might help, if he can manage to keep it down. The paracetamol are taking effect, so he's hopeful.

In the breakfast room – ornate timber panelling and gaudy burnt-orange carpet – he stops near a table where a grey-haired couple dressed in matching white shorts and blue polos chat amiably about their sightseeing plans for the day.

Just who the hell, Ben ponders, would willingly choose to come to this place, given all the enticing places the world has on offer?

He certainly wishes he was anywhere else. He stands still and briefly closes his eyes, willing this to be some sort of waking dream.

'Hello, look what the cat dragged in!'

Ben opens his eyes. Waddling across the carpet before him in his orthopaedic footwear, a grimace with every step, is the ruddy-faced Blunt, his rheumy eyes resembling shell-less snails suspended in pink aspic.

'How're yer feeling today, mate? Looked like you were tying one on last night with Saucy and the niece. I coulda told yer not to drink with Saucy. Good bloke – flash as a rat with a gold tooth. But everyone knows he's got a problem with the piss. Though that's not what you'd call unique around here. Not that he can't hold it or anything but.'

When Ben says nothing, Blunt asks, 'Want brekkie? There's the continental stuff all laid out over there. Go for yer life – just no seconds. Or if it's à la carte you're after I can whip into the kitchen and do yer bacon and eggs. Or kippers. Or maybe you want a plate of kidneys or brains or lamb's fry. Good if you're feeling a bit queasy after a night on the tiles.'

'Continental,' Ben says, struggling with his convulsing stomach.

'Righto. Fill yer boots! Coffee, tea?'

'Tea.'

'Take a seat.'

He sits at a table in the middle of the room and places his elbows on it. They adhere to the plastic tablecloth, sticky with years of spilt and hurriedly wiped foodstuff. He puts his head in his hands. He's aching for a cigarette. He instinctively reaches for his shirt pocket. No cigarettes. But he does feel through the fabric a small lump. He retrieves the second blue tablet the pharmacist gave him last night. He recalls, now, having popped the spare in his shirt pocket. 'For Ron, eh mate, just in case!' the pharmacist had declared.

He holds it on his open palm and regards it closely, closing his hand as Blunt places before him a small aluminium pot of scalding water, the string and tag of a teabag dangling from under its lid, and a little plastic container of UHT milk. Ben manages to tear open the milk with trembling fingers and pour it into his tea.

He sips. Without too much thought he puts the pill on his tongue. He leaves it there a moment, undecided. Then washes it down with another mouthful of tea.

How much worse could it make things?

The temperature outside the Buena Vista is already in the thirties. He looks at his watch. Nelson is late. Ben leans against the stone facade under the shade of the verandah. A subtle breeze has today delivered a thicker, blue-grey haze of smoke dust. People are going about their Saturday business, popping in and out of shops and stopping to chat in the street. Is it just him or are there far more men than women in this place?

As the blue pill starts gripping him, Ben becomes suddenly and acutely aware of all that goes on about him, his senses attuned to every sound, scent, sight. He feels almost good now, certainly very alive, and wonders if he might yet secure more of the pills.

He can hear every ball at the cricket oval a few blocks away, each *bomp* and *thwack* on the pitch and bat. Also – or surely he imagines this? – every wheezy exhalation and exertion of the bowler, the batsmen and the fielders. It is as if the game is being played right here on the road before him and not 500 metres away.

Such sharpened sensibilities cannot be easily controlled, switched on and off. They are, rather, quite at the whim of the minutiae all about him. And the initially wondrous might quickly transmogrify to malevolence.

The cacophonic sound of the heaving breaths and slurping of the two blue cattle dogs sheltering under the verandah and drinking from a big tin basin of water is frightening, deafening. There is the warble of magpies, a sound he once found joyful but that now rings with a sombre, mournful longing, and the mad flapping of their wings, the scritch-scratch of their talons and the mad tapping of their beaks as they bounce about the gutters, snacking on insects and leftovers – the sandwich crust that didn't quite make it to the bin, the little flakes of pastry that flutter to the ground as a corpulent young man with cystic acne gorges on his meat pie from a paper bag on the bench near the trough. The sucking and squelching noise as the man masticates is multiplied a hundredfold, while Ben's vision hones onto his cracked lips and stained teeth and lizard-like pink tongue as he negotiates the grisly meat in oleaginous grey-brown gravy; as he licks the scalded webbing between thumb and forefinger where gobbets of the molten goop have flowed out from the too-soft pastry.

The pie filling reminds Ben of something organic he stepped in after the wave.

His stomach turns; how utterly disgusting, he can never forget, the human body and its functions and remnants can be.

He looks to the street for distraction. Where the hell is Nelson? What sort of time is he working to? Ben can't be late for such a critical meeting. Two teenage boys shimmy past on skateboards, jeans hanging low, arse-cracks exposed, snapbacks on backwards. The T-shirt on one reads: *Skate, Sleep, Repeat*. Ben keeps his eyes on them as they careen across the various lanes and side streets before stopping at the church, where the footpath ends in gravel. They turn around and skate back towards him.

As they pass, something possesses Ben. 'Skating nirvana,' he comments. He's most unsure why he says this.

'Go fuck yourself,' Skate, Sleep, Repeat retorts. 'You a bloody pedo or what?'

Outside the lotto-and-newsagent-cum-vape-shop-and-tobacconist across the road, a poster for *The Irrigator* reads LOCAL DAD: MY GIRL'S KILLERS MUST DIE.

He wanders over, thinking maybe he'll buy the paper. But he's little-blue-pill distracted by a stand of battered used paperbacks and instead chooses one about an Australian truck driver who murdered a British backpacker in 2001 in the Northern Territory. He has no idea why he buys the book, but he adds two packets of smokes and a lighter, crosses back over Gallipoli Way.

Though Ben's headache – and the pressure behind his eyes – has dissipated, he is twitchy amid all the sensory overload. He is sweating. Agitated. Not happy.

A horn beeps in front of him. Nelson has pulled up in a car Ben hadn't recognised, a very old green Valiant. Leaning across, Nelson slings open the door, raises his aviator sunglasses and looks closely at Ben.

'Geez, you look like absolute shit, mate.'

'Thanks. I don't feel too bad now.'

'You drink at The Buena?'

'For a time, yes.'

'Well, that's a trap for young players. Bit of an eclectic clientele, you might say. Only less civilised pub in town is The Pioneers' Arms. Wouldn't drink at either for quids. But then again, they wouldn't have me.'

'What do you mean?'

'Around this town, different peoples tend to keep to themselves.'

Nelson slows as they near the end of Gallipoli Way. On the left is an elaborate, though dry, fountain and horse trough carved from grainy white marble, its centrepiece a war memorial atop which sits a soldier on horseback, the animal rearing on its hind hooves, the rider leaning towards the enemy with drawn bayonet in hand. There's an honour board beneath, listing the names of the fallen.

'That's a big war memorial for such a small town,' Ben says as they pass.

'Yeah. Whitefella war memorial. Anzac Day's the biggest date of the year round here. That and twenty-six January. Bigger than Christmas.'

Nelson drives on past the Masonic Lodge, and the imposing facade of St George's Protestant Church. 'That memorial – the statue on it is a light horseman. You know, mounted infantry. Besides Turks, they sure killed their share of Bedouin and Arabs over in the Middle East. Little wonder, that. Brought up learning it was okay to do the same thing here. Kill Blackfellas, that is.'

'I suppose civilians always come off worst in war. It's an unfortunate fact. Anyway, I hear the Aussies have a reputation for being hard but fair soldiers. Egalitarian. Hard as nails but compassionate. Special mates. All that.'

'Yeah. All that bullshit. Not always. Not then. Not now.'

As they head west out of town on the unmade road, Nelson

says, 'Fun fact, Ben: there's three men named Sloper on that memorial. Three of Cecil Sloper's great-uncles.'

'How terrible.'

'Someone kept sending all the brothers white feathers, see, when they didn't join up. Everyone else was going to fight. White, yellow, Black, brindle. But the Slopers were acting like they were some kind of exempted royalty. Eventually three of 'em signed up due to the shame of the white feathers because *The Irrigator* somehow found out and kept writing stories about how others in town thought they were cowards. The shame of it! And those three brothers, they never come home. Bad luck, that is. It was a tragedy for the family to lose three of the four brothers. Old Cec's granddaddy was the only one who didn't go. He had just one son, and that son has only one as well. That's how all the land ended up in Cec's hands. Most farms round here've been broken up so each brother gets a bit. Some bits and pieces even got handed back to us mob with land grants. But not Hurlstone – that's what the Slopers call the place – it's intact. And it all stands to go to Cec's gentle, not too bright boy when he dies. But Kenneth isn't interested in anything much 'cept the birds and the seasons – he's not much into farming.'

'What's wrong with him, do you think?'

'Bit touched, everyone reckons, like he was dropped on his head as a baby or something. But maybe that's just a story. Also, bullied senseless by the old man by all accounts. Terrified of him. And you would be, right? The daughter was Cec's favourite, til she took off after high school. Just shot through and never came back.'

The further from town they go, the more dramatically the landscape changes. The road traces The Babylon, with the land rising gradually above the river, and they drive along a narrow ridge with a sheer, lethal fall to the water. Ancient-looking eucalypts grow from crevices in the cliff face, their roots stretching down towards the water.

Eventually the road veers inland and descends, and the Slopers' land comes into view.

The entrance to the property is unmissable. Two great stone plinths, more suited to a grand British estate or commons, stand sentinel each end of a pair of gothic, wrought-iron, rusted-open gates. As far as the eye can see, white wooden fences of about chest height stake out the Sloper claim. City cars – Range Rovers, Audis, BMWS, and several news vans with satellite dishes – are parked at the gates. As Nelson drives closer, Ben can see a jeep with *Leap into The Leap Rent-a-Cars* stencilled on the passenger door. Journalists huddle under a shade tree, ordered to stay outside the gates and waiting to be called up to the homestead for the next entertaining instalment of Cec Sloper's Old Testament rantings.

'I'll drop you at the gate,' Nelson says.

The house is perhaps half a kilometre from the gate, at the apex of a steep gravel road.

'Nelson,' Ben says, 'whatever your reason, I respect that you don't want to go too close to the homestead. But can you please just take me through the gate, even fifty metres, so I can avoid this lot?'

'Fifty metres. Hmm. Can do. But no more.'

'Absolutely. And one more thing – can you wait for me? I'm not likely to be long.'

'I'm on double-time, remember. For a Saturday. And I've got a gig tonight.'

'Sure. Whatever you charge is fine.'

'It's alright. I'm taking the piss, mate. I can tell you're good for it. Strikes me you're too naive to be a huckster.'

Nelson accelerates through the gate. TV cameras and a stills photographer train on them as they pass. He soon stops the car abruptly. A cloud of the Valiant's own dust envelops it.

'Bugger 'em,' Nelson says. 'They won't be able to see you now. You should hot-foot it up to the homestead. I'll wait outside the gates. Don't worry. I won't say anything to them pricks.'

Ben's legs are weak and unsteady as he gets out. The driveway is rough beneath his boots. He can now see little through the dust cloud and smoke. He's walked barely a hundred metres when a red ute approaches from the house. It slows and turns diagonally so as to block his way along the drive. The front passenger door flings open.

'Get in, Ben.'

Saucy looks unaffected by last night's titanic blow-out, which is to say, still haggard, with a deathly pallor and flaking skin. The air-conditioner is on full pelt. The car stinks of sweat, hamburgers, Old Spice and stale tobacco smoke. Also dog.

'Look at you – fresh as a daisy,' Saucy says. 'Wouldn't know you'd been on the ran-tan at all.'

'I'm alright, thanks.'

'That's not what Dorinda says. She said you couldn't tell your arse from your elbows last night. Started reading the bloody Gideon Bible to her. Said you had a chunky chuckle – a big fat chunder – too. You were something of a disappointment to her, I think. She gave up on you.'

'Nonsense, I —'

'She reckoned she couldn't have woken the old trouser snake with all the Viagra in Surfers Paradise. Not that you showed any interest at all. Kept talking about your missus. Until you passed out. Don't worry, she'll get over it.'

'That's not true, I —'

'Get a grip, son. I'm taking the piss. All she did was help you to your room on my instruction. She's thoroughly dedicated to her old Uncle Howie, I'll have you know. Not truly interested in other men.'

'Look, whatever,' Ben says. 'Sloper – he's here, right? He's going to talk to me?'

'Said he would. It's why I'm here. I've got to tell you, though, he's in a filthy humour.'

'How so?'

'How so, Ben? How so? His baby daughter has just been murdered – understand? Snuffed out. His pride and joy. The dux. Almost. The world at her feet. Acting career still ahead perhaps. How would you be, Ben, if that'd just happened to you?'

For a moment Ben does actually feel something for Cecil Sloper. He's conscious that he's neglected to consider Sloper's feelings in all this. He *has* lost a daughter terribly. Violently. He must be traumatised by how she died. Ben has seen so much violent death and its ensuing grief and he knows it can make people irrational. Send them quite crazy. He thinks of all the people in Thailand and Cambodia who simply could not believe, would not believe, that the body there before them on the gurney, so disfigured and decomposed it barely resembled a human, could possibly be their beautiful daughter, their son, their parent or partner. Despite the DNA and dental-matching. Perhaps the hideous details of Charlene Sloper's corpse accounted for Cecil's behaviour.

Ben is determined to be compassionate. To acknowledge Sloper's pain. To empathise.

Saucy, having done a laborious U-turn and driven back up the drive, stops between the barn and the house. The harvester, the rusted cars, the dilapidated plough all look so familiar from the TV. The homestead, built from heavy blue stone, has small, deep-set windows that peer like black eyes from beneath the verandah, and the shingle roof hangs crookedly over the walls. Its gutters are rusted through, sprouting weeds like unsightly facial hair. The flywire on the front door is torn and flaps back and forth on the jamb, despite the absence of apparent breeze. There's an air of advancing, unstoppable decrepitude about the whole place.

When Ben gets out of the ute, he can see a small kitchen garden with a well-tended vegetable patch and a clipped lawn down one side of the house. It's in stark contrast to the lack of TLC elsewhere.

The door crashes open and a blue cattle dog comes growling over to Ben. He freezes.

Saucy warns, 'Stop still, Ben. Let him sniff you and he won't bite.'

The dog's lips peel twitchily back over its fangs as it sniffs Ben's crotch, arse and impassive hands. Then it goes back inside.

'Atta boy, Earl.' says Saucy.

Ben follows him into the house. They walk through the kitchen, where a long wooden table that could easily seat twenty is set for two – knife, fork, spoon, bowl – on opposite sides of the middle. An elderly woman is busy at the sink, washing salad leaves, peeling cucumbers. Saucy introduces her as Mrs Morcombe, the housekeeper. She ignores them.

Leading Ben into the heart of the house, Saucy stops at a heavy wooden door. Knocks.

'Come,' says a voice that Ben recognises as Cecil Sloper's.

The room is all wood-panelling and dark lacquered floorboards with patterned rugs. As his eyes adjust to the light, he finds Cecil sitting on a red leather sofa in front of the coffee table. He is mostly bald, without the comb-over for the cameras, and his scalp is flecked all over with liver spots. There are long, stringy tufts of hair around his ears and neck. Muttonchop sideburns.

'Mr Fotheringham-Gaskill, welcome to my humble abode,' he says, standing and extending his hand across the table. 'These are terrible circumstances under which we meet.'

Ben briefly wonders how the man knows his full name, before saying, 'Mr Sloper, my sincere condolences. And please, call me Ben.'

Sloper beckons him to sit in the armchair opposite. Saucy remains standing silently somewhere behind, where Ben can hear his wheezy breathing. Ben's own breathing is shallow. The blue pill, coupled with the freight of responsibility, has his heart beating faster. He can feel the pulse twitching in his neck.

His eye is drawn to the hearth of the fireplace, which is wide enough for a man to lie comfortably in. The fireplace itself is elaborately carved marble – little gargoyles and serpents, kangaroos and birds – and the mantlepiece displays an array of memorabilia. Photographs, an upturned horseshoe, a clock in a glass dome, an old revolver . . . Ben has to blink a few times to make sure that the object at the end of the mantlepiece is what he thinks it is. At first glance he thought it was a smooth white rock, but no, it's a human skull, minus the mandible. Two black circular holes and one near-perfect triangle show where the eyes and nose had been. One of the skull's two large top front teeth is missing. A fine crack runs the length of the cranium.

He's aware, amid his shock at the presence of a human skull, that Cecil has been speaking.

'Mr Sloper —' Ben begins.

'No monologues, please, Mr Fotheringham-Gaskill. It is Benedict Fotheringham-Gaskill, is it not? I know why you are here. It is as obvious to me as the nose on your face – you're here to urge forgiveness in me. But I can save you your breath, I am not to be persuaded. These two women who've murdered and stolen from my girl are the worst type imaginable. Cut from the vilest of Ulster Fenian cloth. A manicurist and a nurse's aid no less. Not even a qualified nurse.'

It's true that while the media has referred to the women variously as 'health workers', 'medical professionals' and 'nurses', their qualifications were not quite so impressive. Ben dares not interrupt what is clearly going to be a haranguing sermon. He glances at the wall of portraits, generations of pioneering Slopers by the looks. Men in broad-brimmed hats on horses, surrounded by cattle on the once-grassy and fertile banks of The Babylon. A man on a pheasant shoot with flintlock guns, a pile of dead birds besides shaggy-haired retrievers. In another painting, a Sloper male stands on a tree-lined rise, looking out over a blue-green valley. Crouching at his feet is an Aboriginal man – the way finder? – shading his eyes with one hand and pointing into the distance with the other. No women are depicted.

Sloper is saying, 'You don't have the benefit or the privilege of having met my daughter, Mr Fotheringham-Gaskill. But if you did, I would not have to tell you how special she was to her family and to the world. She was born premature. At thirty-five weeks. Her mother died in delivery. You would know that if you've done your diligence. To us she was more than a daughter, she was her mother incarnate. Mother and daughter in one. She shone like a beacon in the dark from the moment she left the humidicrib and came home to Hurlstone. She blossomed, despite that difficult start, into the beauty of the region. Not only the most beautiful girl in the whole of The Leap, but the entire Central West Downs. Lead in the school play. A natural on the stage. Like all young people, she needed to see the world. We sent her out into it with all the fears that a loving father might have about one so exquisite, so precious. So there was the air-hostessing, to support her acting. It was only a matter of time until she broke through as an actress. She had the world at her feet when they murdered her, Mr Fotheringham-Gaskill. When these witches killed her! And now, the law of God and the land must run its course. I will not interfere. Is that clear?'

Ben allows the silence to linger. He looks the man in the eye, nods at him with feigned warmth. Feigned because this man is impossible to warm to. He is reptilian, in manner and essence.

'Mr Sloper.' Ben gives a smile of confected empathy. 'As a father I can only try to imagine what you're going through. But of course I simply can't, for I've never known such loss. But I do feel most deeply for you and your family. I must also explain to you my country's position in regard to this matter. The British mission in Saudi Arabia has been unable to hear and assess the evidence against Ms Adair and Ms Kilfoyle, but our representatives will be meeting with both women soon to determine their wellbeing —'

'Their wellbeing? Ha! I imagine they'll be feeling guilty.'

'Quite, sir, and very frightened, I would anticipate. Mr Sloper, the British government's position on the death penalty is unambiguous. We are opposed to it no matter the jurisdiction and regardless of the alleged crime.'

'Alleged! There is no *allegation* of crime here. There is a conviction.'

'True, Mr Sloper. My mistake. And my apologies. But the fact remains that our efforts in relation to these two women are being made regardless of their conviction under Saudi law. Sir, I'm here to implore you to consider showing these women the type of compassion that it seems they may have denied – *did* deny – your daughter. The judge in this case, you will know —'

He is cut off by Saucy, who has remained standing silently behind Ben until now. 'Ben, you don't need to explain the intricacies of the Saudi legal system to my client. Mr Sloper understands perfectly well that the judge has urged him to consider *diyyeh* – to forgive, and accept a payment of compensation, likely to be footed by the British government, although nobody has yet done my client the courtesy of providing the precise details of such payment. But the acceptance of any such payment, like the granting of mercy, is, as you well know, entirely discretionary.'

Sloper stands suddenly and points at Ben. 'And I will neither forgive these harlots nor accept any blood money. They will die. And when their skulls are smashed with stones or their heads are sheared from their bodies in the public square, I will cheer. Were it possible, I would cast the first stone or wield the blade myself!' Sloper is yelling now, and jabbing his finger at Ben emphatically. 'So, the answer, Mr Fotheringham-Gaskill, is no. Take that back to your masters. And while you're at it, tell your two witches the same from me.'

'I do understand, Mr Sloper. Unambiguously. But I still implore you to find it within yourself to show mercy.'

Sloper sits back down and cracks his knuckles. He crosses then uncrosses his legs and shifts his expanse into the middle of the sofa, spreading his arms across its back so that, with the light falling on him from behind, he resembles something of a hayseed Christ enduring crucifixion.

'Allow me to tell you a story,' he says.

'Sir, I'm here to listen.'

'The Slopers arrived on these plains in 1818 – more than two hundred years ago. My great-grandfather-times-five, Thomas Mayall Sloper, came fresh off the boat and over the range with bullock and dray, his convict helper and four hundred sheep, to take up his land grant. Five thousand acres. There was nothing and nobody here. Nothing at all resembling civilisation. Grassland and trees as far as the eye could see. Thomas Mayall and his convict cleared stumps and trees, and built a shingle hut and a stockyard by the banks of The Babylon, the river Thomas named. The property he named Hurlstone, in honour of the family property in the Old Country where tens of generations of Slopers had farmed. Thomas Mayall Sloper originally camped just over there.'

Cecil flicks his head towards the window where perhaps he imagined his pioneering ancestor still stood.

'Eventually he built part of what is now this house. This very room was the sum of the original homestead, see? Others followed Thomas from Sydney to settle the district. As I say, there was no one here. Not a damned civilised soul.'

Ben cannot stop himself from blurting, 'Sir, the Aboriginal people, surely?' and immediately regrets it. Sloper's anger visibly deepens, his face reddens.

'God help me! The wretched natives! They'd no rightful claim to this place. No purpose for it but to wander about on it, sit around their fires and yabber on inanely. Steal our stock, and our fish from The Babylon. Thomas was unbothered by their primitive, childish ways. He felt they could coexist peacefully enough on his land. But then they did that which they can't stop themselves from doing. Stealing from the kitchen garden. Spearing our animals. Thomas defended his land and his stock with the appropriate reprisals. He took a spear to the leg while his convict had one shear through his heart. Being from the Old Country, you'd not have heard of the Great Plains Wars – 1820 to 1860. These were no less wars of empire than the world wars that followed. Thomas Sloper eventually died comfortably in his bed in this house. And after him, his sons stayed on this land. One of them died by a spear. The other took his just retribution in 1856. He won the ensuing war with the Aborigines that time, too. We've always kept the upper hand, we Slopers. Civilisation was assured. Then down the generations, they continued to fight. Tough men and devoted women. Three of the four Sloper brothers of my grandfather's generation went to the Great War. None returned. The only survivor of that generation was my grandfather George. That's him up there.' Sloper indicates the painting of the man with the dead pheasants.

A corpulent blowfly emerges from the chimney and bumbles about the room. It hovers close to Ben's face. Repulsed, he shoos it with his hand, and a moment later it lands on the skull on the mantlepiece.

Ben winces. Sloper notices and slowly his mouth forms into an oleaginous, knowing smirk.

'My family has fought for country and for empire, here and overseas. That's why we are still here today – it's our right to be here in generational, familial perpetuity. My son Kenneth – you've not encountered him – is the end of the Sloper line. He's not very likely one for breeding, I'm afraid. But our Charlene would have given me an heir, a son, I feel certain. And this property would then have continued in our family line to be farmed. But now it ends with me. And Kenneth.'

Sloper falls silent. The blowfly is buzzing about his head now. He swipes at it with a cupped palm, deftly entraps the thing. 'Gotcha,' he whispers to his clenched hand.

Then he extracts the fly with the thumb and forefinger of the other hand, gingerly holds it up by a wing to show Ben. Ben is at once disgusted and fixated on every nuance. The little blue pill is still working overtime. The fly buzzes madly, trying to escape. The sound, as loud as a chainsaw in Ben's state, is becoming intolerable.

'So,' Sloper says, still exhibiting the fly between thumb and forefinger, 'if you really do see it my way, Mr Fotheringham-Gaskill, you will understand why my daughter's killers must forfeit their lives. They've not only ended my daughter's life but snuffed out the Slopers' continuing connection to this land.'

'Again, Mr Sloper, thank you for explaining this. But I have to repeat that this in no way changes my government's determination to save its citizens.'

Cecil Sloper breathes in heavily. He holds the breath. Then as he exhales, words vomit forth in a deep baritone. They seem to come almost from someone else, way down inside his guts, blackened with hatred and fury.

'And if by these things you are not turned to Me, but act with hostility against Me, then I will act with hostility against you; and I, even I, will strike you seven times for your sins. I will also bring upon you a sword which will execute vengeance for the covenant; and when you gather together into your cities, I will send pestilence among you, so that you shall be delivered into enemy hands. Leviticus 26:23–25.'

As he speaks, Sloper squashes the blowfly in his fingers. It pops. It's like a gunshot to Ben's ear. A stream of pussy guts squirts onto the coffee table. Sloper wipes the yellowy-pink viscera from his fingers onto a handkerchief.

Ben has four solid years of theology classes under his belt, an undertaking that always seemed such folly to his parents. Finally they find utility.

'Do not judge, and you will not be judged,' he says calmly. 'Do not condemn, and you will not be condemned. Forgive and you will be forgiven. Luke 6:37.'

Sloper wipes the back of a swollen, sun-browned hand over his incredulous face and bellows, 'If I sharpen My flashing sword, and My hand takes hold on justice, I will render vengeance on my adversaries, and I will repay those who hate me. Deuteronomy 32: 41–43.'

He stands once more and points to the door. 'And now, Mr Fotheringham-Gaskill,' Sloper bellows, 'you will leave my home and never return. You have my final answer. Mr Worcestershire, show him out. Immediately.'

Outside, the heat envelops him like a steaming blanket. The cattle dog trails him, snarling and snapping at his heels, as he walks briskly away from the homestead. Nobody warns it off.

He can see Nelson's car near the bottom of the drive. He's driven back through the gates so Ben might avoid any direct contact with the media. Ben lights a smoke. And walks towards Nelson. The journalists at the gate train cameras onto Ben as he approaches. Any action, no matter how passive, adds to the story. For the story of the murdered hostie, her belligerent father, and the women whose lives are in his hands, is a made-for-TV drama.

Nelson slings open the passenger-side door. 'How'd it go?' he asks.

'I need another ciggie right now,' Ben says.

'That good, eh!'

Ben lights up and draws the smoke deep into his lungs, closes his eyes and expels it slowly.

Nelson quickly turns the car around on the narrow homestead road. He wastes no time driving towards Hurlstone's gates. The journalists are either side of the cattle grate. They gesticulate to Nelson and Ben. The cameras are close to the windows as they pass. The electronic drives of the cameras sound like some poisonous insect caught in Ben's ear.

'Hold on, mate.' Nelson guns the car. It fishtails in the gravel. The journalists scurry as he zips over the cattle grid while giving them the middle finger, turning onto the unmade road and spraying them with red grit. He laughs madly. Ben manages an awkward chuckle, clings onto the metal dash.

Nelson, calmly, as if that hadn't just happened, says, 'Old man Sloper – thoughts?'

'Surreal. Aggressive. Bloody unhinged.'

'Coulda told yer. That's him.'

'I found myself searching for his, I don't know, his humanity or some such. Despite everything I've seen of him on TV, I went in there feeling some pity for him. Or at least ready to feel it. I know grief. I've seen so much of it. People can get hysterical to the point of hurting themselves. But this old man is frightening. His anger feels . . . contrived. Cultivated. Performative. And he spoke about his daughter like she was a possession. A chattel stolen from him.'

'You know, Ben, that's not so unusual round The Leap, that attitude. Blokes tend to rule the roost in them old families. The men did the farming and the fighting and the killing – and the fucking. And the women were always there to clean up their shit, including when it came to the Blackfellas made to work for them. The wives enabled them, you could say. And then for their troubles the women got written out of the family story, like so much else.'

'And the way he spat out Old Testament quotes about punishment and crime, all the while giving me a lesson on his family history. It was just bizarre.'

Nelson shakes his head. He sighs. 'History. Crime. Punishment. According to Cec Sloper, eh? That'd be hilarious if it wasn't so ridiculous. Like ironic, I mean.'

'Say?'

'This whole district, especially The Leap, is still one giant crime scene, mate. Past. Present. Nothing changes.'

Ben thinks he understands something of what Nelson means. The stolen Aboriginal children. He knows that British troops killed Aboriginal resistance fighters. It was, he reckoned, a regrettable aspect of British colonialism that had played out all over the globe, from Ulster to India, from Africa to Australia. The British academy and the broadsheets and the BBC were nowadays increasingly preoccupied with the human rights abuses – reckoning with the past sins – of empire, with talk of apologies and even reparations. It was all so bloody confronting for any British person who made the vaguest effort to self-educate about what had happened.

But Ben believes the past has to be scrutinised and acknowledged. In his short time back in Australia, he is already seeing signs that things might have changed somewhat in this regard, progressed a little. During his gap year, there'd been next to no talk of the colonial stain – the killings, the stolen children, the generational trauma. This time, he's beginning to pick up on elements in the national conversation around these things. That event at the gallery the other evening had showcased a cultural acknowledgement of Indigenous people and their timeless association with the continent. Did that represent a transformation, or was it merely 'woke' window-dressing, as the lunatics on Ether would have it, in the country's most progressive city?

'I think I see what you're saying,' he tells Nelson. 'Back in Canberra everyone was talking about truth-telling. Reconciliation. Recognition. There was obvious respect for your people.'

'Mate, I get your heart's in the right place. It's one reason I don't mind you. But The Leap ain't Canberra. Nobody round here's talking truth-telling. Or referendums, which I promise you will never fly. In the same way as they're not exactly talking Me Too, case you haven't noticed. Round here, nobody but my mob is ever talking about the past except in terms of how what was done to us was a good thing. The Leap is proud of what it did to my people.'

'What do you mean? Not sure I really get it.'

'Wouldn't expect you to. That's because you've got to go back to 1856. Our mob had been skirmishing on and off with the invaders, the settlers led by the Slopers, for near on thirty years by then. This time it starts the same way as always. Some of ours spear a sheep because it's on our land. The Sloper man and his boys give chase and kill a Blackfella. Few days later our people retaliate. Kill a Sloper. But it can't end there. It's disproportionate reprisal. Always. Couple of weeks later the redcoats come in with a militia made up of locals. All our mob are out bush, camped along the ridgeline above The Babylon just up there.'

Nelson's timing is coincidentally perfect and he points through the windscreen to the very ridgeline he's talking about. 'Warriors,' he goes on. 'Wives. Old men and old ladies. Little kids. Teenagers. Just before dawn the camp dogs start barking and the redcoats and local goons come charging in on horses, guns blazing, sabres and axes swinging. They shoot all the dogs and as many of our fighters as they can. Hang the dead up in the trees by their necks. Redcoat commanders call it "the terror", see? But killing the warriors isn't enough for the whitefellas. So they form a line and sweep through the bush, where the old people and the women and kiddies have gone hiding. The old people that don't run, they shoot. The others, mainly the ladies with babies and the little kids, they see what's happened to everyone else as they're being chased and they run over them cliffs out of fear.'

'No!'

'True story.'

'I believe you, but I mean, no – how horrendous. And there was nothing like this in the Wikipedia entry. It just mentioned some fabled early pioneer horseman who accidentally chased his stock over a cliff —'

Nelson laughs. He shakes his head. 'Just like one of those stories by the bush bards, eh!'

'What?'

'Never mind. But this big massacre, it happened just as the town's setting up. And the white community, led by the Slopers, they ask 'emselves, Now what can we call this special place – just who or what thing can we name it after? And of course they settle on The Leap because they want to remember how they killed all those people. It's in the diaries and letters of the redcoats, the way my people were chased over those cliffs out of terror, into the ravine. How they were rounded up and chased and then leapt off those cliffs rather than be murdered where they stood by the soldiers and the militia. I can quote you from old man Aloysius Sloper, Cec Sloper's ancestor, who took part in all that murdering. His diary's in the Mitchell Library over in Sydney. I've read it. Held it in my own hands and read from it. Felt like I wanted a shower afterwards. I got one sentence burned in my brain: "We slayed the warriors with gunshot and blade and instilled into the stragglers the greatest terror so that they ran like so many lemmings and leapt off the highest cliffs, a pitiful procession one after another, whereupon their bodies were dashed on the stony ravine floor far, far below." And then they go and name the town after the massacre! The Leap! We reckon seventy-seven of our people died that morning. Many never got recovered. But the soldiers and settlers took body parts for trophies. Skulls and such like.'

A searing realisation jolts Ben: the skull on Sloper's mantlepiece.

'I'd no idea. I mean, the name, The Leap. It's hideous . . . To name a town in celebration of murdering all those . . . It's just extraordinary!'

'That's something we tell them every time we argue the name of the joint should be changed. But then not so extraordinary at all either. Half this country's named after men that killed our people. We've got eight Skeleton Creeks in one state. Murdering Creek. Butchers Creek. Where do you reckon that came from? Massacre Bay. Murdering Gully. There's no end to them. White people don't much notice. But it taunts us. First they steal the land and rename the landscape in celebration of the massacres. Then they fuck up the country, vandalise it with their cattle and sheep and weeds, and then with their mining and now the bloody fracking. Get it?'

'Yes. I do.'

'It's not that tricky. Thing is, it doesn't end back there but. I got cousins died in the local lock-up. One of them from an epileptic seizure because they wouldn't call a doctor or listen to him when he said he needed his medication. If that happened to a white bloke there'd be shit to pay. And three years ago, the pigs shot one of the uncles. Three times in the chest. Ernie was running away from them – resisting arrest for D and D, they reckoned. Tried to book him for having a piss in Gallipoli Way. He pulled a screwdriver from his pocket when they cornered him in the lane behind the Buena Vista there. Didn't even taser him first, just shot him dead. The inquest basically found Ernie asked for it. Can you imagine a white bloke getting shot for being drunk and disorderly around The Leap! Drunk tank's full of 'em sleeping it off every Saturday night. Pigs don't just shoot them dead in the street, though. And Ernie was even too rat-arsed to scratch himself with that screwdriver.'

'Surely the police can't get away with that? I mean, there are laws . . .'

Nelson is silent.

Ben is mystified. He wonders if he's somehow insulted him – the last thing he wants to do given Nelson is the only person in town who's shown him warmth or kindness.

'What's up?' Ben asks at last. 'Have I said the wrong thing?'

'No. You can't help it if you want to see the best in people. But round here it won't help you much. Because you need to understand that in The Leap there're two sets of laws. So I'll tell you another thing that happened.'

'Go on.'

'So, there's one of the young cousins in our community. Aaron Tyson. This is twenty years ago or somethin'. Lovely young fella. About to get out of this place for good, half his luck. Aaron'd just finished the HSC. Among the first of ours to do it. Did well at it too. Was doing some labouring at the feed factory, making some dough before he was off to uni in Sydney. And then he's run down, knocked off his bicycle one night riding home on the Old Babylon Road. Killed stone-dead. Terrible head injuries.'

'That's too awful. I'm sorry.'

'I know, right. But his head injuries are more than someone's accidentally run him over, they're more like they ran him down then smashed his head in with something to finish him off. Cops looked into it. Not that they ever tried too bloody hard. White cops, Black kid!'

'Did you ever find out what happened to – sorry, what's his name again?'

'Aaron. My cousin Aaron. We pushed and pushed to find out. Went to the big city papers. Cops even sent a detective in from Sydney for a week or two. But they didn't discover nothing. Coroner made an open finding. Seems nobody knew or saw anything at all.'

'Small towns, big secrets, no?'

'People say that all the time. But it's all bullshit too, eh. The Leap is a medium-size town with no secrets, just deliberately forgotten truths. There's just this bloody massive blind eye about a whole lotta difficult stuff that's been purposely disremembered by the so-called pioneer families, and then afterwards by everyone else from the cops to the papers and the politicians. And that's to do with how the settlers murdered the Blackfellas and stole their land and named the place in celebration of it – and they've never eased up on us descendants since. It was a war from the very beginning and there's been no peace. No settlement. Reconciliation – *pfft!* Aaron is another fatality in all that. And likely not the last.'

'But I mean, who'd do such a thing?'

'Mate, just open your eyes and have a look around this place – plenty of people here'd do something like that to Aaron for just a few bucks. Some men here'd do it just for the thrill.'

'Nice town.'

'Yeah, but it's the only one we've got. And we're going nowhere. Though most of us have been out on the eastern edge there at The Rookery for a long time now. That's our community. When they finally forced us all off our land a hundred years back – those of us they hadn't stolen from our families or shot or murdered with poisoned flour yet, that is – they corralled us into a reserve on the old chook farm. Anyway, that's the then and the now of it. The Leap's rap sheet going back to its very start.'

Ben takes a minute.

'That makes sense when I think of Sloper. Anyone who'd seen him on TV could tell he's hard. And then seeing him up close, looking into his eyes, I got this sense of cruelty, almost sadism, about him. Even that he's sort of enjoying this dreadful thing with his daughter. Relishing the situation.'

'You bet he is.'

'He is actually familiar to me. His type, I mean. I went to school and university with the children of men just like him, always wanting to remind you who's got the power. And the breeding. And the fucking entitlement and the privilege.'

'Bingo, Ben. Privilege. Power. Entitlement. He's got it all over life and specially death right now, like the men in his family's always tried to have with my people. And he'll be just loving that the world is watching. Anyway, it's good for you to know just who that dead girl's daddy is.'

'It is. But it also shows me just how impossible this is. Sloper didn't listen to me at all. And I've got to find a way to save those women, I can't let them be executed.'

'You can only do what you're doing. And it's not your fault you're not going to be able to teach Cecil forgiveness. Sloper men don't listen to anybody. Never have. They've always talked a lot about God. But their God is one they've imagined in their own image. Hard. Violent. Greedy. Mean. His father was a real mean fucker too, by all accounts. And his and his and his. All the way back to when they took our land. Charlene was a sweet girl. She'd've known what a cruel prick he was. Just like Marion, too.'

'Marion?'

'Cec's mum. She and Charlene were close.'

'Right. When did Marion die?'

'Marion's still bloody kicking, mate. Ninety-five or near to. Cec bunged her in a home twenty years or so back. Said he couldn't look after that boy of his and her too when she became immobile. She had polio or something as a kid. Been in a chair for yonks.'

'You know her?

'Course. Everyone knows everyone here, one way or another.'

'Maybe I should go see her . . .'

'Like I told you, she's a very old lady. Unwell. And I'm sure she wouldn't want to get mixed up in all this crazy shit.'

For the first time, Ben can hear impatience creeping into Nelson's voice. But he tries again anyway. 'Could I possibly see her, do you think?'

Nelson sighs heavily. 'How come? What do you want from a sick old lady? Best just let her be.'

'She might be able to change her son's mind. Work on his compassionate side.'

Nelson snorts. 'Like I said, he doesn't have one. And Cec Sloper is about as likely to listen to a woman, even if she is his mum, as he is to an English diplomat, even one with your good manners.'

'But worth a shot, surely.'

'Ben, I don't know why you're bothering. You should just go home. Look after yourself. Be with your family.'

'My home is seventeen thousand kilometres away. And it's my job to do everything to save these women.'

They stop at the ATM on Gallipoli Way. It is in a shallow alcove between two stores. The post office flanks one side. The clothing shop on the other declares itself *The Leap's Finest Bush Apparel, dry-cleaner (we remove the most stubborn stains), and tailor (alterations from S to XXXL).* Tan leather Caterpillar boots, toes to the glass, standing sentinel in the window. Polos, flannel shirts, fleece vests, moleskin cargo trousers, denim and canvas overalls, broad-brimmed hats. But no sign of women's finery. It being Saturday afternoon, these and most of the other shops on the street are shut. The block is empty but for a couple of old men sitting side by side on a bench. A motley brown dog sprawls in the butcher's doorway.

The ATM and its alcove stink of piss. The machine charges Ben four dollars to withdraw the maximum of $250.

Back in the car he asks, 'How much do I owe you?'

'Dunno. Whaddaya reckon I'm worth?'

Ben hands him the lot.

Nelson shrugs. Takes the money. 'That'll do. For now,' he says.

It is almost three when Nelson drops Ben at the Buena Vista.

'Remember, tonight at The Crown – Long Walk Home. We come on about eight-thirty. Your name's on the door. It'll be a chill crowd. Nothing like the Buena.'

Ben has no real intention of turning up. He feels shattered. He wants something simple to eat, another shower, then a good night's sleep. He is intent on avoiding drinking and taking any drugs, especially those little blue pills that he's now crashing down off. He also needs to fill his boss in on the meeting with Sloper. He has several missed calls from Sir Gordon, and one from the fastidious Roderick King. And he must call Lucy. The fact she's not tried to contact him since . . . Well, he can't quite remember. But right now that feels tellingly, onerously negative.

'Yes, definitely see you tonight,' he tells Nelson.

He's about to get out of the car when Nelson says, 'Hey – forget something, mate?'

He's holding the book about the truckie murderer.

'That's some weird shit you're reading.'

Ben had forgotten about the book. He's still unsure why he bought it. It's going to do nothing for his state of mind.

In the Buena Vista's dark foyer there are familiar wafts – the burning fat of meat just on the turn, beer, stale tobacco smoke, body odour; damp dog. It turns his guts. Every bit of him aches, with weariness and a teeth-clenching angst. He's heading to the ornate mahogany staircase when a voice from behind says, 'Afternoon, Benedict. Internet's working, as it happens. So, how'd you like to settle up for the room . . . and the not insignificant bar tab from last evening?'

Blunt. The voice – and the grave double negative it imparts – startles him.

'Oh yes, of course.'

Ben goes to the small reception counter – little more than a lectern really – behind which Blunt looms.

'Five nights comes to eight hundred. And with the bar tab it comes to, let's see . . .' he says, proficiently tapping the keys of an antiquated adding machine that prints a thin strip of paper testifying to Ben's enthusiastic participation in the previous evening's bacchanal '. . . just to seventeen hundred and forty-three dollars, seventy-six cents. Just call it seventeen hundred and forty square.'

'What . . . how on earth?' Ben wonders how his bosses might react to such a monstrous bar bill. Although Sir Gordon had, after all, urged him to have a drink or two with Sloper's solicitor. Meanwhile Roderick King's warning not to be reckless with his corporate card also comes to mind.

'Easy. You really tied one on, Benedict. Not surprised you can't remember. But it's all itemised, see – including the three hundred in cash I gave to the pharmacist on your behalf.'

'But I, I, I . . .'

'And I'll have you know that I've quite generously waived the befoulment – or, as others might say, defilement – fee for your room. The cleaner reckoned someone had quite the old regurgitative episode. Now I'm supposing that was you, Ben. Unless you'd like to tell me it was the covetous Dorinda?'

Blunt hands him the itemised bar tab. It shows multiple rounds of beer, whiskey and milk, Jack Daniels and Coke, 'champagne', gin and lemonade, Bacardi and cranberry juice, plus two rounds of three glasses of aged cognac.

Ben hands over his credit card. 'Did the others – the lawyer and his niece – did they actually pay for any drinks at all?'

'No, Benedict, they didn't. Not as such. They said that you insisted it all go on your tab.'

'Stop calling me Benedict, by the way. It's Ben. Okay?'

'Benedict's what it says on your passport, mate. And listen up, there's no need at all for that sort of tone around here. Why don't you come into the bar and I'll shout you a beer. You seem all in a bit of a bloody pickle.'

'No thanks.'

'No thanks – what? I just said, it's my shout.'

'Thanks, but I don't want a drink.'

'Geez, mate, but you really look like you could use one.'

'I do not want a drink.'

Blunt purses his cracked lips, shakes his head and screws up his eyes as if Ben had just dropped his trousers and shat on the floor.

Reading the man's look of apparently genuine hurt, Ben thinks better of it. He opts for diplomacy. That is supposedly his forte. And he is, after all, due to stay here til Wednesday.

'Okay, yes. Why not. Let me freshen up, make a few calls. I'll be down to the bar presently.'

'That's more like it. Oh yeah, one other thing – some plummy-sounding pommy bloke rang for you. Called himself Lord something or other – said he couldn't reach you on your portable phone. Sounded a bit concerned or agitated or something.'

'Might it have been a Sir Gordon Woodhead?'

'Got it in one.'

Sir Gordon isn't answering his phone. Ben leaves a message and then reclines on the bed to await a return call. He lights a cigarette, begins flicking through the book he bought that morning.

Like so many Brits who'd backpacked in Australia, Ben had been captivated by the truckie murderer, just as they had been by Ivan Milat. A young Englishman shot in the middle of the night on a remote Northern Territory highway. The killer, a long-distance truck driver, had then assaulted the dead man's girlfriend, who managed to flee into the scrub and on that pitch-black night escape his feverish search for her.

It is another reminder for Ben that never too far beneath this country's genteel facade of civilised, culturally rich cities and orderly society, festers an unpredictable brutality. There was something so sinister about intrepid, carefree travellers being preyed upon liked that.

Distant Australia loomed so large and inviting in the youthful European imagination, as a place of light and space and blue waters, of sunshine and possibility, of wide open roads and friendly bucolic towns. But Ben is also cottoning onto a darkness, a malevolence, that wasn't just about murdered backpackers. Not so much a secret as a matter of conscientious evasion, a disremembering at the national heart as Nelson had described it.

He looks at the photos of the smiling, sun-kissed faces of the two Brits, and then at the image of the killer, a gangling, khaki-clad apparition with deep-set eyes. His hands were cuffed behind his back, a cop on each arm, as his mouth twisted out an obscenity at the cameras outside court.

Ben's sweat runs cold under the fan. For he recognises this monster now. He's seen elements of him in the faces and eyes of the citizens of The Leap. Right here in the Buena Vista. In Sloper. In the frackers. In the pig shooters. Even Saucy and Blunt, the vile receptionist.

He tosses the book aside and turns on Ether TV.

There he is, Ben himself, pictured in the passenger seat of Nelson's Valiant, looking straight ahead and studiously ignoring the cameras as he's being driven through Hurlstone's gate. Nelson is smiling and giving the cameras the rude finger.

Then the vision shows Ben meandering up the long driveway in a smoke-and-dust haze, coat jacket slung over one shoulder, a cigarette dangling louchely from his mouth as he walks back to Nelson's car. The story says he was 'on a mercy dash to save the lives of Ms Sloper's murderers amid an offer of blood money for her father's forgiveness'. A strap at the bottom of the report misidentifies him as 'London diplomat Benjamin Polkinghorn-Gaskill'.

The item cuts to media rallying around Sloper, standing between the barn and the house, with Saucy beside him looking like some sort of human wreckage.

Saucy says, 'Mr Sloper will now read a short statement about the murder of his beloved daughter, and the increasing diplomatic pressure on him to forgive her killers and have them escape lawful justice.'

Cecil Sloper purses his mouth and narrows his gaze as he takes from his pocket a piece of paper and unfolds it. He looks theatrically from the paper to the cameras and back, playing the dead air for effect.

'Today the government of the United Kingdom sent its emissary to my home. The home where my beautiful daughter was nurtured and grew into blossoming womanhood. The diplomat urged me to show a compassion to my daughter's killers that was foreign to them when they drugged her and threw her from a window before stealing from her. There was talk of some payment – of me accepting payment from the killers, or the government of

Britain on their behalf, in order to spare their lives. But how can I possibly put a price on the life of my daughter? Compassion, when the law of God and Allah is running its course, is simply not mine to give.'

He refolds and puts the paper back in his pocket as a babble erupts from the reporters.

'Mr Sloper won't be taking questions,' Saucy says as Sloper starts walking back to the house. A flurry of questions trails him.

None move him until a young woman finds the bullseye.

'How do you feel about having the blood of two women on your hands?'

Sloper stops mid-stride. Does a double-take. He turns and focuses his narrowed, snakelike eyes hard on the media pack. He looks as though, if he'd a gun, he'd shoot that woman reporter dead.

'How *dare* you! When my daughter's blood is still fresh, an immovable stain, on the pavement of Arabia!' Then, in the booming baritone he adopts to spit fire and brimstone: 'If a man injures his neighbour, just as he has done, so shall it be done to him – fracture for fracture, tooth for tooth. Thus, the one who kills an animal shall make it good, but the one who kills a man shall be put to death. Deuteronomy 19: 18–21. Now get these people *off* my property, Mr Worcestershire.'

Put to death. How coolly, clinically, benign Sloper manages to make an execution sound when he quotes Deuteronomy. Like saying put to sleep, or put to bed. Ben is aware of the details of public stonings and beheadings in Riyadh. But now Sloper has prompted his recall of stills images he's seen of public executions in Saudi Arabia and Iran.

The condemned had appeared resigned for the most part, though the fear was palpable on their faces. A woman, buried up to her shoulders, was pelted with rocks from a pile a few metres in front of her. Robed men, most with their faces concealed by scarves or masks, have taken careful aim and extended their throwing arms for maximum leverage and propulsion. The rocks in these images are airborne. Ben imagines them striking viciously, their dull thumping and cracking sounds as they collide with soft flesh and bone, the woman screaming until well after her skull is crushed and, then, how her body might twitch as she finally loses consciousness. Another woman is kneeling, blindfolded, hands bound behind her back. The robed executioner, his face covered with a mask resembling one that might be worn by a welder, is frozen in the photograph as he poises to bring the blade down hard. Ben recalls the accompanying text describing how the blade struck her high on the shoulder, and the way her dreadful screams carried over the cheers from the crowd. The executioner had to strike again more accurately so that her screaming stopped.

He wants to vomit. He wants to scream. An intense anger is also welling up. How can Sloper wish this on anyone? No matter what they might have done?

'Ben, you're all over the bloody television. In Australia and back home. I do wish you'd be a little more discreet! And I've been trying to reach you . . .'

The high commissioner's anger is evident.

'Sir Gordon, I'm sorry not to have rung sooner. It's a very challenging situation. The media is camped outside Sloper's property. It was impossible for me to get inside without being filmed. And you have to appreciate the sort of town this is – everyone knows what I'm doing here.'

The Leap, he thinks, is a fishbowl where discretion is unheard of. Where a stranger is a cause for curiosity, and one with Ben's name, accent and quest, is a cause for alarm. Added to this, more media seem to be arriving in The Leap by the hour. Through the window, he can see an ABC broadcast van, its satellite dish straining heavenwards on its robotic arm, a reporter strolling along Gallipoli Way doing a piece to camera.

Ben has become the starring actor in this mess, like it or not. Getting plastered with Cecil Sloper's lawyer was not exactly in his best interests from a public relations perspective, to be sure. He wonders whether Sloper has heard about that too. If so, it's hardly likely to have enhanced Ben's chances. He can feel his guilt returning.

'Ben, you misunderstand me. It's not a problem that people know you're a British diplomat trying to save our citizens. That is something we ought rightly be proud of. No, it's the way things appear. I mean, you in that beaten-up old car with a . . . fellow like that. Looking a little, how shall I say, bedraggled. With a cigarette in your mouth. Do you understand me, Ben?'

'Sir.'

'Good. Now, I think things could get rather more complicated. There's a great deal of digging being done on the two Ulsterwomen. Let's just say they have rather interesting, quite dark, backstories. It won't engender very much public sympathy, I'm afraid. I'll email the file on them. But regardless, we really must conduct ourselves with the utmost propriety in respect of saving them. The Australian government is working towards that too, though not as vigorously as one might hope. But I digress. And as I say, appearances are everything.'

'I see that,' says Ben, and goes on to debrief about his meeting with Sloper. He finishes by saying that he believes the old man is a lost cause.

Sir Gordon says that the British ambassador to Saudi Arabia has visited the two prisoners in Riyadh.

'It's not good, Ben. Seems each of them signed a statement claiming that the other killed Ms Sloper. But both have also told the ambassador that they only confessed after being tortured. Both were further threatened with rape, it seems. It's beastly.'

'Indeed. I agree it's barbaric.'

'They each say there was a party on the night of the death. Ms Sloper had been drinking, as had everyone, and took some sort of party drug. As is common with the expatriates there, it seems. She apparently had some sort of an episode, a drug reaction perhaps, and threw herself out of the window. The autopsy shows she had high levels of OxyContin and alcohol in her blood. As did both the Ulsterwomen when tested. This doesn't explain how they came to have Ms Sloper's banking key card and withdrew more than ten thousand riyal between them.'

'Well, sir, they might be difficult and unsavoury types. Thieves, perhaps. But it doesn't, of course, mean they murdered Charlene Sloper. And even if they had they certainly don't warrant such brutal treatment.'

'It's a veritable can of worms, as you can see. And still, we must do our best to save them. Understood? You must get to this Sloper man somehow. Everyone has their price, Ben. So find his. What about the son?'

'I haven't met him, sir. But he's by all accounts a bit simple.'

'Then is there anyone else who might help persuade Mr Sloper?'

'Not that I can think of. But I'll investigate.'

Ben doesn't mention Cecil Sloper's mother, Marion, to Sir Gordon. He doesn't want the old Tory bastard micromanaging him even further.

'Please do, Ben. Initiative. That's the go.'

The high commissioner pauses for emphasis. He resumes in a slightly softer tone. 'And now tell me, Ben – are you okay? I realise this is perhaps stressful for you. And that you can find stress rather . . . difficult.'

'Oh I'm battling on, sir. But thank you for the pastoral concern. I'm very much looking forward to leaving here, I won't deny.'

'Yes, well, I do think though that you ought be prepared to stay on in The Leap while-ever there's any chance at all of saving this pair.'

Ben groans inwardly. There's the new home to set up for his family.

'Sir Gordon, I'm doing my level best here.'

'Yes. Now stand by. I'll email what we've established about our Ms Adair and Ms Kilfoyle presently. And Ben?'

'Sir Gordon?'

'Do try to stay out of the press while looking such a dog's breakfast.'

He goes to his emails. There are dozens of unopened messages. At the top is one from Sir Gordon marked CONFIDENTIAL. It's a matter-of-fact precis of what the British have compiled on the lives of the accused women – Vronnie Adair and Betty Kilfoyle.

Both had worked in 2014 at the same aged care home in Ealing, South West London, Adair as a nurse's aid, and Kilfoyle as a hairdresser and nail technician; the latter also helped occasionally with meals. They were initially regarded as good workers, patient and kind with the residents. Until odd things began happening. The children of one old man reported the disappearance of a gold watch he'd been given as a retirement present after fifty years at British Rail. Next, an elderly lady's black-pearl earrings went missing. Another woman reported losing a diamond wedding ring. The list of disappearances included a digital radio, a camera, an expensive pair of binoculars. Residents also complained that small amounts of cash, kept to purchase sweets or cigarettes, toiletries or newspapers, kept vanishing.

Then an old lady told Adair that she'd lost her ATM banking card. She'd no idea how to cancel it or inform the bank. Unbeknown to the old woman, Adair had taken the card. She'd also made an offer to the old woman to call the bank herself and have the account closed, and in order to do so she would need the card's PIN. When the woman later told her daughter she'd given her PIN to the nurse's aid, the daughter checked with the bank. The account was still open. Several thousand pounds had been withdrawn in small amounts over several weeks. The bank cancelled the card and referred the fraud to police. Security footage showed both Adair and Kilfoyle making withdrawals at the corresponding times. Police informed the nursing home ahead of interviewing them.

Meanwhile, the infirmary at the home had reported irregularities in the inventory of pharmaceuticals, notably Valium and OxyContin. When informed of the police interest in Adair and Kilfoyle, the infirmary manager confronted them about the missing drugs. Adair remained calm but Kilfoyle physically attacked the manager. She was arrested and charged with assault. On searching the flat the two women shared, police found a stash of residents' belongings, thousands in cash and a range of pharmaceuticals. Both women were charged with fraud and theft. Both agreed to drug rehabilitation for their OxyContin habits. They had no convictions recorded and were released on good-behaviour bonds.

Within the year both had left the country for Saudi Arabia, where there were lucrative opportunities for people with their skills. Wealthy Saudi women invested enormously in their appearances. Adair easily found work in a cosmetic surgery practice, and Kilfoyle in a beauty parlour.

They apparently resumed their drug use.

The women shared an apartment in the same building where Charlene Sloper stayed on layovers and soon got to know her. The block was home to many other expatriate workers and there were constant parties.

At the bottom of the email, Sir Gordon had inserted his own observation: *These women emerge as hard, ruthless, calculating and dangerous.*

My god, thinks Ben. These are the women I'm busting my arse to save? The reason I'm in this shit-forsaken place? My sanity for their lives.

He must speak to Lucy. Must. He needs her to tell him it will all be okay. That he's not letting anyone down. That he's much loved. A good and worthwhile, useful person. In a week or two they'll all be together.

It's very early Saturday morning in London. Lucy will probably be awake, ahead of a road trip to Surrey where Jerome is playing football. But she doesn't pick up when he calls. He tries again; same thing.

Fuck it! He tosses his phone onto the bedside table where it clips the complimentary notepad. It catapults the plastic biro to the wooden floor.

It makes the smallest sound as it lands, *clack*, but it's as if someone has fired a gun or cracked a whip. He clenches his eyes shut.

Make. It. Go. Away.

I. Have. The. Power. Not. To. See. It.

But it synthesises, that innocuous *clack*, with the memories of all those foetid bodies of humans amid the detritus of the wave. And those damned dogs! Everywhere. Frenzied over the plenteous corpses.

And now he and Sonny are back inside that cavernous room, the guesthouse devoid of walls, and of people – sucked out to God-knows-where by the retreating surge.

Unless they somehow escaped further inland? Yes, dear Jesus, let it be that. But the stench is too strong. It says, undeniably, that death is all around them. They are standing in the middle of the building, which is as vast as the stage of Royal Albert Hall. There is nothing to be seen but an empty floor and bare walls. They look about. But there is no one.

He and Sonny exchange glances. Sonny shrugs, says, 'Nobody.' They turn for the entrance. As they do something falls in front of them and strikes the concrete floor. *Clack.*

It is a disposable pen. One of those nerd pens just like back at school. Ben and Sonny look at one another again. This time they hold each other's eyes for a few moments. Then, as one, they look slowly up to the ceiling.

Countless bodies. In all states of dress and undress. Strewn in the rafters, some hanging over beams, others piled on top of them. Some in death still hugging the beams onto which the great surge of water had forced them. Others pushed way up into the roof cavity. Rats scamper amongst them, stopping here and there to do that which nature impels.

Ben crumples onto the floor and screams. But no sound comes out. A silent scream from his overloaded senses. Sonny stoops to pick him up. Straightens his mask. Half carries him back to the car.

The sight and the stench remain with him daily.

The counselling was useful. To a point. Once all of the dead who could be found had been identified and all of the consular business seen to. All the loose ends – the dead ends – tied up, those that could be. So many people just listed as permanently missing. The therapy sessions helped him steer his thoughts to better places. To breathe them away. He started running. His sense of control increased by syncopating breath with stride and footfall. He had kept the monsters largely at bay for so very long. Through the other stresses of life and work. Through the many sleepless nights with babies and toddlers and, later, sick kids. Through occasional tensions with Lucy. There were always little sounds – the washing machine clicking onto the spin cycle, the almost inaudible click just before the alarm of the clock radio sounded – that could bring the screaming back into his head. Or it was a smell – rotting garbage, a decomposing animal in the common. But he managed it. And largely hid its near-constant spectre from those closest to him.

Then came Cambodia. The tragedy at Kampot. More bloated, damaged people he'd been unable to identify.

And afterwards, back in Phnom Penh, rattling around the apartment by himself, without his family. The time of his true, inevitable untethering. Bar-hopping alone downtown. Half a bottle of Mekong whiskey. A gram of coke scored at the Napalm Bar. Swatting off hookers. Beer chasers. Back to the apartment. Alone. Still. The aloneness – except for all the dead – crowding in on him. More coke and booze.

He shaved his head in the bathroom mirror. Threw all his clothing, every item he'd had in Kampot and every other piece in his wardrobe, off the tenth-floor balcony. Because that stench was indelible and it had infested everything. Then he sat in the bath and used a scrubbing brush on himself. Scrubbing his arms and legs and torso and face and bald head until he was raw and bleeding all over. Until the smell was gone. He drank still more whiskey.

The maid found him bloodied and unconscious on the lounge room floor the next morning. Then came hospital. Medivac to London. Rehab and intensive psychological counselling where he was coaxed to discuss it all, relive it, repeatedly. He talked. Endlessly. For month after month. He wanted to get better. And the accident wasn't his fault. They told him that over and over.

This was not just post-traumatic stress, they said. No. Moral injury, they called it. The sense of helplessness, of uselessness, that comes with not being able to help someone. To save them.

Yet he still sometimes blames himself. For the wave too. For all its dead. For all the grieving families.

And even after all the therapy sessions, there are things he's never been able to talk about. Will never talk about. Such as why he ended up on the lounge room floor. Just a short stumble to the balcony and then ten floors down to the street. Leaping over the rails would have drawn a permanent line under it all for him. And that's exactly what he'd planned. But then he lost consciousness. And accidentally saved himself, if no one else.

And now here he is, in this dreadful town, trying to deal with the upshot of a woman falling herself, or leaping, or being pushed or thrown or chased over a balcony in a multistorey building, and then smashed into an unrecognisable pulp on the footpath below.

Part III

The bar is quiet for a Saturday late-afternoon. As always, though, the televisions are on. Ether. The racing channel. Only Ether has volume, a constant osmotic soundtrack for whatever might pass for contemplation in the saloon bar of the Buena Vista.

Ben watches in fascinated horror while waiting for Blunt to appear. It's the same hackneyed, inane, brain-dead rant on Ether. The bushfires have been caused by arsonists. Global warming is a conspiracy of leftists, one that only Trump and Australia's straight-shooting prime minister and his adjutants are standing up to. Electric vehicles are the devil's work, they will end the weekend and put tradies out of work. Solar panels are for elites only. Schools are turning our kids trans. The societal evil of gender-neutral toilets . . .

He wonders how they can bear to keep repeating this stuff, though there's a different anchor today – a liver-spotted fellow, patchily bearded, whose black eyes seem far too close together. He resembles nothing so much as a grizzly bear, shirt buttons strained to the point of propulsion on the tailor's miracle that constrains like an overfilled black pudding such burdensome guts.

Grizzly bear laments that it's still early January and yet the left, with all its woke virtue signalling, is already coming for your Australia Day. Yes, they want to ban it! Is nothing sacred? Then he returns to rave about demented Biden and his criminal son. Me Too being dead. Lattes and lefties and chardonnay and urban cyclists who deserve to be run off the bloody road for their aggression; and how off-shore wind farms steal the precious breeze that belongs to all of us and not a privileged few, and which are the true cause of continental warming.

Blunt comes to the bar. He's carrying a bowl of hot chips and licking gravy from his fingers.

'There you are, Ben,' he says.

'Yes, indeed I am.'

'No, I mean up there. On the telly.'

Ben glances at the second, silent monitor in the corner. And sure enough, there he is. It's the same footage of him in Nelson's car at Hurlstone that he's already seen.

'We're not used to all this attention here in The Leap,' Blunt says with a dismissive shrug. 'We're a private lot, see? Anyway, what're you drinking? First two're on me, remember.'

'Beer, please.'

'Not some poofter fancy boutique one?' He laughs wheezily. 'I'm sure you're partial.'

'No. Whatever. You choose. And a pie. Which I'll pay for.'

'Pie warmer's bung, mate. Sorry. Got chips 'n gravy here, though. Straight from the kitchen and happy to share if you'd like some.' He thrusts the bowl towards Ben. Sodden yellow chips sit unappealingly in a slimy congealing matter that looks like dog diarrhoea.

'I'll be right, thanks all the same.'

Blunt looks at Ben like he's quite mad. Shrugs again. 'Suit yerself, mate. Your loss.'

Ben takes his beer to the corner furthest from the noise of Ether. He sits and takes a deep draught of the icy brew, froth from the head frosting his top lip. The beer calms his empty stomach. The alcohol goes straight to his head, at once easing his headache and helping to corral the enervating, exhausting chaos of thoughts and emotions and anguish inside him.

He lights a cigarette. Tobacco and beer will do for him right now. He requires no further sustenance. He drains his beer and feels considerably better – lighter, less anxious, with no pressure at all to think about what next. And before he knows it, he's back at the bar, then at his table with his second beer. He will drink this one slowly, he tells himself. Sit on it a while. People-watch. But it slides down the chute just as quickly. Gloriously. Scarcely touching the sides. He knows he really ought call it quits now. He's acceded to Blunt's shout, been diplomatic. So, now is the time to head upstairs, try to call Lucy and the kids again. Sleep.

Soon there is another table of men. He thinks he recognises them, perhaps amid the previous evening's blur. But there had been so many men. So many men who mostly looked and sounded the same. Tough, wiry, weathered men. Fighters and fuckers and frackers. Tattooed. Mulleted. With dirty hands. Mean, hungry, hard eyes. A primal desperation and urgency about them all.

He remembers by sight a couple of the shooters. How could he forget the cap of one – SHOOT HAPPENS. Two others read GUNS MAKE ME HAPPY BUT YOU DON'T and I STUDY TRIGGERNOMETRY.

'Ferret – schooners?' Blunt yells at them from the bar.

Ben wonders: Would you like a verb with that? He laughs to himself. Drinks up.

'Nah, give us a coupla jugs, Les. And chasers of Jack,' Ferret replies.

Blunt brings the drinks to their table, pronto, on a tray. 'Heading out for some killin'?' he asks.

'You betcha balls. Once she cools down a bit. Too toasty for makin' bacon right now.'

Ben knows he really should leave. He gets up and heads for the door, noticing how much steadier he's suddenly become on his feet. The weariness and the sadness and the terrible anxiety have dissipated a little with the ingestion of that glorious, icy amber fluid. That cold, frothing, refreshing nectar. That was the thing, the almost magical thing, about the hair of the dog, beer in Ben's case. If you drank it to recover from drinking way too much of it the previous night, you entered a zone where you felt so much better. Sober and sharp. The beer catapulted you down a track where mundane, idiotic conversation with boring, detestable and even dangerous people, the type you'd run a mile from or be appalled by when sober, took on new vitality and interest.

But then, very quickly, the drunkenness descended on you again. The question at that point was always: stay or go? Leaving was usually hard, because the beer had this way of making you its prisoner. The worse drunks end up that way because they never know when to leave. Never know how tediously boring they are, nor how inane their repetitive, embellished conversations and preoccupations, nor how dull the company they keep.

Ben loses his internal tussle and stops at the bar, leans on it confidently.

'Another?' Blunt asks.

'Yes, old mate. And one for yourself.'

The receptionist nods. 'Don't mind if I do.' When Ben pulls out his card he says, 'Internet's down again, mate. I'll start a new tab for you. But I see you're getting a handle on the mate and mates thing around here. As I've told yer, we're all mates, and all pretty friendly until someone abuses our hospitality or rubs us up the wrong way.'

Pulling the beer, he says, 'Everyone in this bar is a bloody good bloke, although occasionally there's a sheila. In actual fact there's pretty much an unwritten No Dickheads policy here in The Leap. That goes especially for the bar of the Buena Vista.'

'Really?' Ben says, turning for a moment and casting his eyes about the room. 'And how do you think that's working for you?'

'Well, we like to think it behoves us very well indeed.'

'Well, modest self-belief is good.'

'We like to think so. But I mean to say, Ben, and listen – I don't mean to be rude at all – but the way you talk, it's a little bit like you've swallowed the Oxford Concise. Not so much what you say but the way it sounds when you say it. Plummy. That can put other good blokes off. I mean, why don't you just chillax a little, old mate? To that end, I tell yer what – I reckon you could use some company. So I'll introduce you round. Come on and meet these beaut fellers.' He nods towards Ferret and his table of firearm enthusiasts.

'There's no need, really,' Ben says.

'Ben – remember what I said about hospitality . . .'

He can't recall. Gulping his beer as he walks, he follows Blunt to the hunters' table. They eye him with initial contempt, as they might a straight cop or a fisheries and wildlife officer.

'This here's Ben,' Blunt says. 'He's English. Ben, meet Ferret, Chisel and Knuckle.'

Ferret stands and extends his hand, wearily, warily. It's calloused and brown and strong. The two other men offer Ben mock salutes instead of a shake.

'Have a drink with us, Ben,' says Ferret.

'I'm, uhm, actually, late, to —'

'Ben,' Ferret says insistently, 'have a bloody drink. You'll get yerself in all manner of strife around here if you don't accept when someone offers to shout yer a drink. Grab a seat. Chill out. What else are you gonna fucken do, go sightseeing?'

'Too true, that,' Ben says.

'Too true,' Knuckle says, parodying Ben with an attempted British accent. The men all laugh. Ben manages an awkward smile.

Ferret catches Blunt's eye, gestures an air-circle with his index finger – another round. Almost immediately there are three new jugs on the table. As Ferret fills each man's schooner, Blunt returns with a tray holding eight glasses of bourbon and cola.

'Cheers,' Ferret says. The four men clink glasses.

'Been seeing you on the telly a fair bit,' says Chisel, who looks mean and scary. He has missing teeth, and neck and hand tatts of guns and daggers and pigs' heads and naked women. Painfully thin, with blue-green veins protruding from his arms and neck, and bulging on his forehead. There's a thick pink scar running from just above the brow of his right eye across the bridge of his nose, splitting the left nostril and coming to rest at the corner of his mouth. It is as if someone tried to split his bald head diagonally, like a watermelon, with a sword. Ben tries not to stare in horrid fascination. Something about this guy, his deep-set eyes perhaps, makes Ben think of the truckie-highway murderer from that book.

'Yes, well,' he says, 'ending up on TV is a bit of an occupational hazard when it comes to a situation such as this. I rather think I've become part of the story.' He goes for the bourbon and cola, downs a glass. The sweetness sates his hunger. Right now he feels like he could drink beer and chasers until the cows come home. He's even starting to feel comfortable in the hunters' company. Yes, they're tough and hard men, he thinks. But in their own ultra-masculine way they are welcoming him, a stranger nosing around their town. They remind him a bit of those tough old Anzacs from the bush at the war memorial. That was just the Aussie way, wasn't it? Egalitarian. Inclusive and all that.

Ferret says, 'I guess you're right about that. If you've come here to convince old Sloper that them pair of bitches what killed his darling girl are innocent, you're bound to end up on TV. She was like the princess of The Leap, that one. Everyone says. Cleverest. Most beautiful. An actress. You know, I reckon plenty of people round here would be happy to pull the trigger when them two go before the firing squad.'

'Except,' Ben says, 'they'll be beheaded or stoned to death.'

'Better still! In that case, I'll buy tickets! Or chuck the first stone. Could do with a bit of that sort of tough justice here in Australia – you know, for kiddy fiddlers and crook politicians and that.'

Momentarily, Ben feels almost sober. 'You understand that their guilt or innocence doesn't matter to me? My government is simply trying to save their lives. That it's my duty to do just that.'

Knuckle says, 'Calm the fuck down, mate. Don't get your jocks in a knot. We know you're just doin' yer job. Even if it sounds like a waste of time. And you seem like maybe a slightly above average sort of a bloke. Least you seem to like to have a drink and speak bullshit. But I reckon you've got Buckley's of changing old man Sloper's mind. We know him well as anybody. Do a bit of work for him shooting porkers and goats and the odd wombat. I know – wombats are protected! But you've no idea how badly wombats wreck your land. Fuck up your fences.'

Ben hears all of this and has what seems a very lucid idea. What if he could befriend these men and get them to see things differently, so that they might convince Cecil Sloper to show compassion?

Some things do seem like a very good idea at the time. Especially with beer, and bourbon and cola chasers.

More jugs. Another tray of bourbon and cola. Ben feels on top of the world and relaxed with these men now – Ferret, Chisel and Knuckle, how wonderful they are with their cut-off sleeves and stringy rat's-tails, their three-day growths bristling like needle tips through sweaty pores. And was that the arm of a swastika creeping up Chisel's neck from the top of his collar? What a character he is!

There was no denying they drank too much too, but who didn't drink around this town? Ben could forgive them that, what with the bastard heat and the cloying smoke and the boredom. There seemed bugger-all else to do in this shithole. God, the boredom that must come with living in a place like this. He'd been in town quite long enough to imagine how unbearable it must become. And once you started drinking around here, everyone offered you a drink. It was terribly rude not to accept it. Unmanly. Un-fucking-Australian, apparently. So you accepted it and then you naturally had to buy a round to reciprocate. And on and on and on it went. Until before you knew it you were four or five or six or seven rounds in and as tight as a bloody drum. It was a bit like a frog being boiled alive. As fucked as a fricasseed frog without a notion until it was too damned late.

The conversation was of course utterly inane. Divorced wives, old cars, tattoo choices – what to do with that bloody annoying one of the ex-wife's name – giant boars that had been shot and decapitated, heads mounted, kids who didn't want to know them. The 'bloody black problem', in and around The Leap.

Ben looks at his watch and struggles to focus, checks his phone instead: 5.25 pm. He should call it quits. Go eat something. Retire early. Start his Sunday bright and fresh.

'You're comin' with us, right?' Chisel says.

The man has a curious way of speaking from behind and through his missing and blackened teeth, so that his mouth barely opens. Ben has noticed he drinks similarly, scarcely opening his mouth before leaning his head back and pouring the grog in. Sort of straining it through his dental gaps and down into his gullet.

'Where do you mean?' Ben asks.

'Out to Paradise Downs. Pump some lead into some piggies. They're like plague rabbits out there.'

'Oh, no, I couldn't possibly —.'

'Nah, come on – you'll love it. It's hilarious. The best fun you'll have perpendicular.'

'No, I can't . . . I've got a concert to go to.'

'A fucken concert? In The Leap? Not likely.'

'Yes, at the other pub. The Crown. A band. I promised a friend.'

The others exchange knowing glances.

'Listen,' Knuckle says emphatically, 'you really don't want to be going to The Crown. The Animal House, we call it. Full of blacks and losers from the other side of town. Very poor class of clientele. Come with us. Or if you're really dead-set on hanging out with that lot of fucktards, we'll have you back in time for the band.'

Ben is prevented from protesting further by the creepy apparition of the pharmacist. The transaction between him and Ferret is so lightning quick and practised (a small baggie of blue pills deposited in Ferret's hand as he shakes with the pharmacist, after which Ferret places a cigarette packet with cash in it inside the dealer's breast pocket) that Ben almost misses it. He feels suddenly very pissed again. Pissed as a newt. He could sure use another one of those little blue pills.

Ferret puts one on a beer coaster in front of Ben. He snatches it up, pops it straight in his mouth and doesn't hesitate to wash it down with beer. He clenches his eyes shut and awaits its magic.

The bar is starting to fill with the Saturday evening crowd when Ben follows Ferret, Chisel and Knuckle out onto Gallipoli Way. Knuckle carries a slab of dark and stormy on his shoulder. In his free hand he has a large bottle of lemonade and a packet of salt and vinegar chips. Chisel has an unopened bottle of Jim Beam.

The sun is still up. In the grimy smoke haze its light is milky and soft. The street is empty save for the skater boys, slouching against the stone wall of the pub, and two figures on the opposite side of the road: Saucy and Dorinda. He's holding her upper arm as he steers her across the road to the Buena Vista, heads down and deep in animated conversation. She looks sad and lost. And, as yesterday, slightly afraid. Ben desperately wants to avoid them.

'Here comes ya girlfriend,' Ferret says. 'You wanna ghost her then ya best hurry up and get in.' He opens the back door of a double-cab ute parked out front of the pub. It's already unlocked, engine running. The cool from the air-conditioning spills into the street.

On the back tray is a cage with three dogs – great slobbering, panting brown and white mastiffs. They bark as the men climb into the cabin. A sticker on the back window shows the Australian flag with a hunting rifle next to it and reads: TRY BURNING THIS ONE! Behind the tray, on a trailer, sits some sort of buggy with huge wheels and deeply treaded tyres.

Ben gets into the back seat. Where he realises he is sitting next to a child, a boy of ten or eleven. The kid is watching something on an iPad. It looks to be an animation about a blue dog. Knuckle turns round from the front seat and hands the kid the lemonade and chips.

'There you go, Boy,' he says. 'Fill yer boots.'

Boy takes the chips and the lemonade and rests them on the seat between himself and Ben. He ignores Ben and the others, remaining glued to his screen, smiling and giggling to himself.

Chisel gets in behind the wheel. He revs. The engine burbles. Knuckle, sitting alongside, hands the driver a tinnie of dark and stormy. He tosses tinnies into the back for Ben and Ferret.

'Get these inter yez, cunts.'

The tyres screech as Chisel jerks the car out from the kerb, just as Dorinda reaches the vehicle. With her face inches from the darkened window, eyes wide open, she knocks and waves and forces a grimaced smile. Or is Ben misreading her? A contorted melange of emotion surges through him – sorrow at her sadness and her humiliating desperation, and guilt at his own inability or unwillingness to help her, and pity, yes, mostly pity. All heightened by the little blue pill he just swallowed in the bar. Ben raises a limp hand, forces an awkward, pointless wave.

Her eyes reveal her hurt and disappointment as vividly as the purple and yellow and blue bruises on her upper arms.

'Seems you've made quite the impression on Dorinda,' Ferret says. 'Guess she's only human.'

Ferret and his mates guffaw raucously.

More cruel laughter and ribald jokes as Knuckle ponders how many local men Dorinda might have encountered, and how she has never yet managed to land 'the unicorn' – the gallant stranger passing through The Leap who'd whisk her away from all the pain and disappointment.

The yowls and guttural shrieks that follow sound like starving dogs ripping into a lame lamb.

Ben yearns for the drink. Like he could knock off that whole slab of dark and stormy himself. He glugs from the can. All his senses are waltzing. While he no longer feels drunk, he does feel twitchy, full of restless energy and anticipation – or perhaps fear. There seems no difference right now. He is quick to laugh and swallow, and his mind is darting about, one moment jumbled, the next focused intently on the kid's iPad.

Chisel slows the ute as a cop car approaches on Gallipoli Way. The police car flashes its lights and emits a brief siren blast of acknowledgement. Chisel winds down the window and offers a thumbs-up. Then he puts the foot down, propelling the big rumbling V8 west out of town into the descending dusk. Towards Paradise Downs.

Once they cross The Babylon, the land becomes flat, undulating like a moonscape studded with boulders. Ben has never seen such remarkable country. He wants to stop and prostrate himself on one of the smooth giant rocks. He thinks them beautiful. Somehow unearthly and ethereal. Or cathedral-like. He doesn't know. But they seem special. He wants to connect with them.

Chisel tells him to fuck right off when he suggests stopping, they've no time. Best time for feral pigs, it seems, is the hour or so before sundown when they venture out to feed and forage with their young'uns.

'Anyway, bad juju round here. The Abos reckon it's their sacred ground or some bullshit. That them rocks are giant snake eggs or from emus or some crap. Whatever – we don't never stop here.'

The dust and rocks soon give way to fenced-off paddocks of grass interspersed with towering ghost gums, their twisted arms and fingers black and grey against the pinking sky at the horizon. As they drive further west, the pasture transitions to open scrub, and here the earth is thinly veneered with ash, dotted with bracken, and anthills tall as portaloos.

Chisel edges slowly off the road, parks on a flat clearing about a hundred metres into the scrub. He gets out, leaving the engine running, lowers a ramp at the back of the trailer and reverses the buggy onto the ground.

'Let's go,' he yells. 'Jump on. Boy, lose the iPad. See to the doggies. Woof!'

Boy sighs. Alights wearily. He releases the dogs from the cage. They snuffle about, locking onto porcine scent. They sniff Ben. His crutch and his backside and his hands and his feet. He stops still. Anxiously raises his hands. Repulsed by their slavering mouths and their thick, gummy slobber on his pants.

No dog has been the same to him since the wave. He even has his triggering moments with Nancy the labradoodle.

The mastiffs hare off into the scrub, but return instantly when Boy whistles. The kid is now sandwiched between Chisel and Knuckle in the front seat of the buggy; Knuckle nurses a hunting rifle across his knees. Ferret, a rifle slung over his shoulder, stands with Ben on the rear platform, behind a roll-bar with a spotlight the size of a schoolroom clock. Boy speaks his unique language to the dogs in a castrato-like voice, a combination of whistles and grunts and commands, barely discernible to Ben.

'Wazzit, wazzit – Gypsy, Dane. Yo, Prince – eee boy. Back now. Goooodawgs.'

The dogs mill impatiently around the buggy as Chisel, open bottle of Jim Beam in one hand, starts the engine and lurches forward into the scrub. He's a dexterous driver, careening through brush and thin scrub, smashing down small trees while avoiding the anthills, all the while necking the liquor. Ben clings onto the roll-bar for dear life. Ferret yowls, 'COOOOEEEEE,' into the dust and flying detritus about them. Chisel slows to a crawl as they reach the edge of a clearing, the buggy idling to a metronomic rumble. The dogs, panting madly, frantic on the scent of as yet unseen quarry, turn circles on themselves while Boy calms them.

'Eaaaasy. Staynow daaawgies,' he sings.

When the buggy stops completely Ferret raises his rifle and shoots into the bush. There's a tremendous crack. Cockatoos and magpies ascend from nowhere, screeching and warbling, the collective sound of their wings like canvas flapping madly in a gale.

Now comes the sudden high-pitched squeal of a sow and the baritone grunt of a boar as they break into the clearing. Long brown-black bristles, contorted tusks protruding from the sides of their mouths.

'Look at that motherfucker, will you!' Ferret yells. 'He's huge. 'Fucken mammoth beast!'

Chisel and Knuckle hoot ecstatically.

'Ggogeeeetemandgo,' Boy commands, and the dogs fly after the pigs, across the clearing and into the scrub on the other side.

'Let's go,' Chisel yells. He bolts after the dogs. Knuckle, Ferret and Boy, a backpack on his back, on his heels.

Ben, with all the booze and his brain buzzing with the blue pill and the electricity in his legs, doesn't want to stop still. And he needs to know. He just must know. What now? What next? It feels menacing and acutely existential but he can't bear to stay here, alone, while it's all going to unfold ahead of him. He's terrified. But the terror, counterintuitively, is impelling him to follow rather than freeze, even though he's never been a follower. He's terrified of the guns. Of the crazed, drunken, drugged-up, maleficent men wielding them. Of the vicious dogs and their fucked-up, creepy kid handler. Of the wild pigs; he's seen *Razorback*. He now shares the Englishman's seemingly innate terror of any wildlife – animal, bird, fish or insect – on Australian land or sea. Then, an unexpected rational spark chills him: wasted, criminal-looking blokes with guns everywhere and he's the only one unarmed! This is anathema to all his situational awareness training. Suddenly the circumstances feel acutely dangerous. Treacherously foreign. Potentially lethal.

Ben watches closely as Knuckle, Chisel and Ferret stop abruptly at the clearing's edge, rifles raised. A conga line of piglets – one, two, three, four, five – squeal into the open, trailing their parents. The three men raise their rifles. Fire. The piglets scream as the hollow-point bullets explode into their soft pinkness, expelling little puffs of bloody viscera into the dirty air.

The men high-five.

'Rotten little cunts,' Chisel says. 'Nice shooting, bros.'

The men now run through the scrub after the dogs and the adult pigs, with Boy on the heels of the mastiffs. Ben momentarily thinks again about staying closer to the vehicle. But that fear and elation and curiosity direct him to charge into the scrub after them all. The men are shouting incoherently and Boy screams commands to the dogs: 'Ontatheears, put 'em doooown.

Gooddawgs. Gypsy geeet innere. Ripinto 'em girl. Dane good boy.' Ben feels the excitement in his stomach and loins as he dodges the low bushes and weaves about the ant mounds. Sharp twigs tear at his clothing as he smashes his way through the brush behind the others.

He is breathing hard, his heart pounding wildly from the booze and the drugs, and the chaotic human and animal desperation, and the blood of the piglets and the way they kicked up from the ground and pounded dead onto the earth like birds blasted from the sky, and the raw, rank stench of such excitement, cordite, existential peril and hyper-masculine violence. And then there is the noise – a malevolent symphony of the screaming men and unnervingly high-pitched Boy, of the scrub being smashed and crushed as they careen through it after the animals, of the crack of gunfire and dogs yowling and growling for flesh and barking, and now, the sow and the boar crying out, wailing in distress.

There is an unaccountable, terrifying pleasure in it all for Ben. It is visceral. So acutely that his addled neurons buzz about, questing to define all he senses. He lands on a word: 'groinal'. It's freighted with guilt, too, like some sort of illicit sex that's taken him to the brink, only to hold him there giddily, in a wonder of performance anxiety and anticipated relief. It all reverberates through him, resonant of those irrational, pang-like, physical, drug-and-booze-inspired responses – fleeting, illogical urges – he had towards poor covetous Dorinda. It is the thrill of engagement, of going to the edge and hovering over, without leaping into, the ecstatic abyss.

And so, as he sprints through the scrub now, he desperately wants – needs – to tango cheek to cheek with, to embrace as tightly as possible, this primal savagery. To flirt with it and perhaps even welcome it into himself. And as he does this, panting and half choking on his own breath, he is asking himself a question: Could this be who I really am after all?

Up ahead he sees Chisel and Knuckle standing behind the grounded boar, its body the expanse of a lion's, its head the size of a medicine ball, with great gnarly tusks protruding from the sides of the snout. Two of the mastiffs, each with a flappy pink ear of the boar clamped in their jaw, have pinned its head to the dust. Every time the pig moves, the dog's fangs tear terribly at the ears, causing it to scream in terror and agony. Knuckle grasps the right rear trotter and pulls hard on the leg. It submits, panting and squealing, to its fate. One of the dogs eases up, allowing the boar to turn and survey its captors – and its nearby mate who is likewise pinned to the dirt by the third mastiff. Ferret smashes his rifle butt into its head, crushing its skull. But it's still alive. He laughs. The animal is silent. Breathing fitfully.

Ben catches the boar's eye. It is beautiful – a soft hazel flecked with green, orbited by the pure white sclera. It has long, dainty, concave – personable – eyelashes. Its look is so very human. In the dwindling light its eye, barely discernibly, reflects Ben, now staring at it in horror and wonder and sympathy, panting, as he absentmindedly drinks from the can of alcohol he'd forgotten is still fixed in his hand. He drains it. He crushes the empty can in his hand before lobbing it without thought into the bush. He does think: Another.

There is something else in the boar now. Ben wonders if it is perhaps that the animal wishes only for the coming finale to be swift. To be over. For him and the sow.

Chisel pulls a bowie knife from the sheath strapped to his leg, kneels beside the boar. He holds its gaze and smiles, delighting in its fear. Then in a swift, practised movement he draws the blade across its throat. The animal flinches, and closes its eyes.

The blood squirts in a thick purple arc, blackening the red earth where it lands.

'Die, motherfucker,' Chisel says, as the dogs release the pig's ears and move over to snap at the sow. It is smaller than its mate, though it still has the length and girth of a fat, unshorn sheep. Ferret has it by the hock and it, too, has ceased struggling, submitted to imminent death.

Chisel offers the knife, handle first, to Ben. 'Go on, mate. Finish her off. Let's see what you're made of.'

His protests fall on deaf ears. 'Go on. Don't be a piker. You'll never get this chance again.'

'But why would I want to?'

'Ferret,' Chisel says, 'what's the best thing about offing a pig?'

Ferret pulls one of the dogs away, so that the sow turns its head to observe its killers. 'Because it's the closest you'll ever come to killing a person without committing murder. Believe me.'

'Yeah, and he knows,' Knuckle says. 'He absolutely does.'

Ben has no problem believing that Ferret has killed a man. Or a woman. All of these people, he thinks, are capable. Might they kill me, then, if I don't cut the animal's throat?

'So listen up – you take this knife and you do it right now,' Chisel orders.

All three men and Boy look upon Ben. Boy smiles as Ben reluctantly takes the knife. Ben sees the utter terror – and personable intelligence – in the sow's expression.

He kneels beside the animal and, aping Chisel's action with the boar, puts the blade under her throat. Swiftly draws upwards and across. He feels the skin beneath its gullet split. The sow blinks once and expels a deep moan. As its head drops to the earth, its open eye remains fixed on Ben. Blood sprays across Ben's face and hands, misting his shirt and pants.

'You beauty!' Ferret yells. 'How good did that feel, mate?'

Ben can't respond. His heart beats so loudly in his ears he can scarcely register the men and the boy cheering and patting him on the back. The dogs circle the sow, sniffing at its head and orifices, tails wagging madly. One of them slurps at the blood spilling from its throat.

Ben stands up. He has the knife in one hand. He wipes the blood off his other hand onto his shirt.

'Well done, killer,' Knuckle says. 'Here, have a bloody drink.'

He hands Ben the half-empty bottle of Jim Beam. The warm, sugary, spicy liquor burns his throat and settles warmly in his guts. Knuckle takes out his phone. Photographs the carnage.

'I think I'm going to be . . .'

But he swallows the vomit back down, takes another swig from the bottle.

Knuckle takes the backpack from Boy. He unzips it and pulls out a thick nylon rope, looped nooselike at one end, and searches for a suitable tree. They are elusive in this landscape of low scrub and ant mounds. He spots a ghost gum, and throws the rope over a bough. The noose dangles. The three men and Boy regard Ben with bemusement.

A chill runs the length of him, finishing in his head like a volt of electricity. Now the fear freezes him.

Ferret takes a long swig of Jim Beam. Clears his throat.

'All rise,' he begins. 'This court is now in session. Ben, the Englishman, you are herewith charged that on the . . .' Ferret pauses briefly to contemplate the month. 'That on this day in January in this year of the Lord 2020, you took a blade and fatally cut the throat of our sister, Miss Piggy. How plead you, Englishman Ben? Guilty or not guilty?'

In this moment, as night envelops them, Ben genuinely fears for his life. He realises that these men – and this boy – dwell on the edge of another civilisation. That they kill not because pigs are a feral pest, but because they enjoy the act of extinguishing life. He does actually briefly think the noose is more than just a macabre joke – that he might indeed be imminently hanged out in the middle of the remote, fabled, bloody Australian bush. At the hands of these blokes, drunk on blood-lust and booze, and crazed on blue pills. They'd easily do it just to watch him die. Just for a laugh. For the thrill of it. To ease the boredom. To show off to Boy. Then bury him deep in the bush, like a victim of the Belanglo backpacker killer or that murderous highway monster in the Northern Territory.

Ferret passes the bottle to Ben. 'Hold this,' he commands.

Ben does as he's told. Takes another drink.

They tighten the noose around the hocks of the boar. It takes the strength of the three men to hoist it off the ground. Dangling there from the tree the animal, its limbs fully extended, is physically mammoth. Blood and viscera stream from its mouth.

Boy uses one of the men's phones to photograph the hunters and their pig. Ben is pictured standing idly by the tree, bottle in hand.

'Would you look at the size of this fucker,' Ferret says. 'Gotta be close to a record.'

They crash the animal to the ground with a thump and let the dogs at it. They collect the rope and wander back to the clearing. There, Ferret butchers the piglets with a tomahawk, taking only their hocks.

With their forward trotters extended and minus their back legs, they look like some sort of parody of swine – an art installation of the likes seen at Tate Modern or The Met – swimming in red dust.

Back at the buggy they dig a hole, light a fire and roast several of the hocks on a grill over the hissing flames. By the time they start gorging on bush pork the night is pitch-black. Sparks disappear into the starless darkness above them, illuminating the faces of malevolence around the fire pit.

Ben eats ravenously. The meat, adorned only with salt, is barely cooked, but it sates the hunger Ben barely recognised until he began chewing. The hock is sizzling hot, greasy and slippery to the touch as he juggles it from hand to hand. He takes a handkerchief from his pocket to more easily clench the hunk of flesh. The rich meat and fat burn his lips, the interior of his mouth and his throat, the bloody juice dripping down his chin and onto his shirt. He wipes his mouth on his sleeve.

The men all crack more cans, wash the meat down with dark and stormy. Fart and belch. A kangaroo, inquisitive, deeply unfortunate, bounds to the outermost edge of the firelight. Chisel, vigilant, shoots it between the eyes for fun and all but Ben laugh.

'It doesn't get better than this,' Knuckle says. 'No it does not.'

'Best thing that happened to you today, Boy?' Chisel asks.

Silence, as usual, from the kid, who Ben's only ever heard talk in dog language. Boy contemplates. After a while he nods at Ben and in his eerie, high voice says, 'Seeing him shit himself when he thought we was maybe gonna hang him, eh!'

The Crown Hotel. Chisel pulls the ute up out front. Ferret and Knuckle shake Ben awake. He lolls about on the back seat, jammed between Ferret and the door, head resting against the half-opened window. Boy is in the front seat now, glued to the iPad again.

'I think I'm going to be ill,' Ben says.

'Chunder in my car, soft-cock, and we really will have to hang you,' Chisel says. 'Out you get. Still in time for the fuckwit band, see?'

Ben can hear them playing from the street. 'I'm not sure my legs are working.'

Knuckle gets out and comes around. He opens the door and grabs Ben roughly under the arms. Extracts him. Ben has to hold onto the man to steady himself – he stinks of bourbon, cigarettes, sweat, blood, and ever so vaguely of piss. And barbecued pork. Or maybe that's just Ben catching his own odour.

He wonders if he looks a fright. His hair is crusted with sweat and ash. The pig grease and soot on his skin. The blood and viscera sprayed over his clothing and boots.

Knuckle steadies him. Fixes his collar and brushes the front of his shirt, as if removing a few breakfast crumbs from a kid at school drop-off.

'There you go, mate. Good as gold. Sure you don't wanna come back to the Buena with us for a nightcap?'

'Nah. Gonna see the band.'

He doesn't care if he catches the band or not. He only wants to be away from these men.

'No worries, mate. Suit yerself if you're set on watching that lot of drongo losers. Let's get together for a drink again real soon. And here you go, take this one for the road. Pep you up in case you're falling down.'

He puts a blue pill in the breast pocket of Ben's filthy shirt. Chisel accelerates and Ben is left swaying on the footpath.

Ben pops the pill in his dry mouth and struggles to swallow it down. He stumbles towards the pub, whose windows emit inviting red and yellow and silver light. The music is thumping.

Ben can recognise Nelson's voice. Punters sing along tunelessly to the chorus: 'It's a long walk home / When you're all on your own / Yeah it's a long way home / When you're sad and alone.'

At the door, the phone he'd forgotten about vibrates silently in the back pocket of his trousers. It's Saucy.

'Well hello, Ben. I have been attempting to locate you all evening. But to no avail.'

'Went sightseeing.'

'Yes, we did observe you heading out with the pig hunters. And a lovely bunch of blokes they are, too. Earthy. Friendly. Welcoming – they're among my best clients.'

Ben is struck by the weird new formality of the solicitor's tone. He leans back against the wall of the pub and slumps down to a squat, knees up against his chest. He feels wretched. 'You called to tell me that?'

'Not at all. I'm calling to tell you that Mr Cecil Sloper has some questions for you.'

'He does? Odd, given he said he never wanted to see me again. Questions about what, precisely?'

'Oh, I'm not at liberty to disclose that, as such. My client keeps his own counsel. And he wishes to speak to you about his daughter, the apple —'

'Yeah, yes, of his eye. I know. When can he see me?'

'Dunno exactly. Next few days.'

'Fine. I'll be gone on Wednesday, so tomorrow or Monday or Tuesday. Sooner the better for me.'

'Ben, I hope that gives you some time to recover. But you ought know in advance that my client has not changed his mind. He's resolute when it comes to the execution of those murdering vixens. He simply wants to hear what you've got to say because, well, he's a . . . fair man. I'll confirm the time.' With that, Saucy abruptly ends the call.

Even in his wretchedness and brain fog, Ben recognises Sloper's curious overture as a potential advance. Any communication is better than none. Of one thing he is certain, though: Sloper has no genuine interest in any arguments for mercy that might be put to him again. Ben must appeal to something else in him. Maybe the man wants nothing but to toy with him some more? It's impossible in this state to anticipate anything much at all.

Ben uses the wall to hoist himself upright, back onto unsteady feet. The music has stopped now and people have begun leaving the pub. Some are laughing. Others singing in the afterglow of the music. The Crown seems rather more sober and friendly than the Buena Vista. He wonders if he really ought to have stayed here instead.

He searches himself for a cigarette. What he'd do for one right now. He'll quit soon. Tomorrow. Or whenever this thing is over. For it must end. One way or another.

A young man and a woman – white, city clothes – come out of the pub chatting animatedly. The man lights his cigarette.

'Could I trouble you for one?' Ben asks, slurring slightly.

The man hands him a cigarette and lights it for him, and the woman says, 'I recognise you. You're the —'

'Nah, I'm nobody,' says Ben. 'But thanks for the smoke.'

The woman takes a photo with her phone and he raises a hand in protest. But she gets in a few more before Nelson steps outside with another man, both carrying guitars.

The couple leave and Nelson stops. He peers into the darkness, does a double-take when he recognises Ben. 'Holy snapping duckshit, mate. What in hell's happened to you?'

'Pig hunting.'

'Aw, Jesus, Ben, you want to mind going out with those fucken evil rednecks. There's some bad pricks round about this place. I already told you.'

'I was trying to get them onside. Understand how they think. Thought maybe they could help me convince Sloper, get him to change his mind. Saucy told me they work for him sometimes. But in the end . . . I didn't even get a chance to ask them to help. And look, they didn't seem all bad. At first.'

'Through the beer goggles, right? Mate, what you actually need to understand is that most of these dickheads don't help anyone and they certainly don't think about anything much, 'cept how to day-drink and kill shit. You don't want to fuck around with them. Or with that creepy solicitor and that poor oddball girl he's got under his thumb. And you don't mess with the Slopers either.'

'Okay. I just needed to find another way into Sloper's ear and I thought those blokes might be it. But now Sloper's agreed to see me again anyway.'

'That's something, I spose. When?'

'Saucy will let me know.'

'I'll give you an A for persistence at least. Want me to get you there again?'

'That'd be good. Thanks. And Nelson, you mentioned his mother. Mary.'

'Marion. It's Marion.'

'Could you take me to her? Please.'

'Maybe. But that won't help for shit. I told you he doesn't listen to her. He good as banished her a long time ago.'

'Please, Nelson.'

'Jesus wept, mate – I'll see what I can do. But right now lemme get you back to your room, like I'm you're bloody nursemaid or something, you dick.'

'Let's go for a drink first?'

'Get your hand off it, Ben! How's about I take you to the Betty Ford Clinic instead? Last thing you look like you need's a drink. If I don't take you home and the coppers find you wandering round sacred Gallipoli Way they'll chuck you in the drunk tank. Get in the car, Ben. I'll drive you down the Buena.'

Ben, humbled, concedes. 'Sorry I missed the band, I just —'

'I knew you wouldn't come.'

'I'm really sorry. I wanted to.'

'Ahh, don't shit me, Ben. But you've got another chance. It's family and friends night tomorrow. An early start – six o'clock – for the littlies.'

He wakes to the whispering patter of light rain on the corrugated-iron roof. The ceiling fan rotates lazily. Both windows are open, and with the rain comes a fresh breeze. The curtains swish and sway, circulating the sweet, vital scent of new rain.

In that briefest moment before his eyes fully open, Ben is cruelly deceived. He is back, years ago, in the magically decrepit grounds of Fulham Palace, where a misty spring rain settles on the recently cut turf and the tree canopies as he and the kids wander about the gardens and eventually take shelter under an ancient holly oak.

The rain and the breeze cease emphatically. He closes his eyes again, hoping to stay in the damp fragrant grass of home, but it's quickly suffused with the noxious cocktail of campfire and stale alcohol, and the breakfast stink of bacon, lamb fat, and frying eggs and offal wafting up from downstairs.

He feels as if someone has surgically opened his skull, poured in wet cement and sutured it up. His mouth is blistered and foul-tasting, his throat sore. He tries to focus on his stinging hands, flecked with blood and scalded from holding the searing, greasy hock of slain piglet he'd so bestially torn into with his teeth. He is still in his clothes, which are stained beyond repair.

He showers under cold water. Shaving is again a struggle. So, too, is trying to avoid his bloodshot eyes following him about in the mirror. Anxiety is a python curled around his midriff, squeezing the breath out of him, paralysing him. He has a sudden, urgent instinct to flee. To go downstairs, settle his bill, check out and fly back to Canberra. There he will quit the foreign service and return to the UK, to his wife and children. He will cut and run, put this whole pointless misery behind him.

Instead he dresses in running shorts and a T-shirt, drinks glass after glass of water, and sits on the bed to call Lucy.

She is sitting on the sofa, in the familiar, comfortable, comforting, safe interior of their home. Through the French window behind her he sees the maple tree they planted a few years ago, its delicate, denuded wintertime branches dancing with fairy lights. The TV is muted. But he knows she'll be watching *Midsomer Murders* or *Vera* or something (they all sound soothingly similar to him and they both watch them never really for the storyline, but for their reassuring familiarity and patois). Lucy has a glass in her other hand – a French white from their 'cellar', which is really just a small underground cupboard in the floor of the walk-in pantry. What he'd do to be there with her, next to her on the sofa, for a calm Saturday night in.

'Darling, you're alive. I thought you'd gone missing somewhere in the wilds.'

Ben thinks she looks quite beautiful. More so perhaps than he ever noticed previously. Or at least in recent years. Her tone is warm and caring tonight. Concerned.

'Yes, well, the time difference, you know. Sorry. Makes it hell to communicate.'

'What've you been doing – besides trying to save those poor women? As if that isn't enough.'

'Oh, nothing remarkable. A little bit of communing with the locals. Eccentric as they are. I'm in the most godforsaken place, to be honest.'

'I keep seeing that dreadful man on television, Benny. He's all over the media here. Radio. TV. The papers. Calling for the women to be executed. Saying they don't deserve mercy. And you've been on TV too. People keep ringing to say, "I've seen your Benny on TV." I say, "Well, he's just doing his job." I did think you looked quite dashing walking up that dusty road with your coat over your shoulder. And did you have a ciggie in your mouth? I hope you're not smoking too much. But today you look tired – a little puffy around the eyes. You okay?'

'Just feeling the weight of it all. It's a lot, babe. I mean, he's going to let them die. And I can't stop him. It's like he's taunting me with his, I don't know, his deliberate intransigence.'

'You feel for them, that's understandable.'

'Dreadfully. I feel utterly responsible.'

'Darling, it's not your fault. You're in no way responsible. You mustn't think like that, you have to look at it another way. You'll be responsible if they live. But not if they die. If they're executed, it's that wicked old man's fault.'

She brings the phone closer to her face, peers into the screen, straining for a better look at something in Ben's realm.

'Ben,' she says, 'tell me that's not an ashtray beside the bed there?'

He turns around, regards the ashtray. Shrugs. 'You got me, babe. It is.'

Lucy doesn't say a thing. But he reads judgement in her expression and is annoyed. She still smokes, and vapes, sometimes.

'Look, it helps with . . . the anxiety,' he says defensively. 'And this shitty damned place. I'll chuck it again soon.'

'Oh Benny, I've been so worried. Don't take this the wrong way – but worried you might not be coping so well. Getting too down under the pressure . . . drinking a little too much, perhaps. I know how you can become when things pile up.'

'I'm coping. Doing the best I can. I just want to get out of here and back to Canberra, set the house up. Then I need you and the kids there with me. I'm missing you all so much.'

'We'll all be there soon enough. The kids are still quite worried about it all. I mean the fires and —'

'The fires are almost out. The smoke's lifting even as we speak.' Impatience and anger have joined the weariness in his tone.

Lucy says, 'Well, the fires were still everywhere on TV back here today. They said that they were still burning. And we saw Sydney Harbour on the news too, it was filled with smoke. And Canberra – it looks ghastly, like the whole place is under a grey pall.'

'The TV exaggerates everything, Lucy. You know that.'

'And then there's the mystery virus thing. The talk that it's a pandemic. Possible international travel restrictions. It just all seems very tense. Uncertain. And everything feels so safe and so certain here in comparison.'

'Luce, this will be an adventure for the kids. It's what we decided we wanted.'

'I know that, Ben. I know.'

Nancy nuzzles up against Lucy, nudges her head into the frame.

'Nancy, say hello to Benny. I'm sure she misses you awfully too.'

Ben goes to speak to his dog but the words jag in his throat. His heart aches. For his family. For home. For his lounge room. For Nancy. He sees the dog paw Lucy's shoulder.

'Okay, she's telling me she needs to go outside for her business. I'd better go.'

'I'll call again tomorrow,' he says.

'Do. Remember we love you, Ben. Very much. Take care. Stay safe, darling.'

She finishes the call before he can say, I'll try.

The phone immediately rings.

Nelson.

'Ben – good news,' he says.

'Say that again. I could use some.'

'Marion. Cec's mum. Charlene's grandma. She's up for a visit from you. Today.'

Ben is surprised. He hadn't thought this would happen. 'That's fantastic. I'm —'

'Hungover to buggery I'll bet.'

'Not at all. I'm up and about. Ready to embrace another day in the wondrous environs of The Leap.'

Pleasant Hills Retirement Village is neither pleasant nor hilly.

The breath-stopping aroma – faintly uric, infused with boiled cabbage and cleaning products – is the first thing he notices. The second is that this is not the sort of place you'd voluntarily retire to. It is where others would put you.

It is a place, Ben realises as soon as he enters with Nelson, that makes you think, Here but for the grace of God . . .

He glances down corridors of scuffed linoleum, where the sufficiently mobile inch about on walking frames or with sticks. From somewhere he can hear the blare of a TV, and voices that sound anguished.

'Hey, sis.' Nelson knows the woman at the desk. She has a blue uniform with *Aretha* stitched above the left breast.

'Cuz,' she says, buzzing open the glass security door and walking around the counter to embrace him.

There is small talk. Family. Rugby League. The smoke and weather. The band. Aretha had been at the gig last night. Nelson introduces Ben.

Nelson has called ahead to tell her they hope to see Marion Sloper.

'Let me check if she's awake. She's sleeping more and more lately.' Aretha looks at Ben and says, 'And she doesn't get many visitors. Cruel, given she's still got family about.'

'Okay, thank you,' he says.

'No worries. And you know, obviously she's had a terrible time lately. Charlene's death hit her hard. They were still in touch. Charlene always made some effort with her nanna. Anyway, wait here a minute.'

Ben does a quick emotional equation: Marion's closeness to Charlene might make her as immovable as her son when it comes to showing compassion to her granddaughter's alleged killers.

'Jesus Christ,' Ben says, surveying the place. 'Getting old has nothing at all going for it.'

The residents are killing time on chairs, in lounges, in beds in darkened rooms, or in wheelchairs in the treeless courtyard. The TV and the voices of people in distress constitute the white noise of Pleasant Hills, but this sound camouflages a disturbing absence. Amid this hubbub of wretchedness there is no conversation among the residents. And what is there, after all, left to say about languishing here? There is but one way out from Pleasant Hills.

Nelson seems to have read his thoughts. 'Well,' he says, 'it maybe beats the alternative, I'd reckon. I mean, just ask Charlene Sloper. Or for that matter, Aaron.'

'Your cousin?'

'Yeah – I told you.'

'And Aretha here's your cousin too?'

'Yeah. We're related. It's not a big community but it's tight. What's it matter?'

'Sorry, just getting my head around who's who in this place. The connections.'

'Yeah, right. So, like, Aretha helps care for Cec Sloper's mum. And Cec's descended directly from the man who took our land and massacred us – the reason Cec has still got our land. It's kind of like the way the snake has its tail in the past but its head in the present, if you know what I mean.'

'But the fact that Aretha helps look after Marion Sloper, I mean, that's . . .'

'Not so amazing, really. She's a kind, lovely old lady. Nothing like her son. Only she could've saved the world some trouble if she'd dashed his brains out at birth but.'

'Not her fault, sure. But her family has always had the upper hand? I mean, the massacre. They won. They've got your land. Still have it. Won it all.'

'Still, my people did even the score somewhat.'

'How so?'

'You know how yesterday I showed you the war memorial? And told you about the Sloper men not fighting at first, and getting sent white feathers?'

'Yeah.'

'Well, that was my great-grandmother sent those feathers and told the paper.'

'No way, Nelson.'

'Yes way, mate. All us Blackfellas from round here were signing up to go fight. But what do the Sloper boys do? Sit on their soft privileged white arses counting their baa-lambs and their wool money. So every month my great-grandma, she was taught to write by the church and then made to work as a domestic for another white family – well, she goes to the post office over in the next town, Whitelaw. And she posts four letters. One letter to each of the four Sloper boys, including the one what turned out to be Cec Sloper's granddaddy. Inside every one of those letters was a white feather. She somehow lets *The Irrigator* know about them receiving the feathers and not wanting to fight. In the end the shame gets to 'em. Three of them four signed up. And all of 'em got killed in France. The only brother left was Cec's grandpa.'

Aretha returns and re-engages them with her summery smile. She says, 'Mrs Sloper is happy to see you, Ben. And she'll be pleased to discuss what it is you came here to talk to her about.'

'How does she know what I want to talk about?'

With an eye roll, Aretha says, 'Jesus, mate, she might be old but she's still got her marbles. It's all over the news. And because Nelson spoke to me about it this morning and I told her. We want to help. Follow me before she dozes off again. She shares a room with another client, so I've moved her into the hallway for some privacy.'

They pad through the lounge room over dense brown carpet. Most of the people in here have a tray table in front of them. The heads of some loll forwards or onto their shoulders as they doze; others are slack-jawed and wide-eyed. The TV, big as a dining table, casts a silvery-green pall over them with an *Antiques Roadshow* repeat, volume down low. Another staff member walks from chair to chair handing out medications and cups of fruit juice to those who are awake. She tries to rouse the dozers to ensure they, too, take their medication.

Ben and Nelson follow Aretha out of the lounge room then past the kitchen and through the dining room, which another worker is readying for the next meal. They turn into a dark corridor at the end of which a skylight casts a small, perfect square of illumination onto the linoleum. Marion Sloper presents as something of an apparition, aglow within this patch of luminescence – her silver hair, pale skin and white cotton shirt. Her legs are covered with a rug. From their opposite end of the corridor she appears to be only a torso, ethereally levitating within a beam of heavenly light.

Marion is looking at them unflinchingly as they approach. It's only as they draw near that Ben realises she is in a wheelchair.

She smiles. It is a young person's smile, broad and white-toothed. Ben is taken by the skin of her face and her delicate, bony hands. She is unblemished and pale, almost to the point of translucence, as if she'd rarely in a long life been in the sunlight that now bathes her. Her thick hair is pulled back in a ponytail, accentuating her high cheekbones. Her eyes, a startling cool blue, are the same striking hue as her son's and granddaughter's. But there the likeness to Sloper's ends; Marion's are clear and wide and empathetic. They lock warmly upon her subjects, where her son's are narrow and evasive.

'Nelson, my darling, it's lovely to see you,' she says, turning her head slightly so that he may kiss her cheek. She exudes elegance and poise.

'Mrs Sloper, this is our friend Ben. The English diplomat, you know?'

'Yes, yes, of course I know! I didn't come down in the last shower.' She says it with mirth, absent of reproach, and shakes his hand, her grip surprisingly firm.

'Mrs Sloper, thanks for seeing me. Let me just say, I'm terribly sorry for your loss. Your granddaughter sounds like she was a special young woman.'

'Charlene was special in that she was my only granddaughter. But the truth is she was a bit of a lost soul too. She could not get far away enough from this place as soon as she was able. She spent the rest of her life looking for a home, and I don't think she ever quite found it. But I don't blame her for that one bit. Me, I stayed. And I stayed and stayed. Until it was too late for me to go anywhere except in here. More fool me. Now I'm stuck in this place. I was a burden to Cecil on the farm, which he inherited because, naturally, the land will only ever pass from father to son and he had no brothers. Anyway, I know exactly why you're here. But I'm not sure I can help you.'

'I've seen the photographs of her,' Ben says, picturing, for a moment, not the vivacious, physically striking and very much alive Charlene, but the terrible death scene images from Riyadh. 'She was remarkably beautiful.'

'She was that. But also intelligent. Though her father only really valued her beauty. She was also adventurous. And always a risk-taker. Kind and gentle too. She made an effort to visit me here most years after she left. Usually around my birthday. She'd come in and out of The Leap and visit me without seeing her father. I'm sure he knew, though. Nothing has ever been secret for very long around here.'

'This might seem a rather odd question,' he says, 'but . . .'

'Goodness, Ben, ask me, go on – I can handle it, I'm sure.'

'Charlene was kind and gentle, you said. How would she – I mean, what would she do with the women charged with murdering her?'

'You're right. It's a strange question – a rather pointless hypothetical, really.'

'Um, okay, Mrs Sloper, I'll get to the point. Is there any way you could imagine that your son might be persuaded to change his mind – to show mercy to the two women charged with murder?'

Marion thoughtfully fingers the small brooch on her shirt. It's a platypus made of silver and mother-of-pearl. He wonders if it was a gift from Charlene. 'You need to understand that my son and I haven't been close since he was a little boy. And not even then, really. He was an unusual child. And he grew into a difficult man. But that's been the pattern for the Sloper men. Tell me, do you have children?'

'Three.'

'A son?'

'Yes. Jerome.'

'Such a lovely name. And what's for you the most important thing when it comes to fathering him?'

'Oh, it's to make sure he feels safe, secure. And confident. But I don't treat him any differently than I do my two daughters.'

Marion nods. 'Exactly. And that's just the way it ought to be. Boys have to be loved. Have to be petted, just like girls. By their fathers and their mothers. But the Sloper men are different. From the moment Cecil was born his father was trying to wrest him away from me, just as his father had done to him. My husband, Donald, believed that the only thing Cecil needed to understand was survival. How to be the toughest, the hardest, the most resolute. With animals. With other people. With the universe. That meant eschewing compassion. Closing off feelings. Only that way would the Slopers remain where the Sloper men felt it was their destiny to be for all time. On Hurlstone.

'By the time Donald died, the damage was already done with Cecil. And yet somehow he found a beautiful woman, Mary. Charlene's mother. But he bullied her. Squashed the life and the passion out of her. Wrung her out like a wet tea towel, he did. He'll tell you that Mary died in labour with Charlene. Nonsense! I say he – my own son – bullied her to death. She had a terrible case of the baby blues. Couldn't feed or connect to her daughter. Cecil told Mary again and again she was a failure as a mother, useless – told her that until he finally defeated her. She took pills . . . then she waded into The Babylon with stones in her pockets. That was one more funeral for a Sloper woman who discovered the hard truth about the family she married into. And when Charlene's body comes home next week she'll be buried in Hurlstone's sad, lonely little cemetery too, I suppose. To think I always assumed I'd be next.'

Despite all Ben has learnt about Cecil Sloper's character, and his personal experience of the man's sinister coldness, this still shocks him. He finds it unfathomably sad. For Charlene. Her brother. For Marion.

'Mrs Sloper, I'm so sorry. How awful.'

'After that I always tried to care for Charlene. I brought her up from a toddler, see? Tried to protect her from her father. And tried to protect Kenny too. That boy! Kenny knows no other way but kindness too. And he's been mercilessly put down by Cecil. He's a big boy. Big and affectionate, soft and gentle, if not at all academically inclined. He's terrified of his father. And he's the very opposite of him. He'd prefer to cuddle a wild animal than shoot it. Cries when the lambs are trucked off to the knackery. But unlike Charlene, who had the gumption to get away, he's not got the wherewithal to make an independent life for himself.'

The old woman sighs. Her brow furrows. She clears her throat and runs a hand across her brow. A gossamer sheen of perspiration has appeared on her forehead and upper lip.

Aretha says, 'Mrs Sloper, shall we move out of the sun?' She wheels the chair to the side of the hallway. They sit opposite her on a wooden bench.

There is silence now. Marion Sloper glances at Nelson and Aretha. She looks into Ben's eyes and purses her lips. Her face wears a hybrid expression of grimace and knowing smile. She nods her head several times emphatically. A tear rolls down her cheek. There is clearly more she wants to say. They wait while she composes herself. Aretha gently strokes her hand.

'Well, with all that happened when she was a baby girl,' Marion continues, 'I often think that Charlene was sort of hardened and hollowed out all at once. Emotionally, I mean. She learnt how to shield herself from an early age, but I also tried to protect her as she grew up. Right up until she was a young woman and left. You see, I was already in this chair and I needed looking after myself. And that was increasingly falling to Charlene because, well, my son wasn't prepared to do it. And then she . . . had to leave for the city. She couldn't stay and help me anymore. Just couldn't. And so I ended up in here. There was little choice. That was twenty years ago. I've been here for two decades.'

'That's a dreadfully long time, Mrs Sloper. It must be —'

'Lonely? Sometimes. Though I've good friends here. Problem is they keep damn well dying! Cecil I'm lucky to see once a year. But Kenny still comes. And Charlene always did, as I said. You know, she called me most weeks no matter where she was. And I last saw her just six months or so ago. There has been so much pain . . .'

Ben senses something unsayable. Did Cecil somehow abuse his daughter to the point where she fled and cut all further contact with him? Marion has made it clear that Charlene was not quite so precious to Cecil Sloper as he has been insisting to the world, and that her death isn't the crushing heartbreak he claims.

He proceeds gently. 'Mrs Sloper, why did Charlene leave The Leap so suddenly?'

She sighs once more. 'There was no one thing. Look at it this way: she'd been waiting her whole life to leave. To make her own way. And then there she was, out of school, eighteen years old, with options, and choices to make. She did well at school. She was offered a place at agricultural college. She thought that she'd learn about farming. Land care. How to diversify Hurlstone because perhaps, one day, when the time came, she and Kenneth could manage the place together. But then once she was in the city she started the acting and the modelling instead. And then the flying. She stayed away. And she just kept moving.'

Marion is again fiddling with her platypus brooch as she says this. Her voice is cracking a little. Her eyes, focused on his throughout their conversation, momentarily shift about the hallway.

'Your son told me he intended to leave Charlene the farm. Or at least have it passed down to any child she had in the future – a son, presumably. That's what he said to me.'

'Well, he can't take it with him! And now there's only Kenneth.'

The sudden harshness in her tone makes him pause a moment. 'Mrs Sloper, thank you. But I'm still wondering whether, and how, your son might be convinced to change his mind about the two condemned women.'

'But don't you see? His vanity. His lack of empathy. His cruelty. He's not so much angry at those women because they might have killed his only daughter and denied him an heir, as he insists. No. He's enjoying the attention – all the focus on him.

The "will he/won't he?" The longer that all goes on, the more chance you will have, is the way I see it.'

But Ben needs to wrap this matter up quickly. The thought of not being on that plane out of The Leap on Wednesday is torturous. Surely there must be a better way than just waiting Sloper out, as Marion suggests?

'Mrs Sloper, if only he could be persuaded to accept the money.'

'Yes, I saw that Cecil mentioned this on the television – that some payment might be made by your government in return for his mercy. But how could he possibly put a price on the life of his treasured Charlene, he said. Not that she ever seemed quite so priceless to him in life, mind you! So he was refusing such an offer. Wouldn't hear of it, considered it an insult. The papers have reported that too. I must say I wondered if this was accurate?'

Ben explains the intricacies of the Saudi court's blood money. 'And yes,' he says, 'your son is refusing to countenance *diyyeh*.'

'I do find that a little surprising. I can tell you there's been bad year after bad year on that farm. Drought. Erosion. Soil depletion. Invasive plants and weeds. That land is exhausted. He's going to have to start selling off chunks of it to survive, eventually. "Eating the farm", they call it round here. It's happened on so many of the big properties. So, my advice would be to just keep talking money with him. Money, he understands. The Sloper men have all died with their first dollars – or shillings – in their pockets. Have always cried poor. But money's not the be all and end all for him either, you should understand.'

'What is, then, Mrs Sloper?'

'Control, Ben. Controlling everyone and everything around him. Playing God, you might say. Cecil is not wired like other people. Normal people, I mean. Emotionally. Morally.

He is the sum total of the way generations of Sloper men have been conditioned. But that conditioning has stopped with Kenneth. No matter Cecil's cruelty, his mistreatment of that boy, Kenneth remains good.'

'Mrs Sloper, can you talk to him? Or to Kenneth? Might Kenneth have some influence? Persuade his father that the best way to keep the property in Sloper hands, and to be remembered favourably by the world – and the whole world *is* watching – is to consider the *diyyeh*?'

'Kenny bleeds compassion, as I've told you – despite all appearances, he is only good. But his father will *never* listen to him. Cecil likes to say he gets more sense from talking to the sheep. And he won't listen to me either. I'm a woman, after all. Even if I am his mother.'

Ben slumps in the front seat of the Valiant as Nelson drives him back to the Buena Vista. The light is starting to fade, snuffed out by smoke and dust, even though it's barely mid-afternoon. He feels thoroughly spent. Depleted beyond repair. He loathes the feeling of atrophy, and uselessness, that is crushing him. He can no longer bear waiting around, at Sloper's whim.

'I'm absolutely rooted here,' he tells Nelson. 'In every way. Totally up shit creek with no paddle. I don't know what to do. I can't wait here forever while this psychopath plays with me.'

'Don't take it personally, mate. Cecil Sloper has been like that forever, with everyone. His own family included. As you've just heard. But I'll tell you what to do – get out of this car.' Nelson pulls into the kerb outside the hotel. 'Do not go into the bar. Go straight upstairs. Sleep. And then come to our gig tonight. You'll be welcome there.'

The ruckus from the Buena's public bar wakens him, like some primordial slime seeping up through the floor. There's the nasally voice of Blunt booming out a bawdy tale to his dedicated drinkers; Ben can hear mention of fuckers and goats, undies and pillows and strap-ons . . . It penetrates even the blasting metronomic soundscape of the rugby chat show and Ether's provocations. At the tale's punchline, the bar erupts in screaming, spluttering, mad laughter.

In his early-evening state of half-sleep, weariness and increasingly foreign sobriety, the noise is frighteningly unsettling. Universe, please protect me from this, he thinks, so that I may somehow survive.

And yet, perversely, he feels beckoned. Ineluctably drawn, yet again, to the hideous netherworld beneath the floorboards.

It would be the easiest thing in the world right now – to acquiesce to that societal Hades below. To drink deliciously frosty schooners of gently frothing amber ale. To suck down bourbon and colas and take another of the pharmacist's magical little blue pills. To run straight at danger, to shun caution and self-preservation.

'Save me,' he says aloud. But from what? This place. It's got to be this dreadful shithole. This civic dung-heap, The Leap, with its murderous genesis, its endless reservoirs of booze that must be drunk, its freakish and dangerous men and their guns, its Buena-fucking-Vista portal into a frightening purgatory of . . . me. I will leave The Leap come Wednesday. Fly out for good.

His watch says nearly six. He promised Nelson he'd come to The Crown at six, for family night. It might be just what he needs. He shaves, showers, puts on a clean shirt and heads downstairs.

'Where're you going, then? Come join us in the bar for a coldie or three, eh mate. It's well past beer o'clock.' Blunt's voice snares him as he negotiates the sticky carpet under the grim yellow pall from the busted chandelier, beckoning him into the bar. Ben looks around. But it's his own inner voice that's calling, aping that of the receptionist. 'What are yer, a bloody psycho or something? Some people. I mean they just need their heads read.'

The street is lifeless, as usual, save for a lone dog asleep against the wall of the TAB. The wind has dropped and the smoke has thickened since the afternoon.

He walks slowly, the tension in his body easing with each step away from the Buena. After a few hundred metres he can see the lights of The Crown, and soon it's aglow like a Christmas tree, with red and green lights strobing through the barred windows. He stops outside.

The hum of laughter and chatter drifts onto the street – kids squealing and adults nattering. It is a soundtrack of excited conviviality and accord. Of communal unruliness and fun. The music is not so loud as to drown out the thrum of conversation and merriment, but he can still make out Nelson's distinctive voice, now set to a light baritone as he croons an Elvis cover: 'Suspicious Minds'.

The man on the door, a towering Pacific Islander with tribal tattoos on his arms and face, quickly surveys Ben. He smiles an inviting, gap-toothed greeting, little crow's-feet appearing at the outer corners of his eyes as his face creases with warmth and welcome.

'You're Ben, eh. Nelson's mate. He told me to look out for ya. Come in.'

There is a small table just inside the door of the lounge, on which sits a shoebox of football socks. Ben thinks this curious. Most of the tables have been pushed to the edge of the room so that the floor is clear for dancing. Three tables have been set aside for the older men and women, and several others are laden with food. There is a reassuring aroma from his childhood – it's just like his grandmother's homely kitchen after she'd cooked Sunday lunch of cottage pie and bread-and-butter pud.

Ben breaks into a smile. His body begins to expel tension. His shoulders relax. He could not have imagined such an untroubled oasis of safety and joy, even at his favourite, more sedate watering holes back home. Let alone in The Leap. It calls to mind the Moon Under Water, George Orwell's ideal of the non-existent, perfect pub.

Nelson's three-piece is at the end of the room, opposite the bar, under bunting that reads FAREWELL AND CONGRATS ROY. The ornate architraves and pressed-metal roof are festooned with crepe streamers in black and yellow and red.

Amid the be-socked kids sliding across the shiny, buffed wooden floor, couples are dancing. Black and white, Black and Black, white and white. Men and men. Women and women.

The song ends as Ben is self-consciously looking for somewhere to hide himself. He catches Nelson's eye. Nelson nods and smiles, gives him a mimic of a salute. The band starts up again, begins to massacre a Simple Minds song, 'Someone Somewhere in Summertime', but quickly finds its rhythm and doesn't sound half bad.

Nelson is shimmying around the mic stand. The older people seated at the tables nod and sway, tap hands and feet. The song has a melancholic energy and Ben shivers a little, an involuntary emotional nerve triggered by this anthem of his teens. Ben stands by the tables of food, transfixed. There are plates of homemade sausage rolls and pies, cold chicken drumsticks. There are white-bread chicken and ham sandwiches, crusts removed, and big plastic Tupperware containers of chocolate crackles and fairy bread. Open bottles of cola and industrial-sized pots of tea. Paper plates and serviettes. Paper cups.

When the music stops he takes it as his cue to go to the bar. He's dying for a drink.

As he passes the table of the old ladies, one of them wolf whistles. The other ladies chortle, leaning into one another and covering their mouths with splayed hands.

Ben thinks he hears one of them say, 'Nice bum there – for a gubbah anyways.'

Now they're laughing raucously. One of the men leans across to the women. 'That how you welcome an out-of-town guest, Beryl? Y'old flibberty flirt.'

'Nothing wrong with appreciating the landscape, Danny. The man should take a compliment from a woman as vital as me.'

More laughter erupts. Ben looks awkwardly at them, unsure what to do.

Danny stands up and extends a hand to Ben. 'Name's Uncle Dan. Good to see you. Who are you, though?'

Still blushing, Ben says, 'Ben. I'm Ben. How do you do.'

'Good on you, Ben. Your voice says you're not from round The Leap. Where'd you say your mob's from then, eh?'

'My mob? Great Britain, I suppose,' he says. The women guffaw again.

'Oh, he's from Great Britain,' Beryl says. 'Fancy.'

Dan says, 'Great Britain, eh! You come back, did yer, to take the rest of our land? Only kidding,' he adds. 'Only kidding.'

'I spose you'd be on intimate terms with Queen Betty then, would you?' Beryl asks.

Dan nods to the women. 'Don't mind them. It's just their way of being friendly. Can't take 'em anywhere but, if you know what I mean.'

'Danny, you gettin' full of lip there,' says another woman. 'How many beers've you had?'

'Not a bloody drop. You know it's been twenty years, Val.'

'Well,' she says, 'you're carrying on like you've drained the bloody kegs and then some down the Buena Vista.'

That sets them all off again.

'So,' Val says to Ben, 'you come here to find a girl? There're younger ones than us about. Maybe prettier too. Who knows, you might do all right round here in those fancy boots, with your nice Prince Charles voice and cute behind.'

Beryl is laughing so hard she splutters her tea. And with all their laughing, Ben can't help chuckling himself. He says, 'No, I came because I'm a friend of Nelson's. He's helped me out so . . .'

'Makes sense,' says Val. 'Always helpin' people is Nelson. Kindest boy ever.'

'He's hardly a boy,' one of the other men says. 'He's almost forty.'

The band starts to belt out another cover. Midnight Oil, 'Blue Sky Mine'. Nelson plays the heady harmonica intro before launching into the lyrics.

Beryl's face becomes suddenly serious. She looks Ben over, reading him. 'Listen, love, don't mind us and all our silly banter. You're welcome here. Please fix yourself up with some food. Grab a drink.'

He smiles and says he'll do that. He's hungry. At the food table he puts two bite-sized sausage rolls on a paper plate, squeezes on some tomato sauce. He bites into one. Then closes his eyes in delight. It just might be the best thing he's ever eaten. Certainly in The Leap. He puts a few more on his plate and tucks in as he heads to the bar.

The young bloke behind the bar has an agricultural beard and long blond dreads. A tattooed serpent twists down his right arm, its hissing head resting on his knuckles. He smiles at Ben, asks what he wants.

'Okay,' says the bartender when Ben orders a beer, 'here's the deal. For every beer you order tonight you've got to put the same amount into the jar here for Roy. Metaphorically speaking, that is. Not the actual beer, just the amount it costs. So, you buy a beer for seven bucks, you throw in seven for Roy. He's off to uni in the city, see – and tonight's all about raising some cash to help set him up.'

'Got it,' Ben says. He pays twice.

'You want to enter the raffle? Five bucks a ticket. Second prize is the meat tray. First prize – you get Nelson's band for a night. You know, weddings, christenings, wakes.'

'I'll take four tickets.'

The sound of a didgeridoo cuts through their conversation. Nelson is playing it. The crowd hushes as Dan and one of the other men appear from an anteroom. They're wearing red shorts, their stomachs and chests painted in white and yellow and red ochre. Their faces are covered in grey ash. A line of half a dozen boys, identically dressed and painted, trail the men as they turn circles on bowed legs, sing in their language and signal with splayed hands at the people around the edge of the room. Uncle Dan taps clapsticks as Nelson lowers the volume of his didgeridoo to a low, guttural background hum.

The old man welcomes all the guests to his people's traditional lands. 'Black and white, family and strangers – welcome all,' he says. 'The wayfarer who comes in peace will always be met with our hospitality and protection. We know no other way. We always were and always will be here to welcome you.'

Ben feels directly addressed. Dan's words are like a comforting, lingering hug for him and he shudders as he takes them in. He can't think of a time he's ever felt more invited or accepted. Not at his posh, unaffordable boys' school. Even less so at university. And certainly not at the foreign office. It is at once all-consuming, beyond gratifyingly human, and mournfully alien.

'Now dig deep for young Roy who's off to the uni. Another young one of our mob's going off to make us proud. But may he always return to us.'

The room starts to chant. *'Roy. Roy. Roy. Roy.'*

A gangly teenager with a mane of yellow hair comes to join the painted dancers. His T-shirt declares: AUSTRALIA – DRIVING IT LIKE YOU STOLE IT. He looks down demurely as he speaks.

'Uncle Nelson told me earlier today that, in the words of some great philosopher, or so he reckoned, some bloke I never heard of, that, you know, I can check out from The Crown and The Leap any time I like, but I can never really leave. Well, I'm not quite sure what that all means, but I think it's probably good because I'm a bit scared to be honest, you know. That's because all I've ever known here is love from my community. And it's the only true home I will ever have.'

Ben's bottom lip is quivering and he sips his beer to hide it. Wipes his eyes on his fist. But he can't stop the tears. His distance from home feels other-planetary now.

There is a pre-dawn moment before the pub groans into life and ahead of the first trill of birdsong when the dark and the quiet are cocooning. The only sound for Ben is that of his body. Lungs. Heart. Breath and pulse. But the stillness, even in his half-sleep, sets his mind racing madly down that unavoidable track of anxiety and worthlessness. The previous night at The Crown was a balm. But today the dread grips him as tightly as ever.

The circular breathing he now practises shifts him closer to sleep. He dreams vividly. Several Saudi policemen march Adair and Kilfoyle into a public square, between a mosque and a fountain of dark marble. Chop Chop Square, the expatriates call it. A heat haze blurs the spectacle. Ben hovers above it all with a drone's-eye view. The crowd jeers as the two women are paraded. One of them – he can't tell which because their heads are obscured by hoods – is lowered into a hole chest-deep. Her arms are secured. The other woman is made to kneel before a man in black robes. His face is uncovered, unlike the images of Saudi executioners Ben's seen. This executioner is bold. Proud. The long blade of a *sulthan* glints as he poises it with both hands above his head.

The kneeling woman is perfectly still but the woman in the hole is agitated. Trying fruitlessly to wriggle free. Suddenly Ben is no longer hovering above, but standing in front of this half-buried woman. He steps towards a pile of rocks, each about the size of a potato, and selects one. It is smooth and pleasant to the touch, fitting snugly into his palm. He notices it is streaked with blood. Now the woman is hyperventilating, the cloth of her hood inflating and deflating over her mouth. Ben raises his arm, twists his body and propels the rock. It travels with the direct line of a cricket ball. In that instant he looks over to see the berobed executioner swinging the *sulthan* down onto the exposed neck of the other woman. It is Cecil Sloper. Ben screams in unison with the woman he has stoned, just as the head of the other separates from her body.

He is still screaming as he wakes in his hotel room in The Leap.

His heart beating madly, he gulps water from the teacup on the bedside table. The foreboding inside him becomes more toxic as ashen daylight seeps into the room. Through the window the air appears heavier with smoke than yesterday. Then from down below come the first sounds of an awakening Buena Vista – the metallic thunk of beer kegs being loaded and unloaded.

The nightmare has left Ben with a crippling sense of dread. His phone shows several missed calls from Sir Gordon and a message from Roderick King. There are four missed calls from Lucy, and a text message:

Darling THOSE photographs. Please tell me you're okay. xxx

From King:

When you wake call asp PLS – RK

The chargé d'affaires has sent him two links. One to an article in *The Herald* with the headline: SIX IN 10 SAY FATHER OF SLAUGHTERED AUSSIE SWEETHEART HOSTIE SHOULD INSIST ON EXECUTION FOR KILLERS.

This is most unhelpful. To put it mildly.

The other link is to *The Mail*. It's a shit-show. There is Ben, wild-eyed, covered in blood and soot and grease, smiling feebly while brandishing a knife in one hand and the bottle of Jim Beam in the other. Behind him the massive boar is hoisted up by its hocks, blood streaming onto the dirt from its gashed-open throat and snout, the three grimy pig hunters with their prison tatts and their shooter's merch caps and their faces contorted into malign sneers as they strain at the other end of the rope to keep the beast off the ground. Ben has no recollection of the photo being taken.

In another shot, taken a few hours later on Saturday night outside The Crown, he is wild-eyed and his hair is matted with sweat and grime and blood. His shirt covered in viscera and grease. The cigarette he'd bludged from the nice couple – journalists! – outside the pub hangs slackly from his lips. His hand is raised in protest. The headline reads: PIGS MIGHT FLY: BRIT ENVOY TAKES IN LOCAL SIGHTS IN MERCY DASH FOR KILLERS OF OUR GIRL NEXT DOOR CHARLENE.

He reads a few lines of the article. It recounts how he'd been 'on the ran-tan' in The Leap since Friday afternoon, 'drinking and relaxing' with the locals. This included a 'wild night' on Saturday when he collapsed outside a local hostelry after a 'spot of recreational pig shooting earlier in the evening'. The article quotes various locals, including one of the hunters, unnamed, who waxes lyrical about how Ben proved himself a 'natural born killer'. It also quotes Saucy saying that Ben is 'an affable enough social companion' although 'somewhat unpersuasive' when it comes to Cecil Sloper.

Ben calls King. He answers immediately. Says, 'Ben.' Then nothing more, affording Ben all space required to explain – or condemn – himself.

For what feels like minutes, the silence is complete at King's end. Then Ben hears the carolling of magpies and wonders how The Leap might sound to King at the other end of the line. He takes the phone away from his ear for a moment and holds it up to the room, the better for Roderick to hear. The brewery truck is gone and from an adjacent room Ben can hear the tinkle of someone pissing. Then a trumpeting fart. Outside, there's the warble of what he thinks might be a currawong. It sounds ghost-like. Otherwise, there's nothing but his heartbeat, still too rapid, and breathing.

And suddenly the silence is claustrophobic. And he feels as if he's been struck by an almighty wave, is under water and getting sucked down, deeper and deeper, his body and mind being unbearably compressed. This silence has a colour. It is mauve shot through with threads of black. It has a smell: ammonia and the sickly-sweet metallic tang of pig's blood.

He pulls himself together and sighs into the phone. 'Rod – I mean, Roderick – what can I say? Really?'

There are a hundred things he can say of course, especially if he were of a mind to offer a mea culpa. But he won't give that to King. On that front, King really can go root his boot. Ben is torn between being aware that, yes, he certainly warrants a bollocking – for being such a fool, perhaps for bringing the service into disrepute – and indignation that his employers have put him in this untenable position in the first place. Without a scintilla of support. In a town full of weirdos, racists, drunks, misogynists, druggos, religious freaks and gun nuts.

But there is something else too: for the first time, on the back of his conversation with Marion, Ben has the merest skerrick of hope that Cecil Sloper might just have his price.

King responds with a sigh of his own – impatient weariness, as if dealing with an errant child whose behaviour is so appalling it transcends both punishment and redemption. He says, 'Well, I suppose you could begin by explaining yourself, Benedict. Those pictures have gone all over the world. Viral. Sir Gordon is absolutely beside himself. He has a mind to request your recall to Whitehall.'

Whitehall. Back in London. Would that be so bad? He might put all this down to a frivolous misadventure. A complete breakdown perhaps. Move back in with the family in Putney and abandon the idyllic antipodean revisitation. Count his blessings. Work on his physical and psychological wellbeing. But most importantly, feel safe and secure with Lucy and the kids. No, that would not be too bad at all, if that's how things transpired.

And yet he also wonders if it's just a day or two too early to indulge that possibility, while there remains a modicum of potential opportunity and hope on the back of his meeting with Marion Sloper. Work yet to be done – a final meeting with Cecil Sloper – is impelling him to continue. For now.

'Roderick, yes . . . I can understand. But please, I feel like something may be ever so slightly shifting here. Finally. Recalling me at this point could be counterproductive.'

'Are you telling me there has actually been some sort of development?'

'I've met Sloper's mother. She's a good woman. Not at all like her son. And she's suggested that he might yet accept the *diyyeh* after all. His farm is going broke, apparently. Money might speak his language.'

'Well, she's the matriarch. Can't she just persuade him to take it?'

'I'm afraid not. She's in a nursing home and he barely has anything to do with her. But Cecil Sloper has agreed to another meeting with me. I'm not yet sure when, but it would be helpful if I knew precisely what we might offer him – if I could name the price of his forgiveness. Make it more than merely hypothetical. A concrete offer. A number. I need to put something on the table.'

King says, 'Our government, Ben, is willing to pay a million pounds. That's about two million Australian dollars. An awful lot of money. But no more than half of it can go directly to the father. The rest must go into a fund of some sort. In Charlene Sloper's memory. You must put this to him personally as soon as possible. Nobody wants this to be passed on via the solicitor, who looks – not to put it too delicately – *dodgy* as hell. Unreliable. It's a concrete offer. Nothing hypothetical about it.'

'What sort of fund are you talking about?'

'We must suggest a bequest in her name – the Charlene Sloper Bequest. For something in keeping with her aspirations. Perhaps a subsidy for a would-be actor from The Leap to study drama in the city. Perhaps a coloured person – an *Aboriginal*, no?'

'No. That won't fly. Not in the least. Sloper is basically a white supremacist.'

'Oh dear. Well then, we'll make it a drama scholarship for a non-coloured person. We might call it Charlene's Wish, or some such. Meanwhile, you ought find a photograph of her on the stage in that school play she was in.'

King says he has just emailed through a precis of the latest cabling on Charlene Sloper, Kilfoyle and Adair. He ends the call with a warning for Ben to stay on the straight and narrow.

The email elaborates on what he has already read. Booze, drugs, parties and sex among the expats in the Riyadh apartment building. A well-established illegal trade in Oxy in which Charlene Sloper was apparently involved with Kilfoyle and Adair. A suggestion that Charlene owed them money. A none too credible eyewitness account (it had hallmarks of police verballing) from a neighbouring building, stating that a woman resembling Adair was at the open window when Charlene fell or was pushed to her death. More evidence that Charlene had continued, until the day of her death, making considerable money through an adult site offering 'private shows' performed live online. Charlene's page had thousands of subscribers.

And yet somehow, in The Leap, Charlene Sloper's reputation has remained perpetually unblemished, fixed in the collective memory and imagination as that of the talented girl next door. The wholesome, intelligent farm girl with the adventurous streak who set out to make the world her own and bring her acting talent to it. Even her grandmother seemed to cultivate the trope. But then it is clear to Ben that Marion Sloper may well have been withholding something important about her granddaughter's true reason for fleeing The Leap so suddenly as a teenager.

It only compounds his confusion about the quest he's manacled to. Why on earth, he wonders, are any of these people worth it?

He lies back on the bed and closes his eyes. Images flash across the screen under his lids. Charlene Sloper, shattered and unrecognisable on the footpath. The two Ulsterwomen being at once stoned and dismembered. The wave. Mardie Clarke and her daughters and her inconsolable husband.

He falls back into a fitful doze, tossing and turning in the sweaty heat of his room in the Buena. He descends into a deep, coma-like sleep. He doesn't wake for several hours. Soon after he does, his phone rings.

'It's Dorinda. I'm in the bar. I've got something for you. Hurry. He doesn't know I'm out. And once he realises, he'll come after me.'

He wonders what on earth Dorinda has. On his way downstairs he decides he'll have just one beer, a small one, with something simple to eat. He is, after all, waiting to hear when he might again meet Cecil Sloper. So he'd better stay nice.

There are only a few people in the bar on a Monday mid-afternoon, a couple of frackers in hi-vis, the two regular old chaps in pork-pie hats huddled over the form guide. There's also a cop in uniform. Drinking. He doffs his cap to Ben. Dorinda is in the far corner beneath the TV, from which blares the ubiquitous bellicosity of Ether commentators: the China virus cover-up, the Marxist ABC–Green conspiracy, absolute outrage over the installation of gender-neutral toilets in another Commonwealth department . . .

A fracker is speaking at Dorinda, voice raised.

'Jesus Christ, Baz,' she says, 'I'll tell you again – I'm not bloody interested.'

'Well piss off then, you frigid mole.' Seeing Ben, he adds, 'Spose this poofter's yer boyfriend or something, eh! Hope yer fucken happy together.'

Dorinda gestures to the chair opposite her.

Ben, indicating the TV above, says, 'Should we move to a quieter table?'

'No. I don't want them to hear. They're all watching us anyway.'

When Ben sits she hands him a piece of paper. Nods at it. He unfolds it to find a clumsily photocopied letter, the edges darkened and the type slightly smudged. It bears the letterhead of Howard Worcestershire & Associates and is addressed to Charlene Sloper at an address in Sydney. It's dated September 2002. In red ink on the top corner is handwritten: *Sent, registered post, 19/9/2002 – copy forwarded to Mr Cecil Sloper.*

Dorinda says, 'Check the date. Year after Charlene left school. Right?'

Ben reads:

Dear Ms Sloper,

I act for Mr Cecil Sloper, of Hurlstone, via Sloper's Blvd, The Leap.

I write to inform you that Mr Sloper advises that he wishes to formally sever all contact with you, and he asks that from this day forward you cease all physical and other forms of interaction with him and all other members of the Sloper family. Should you contact him or any member of his family he will have no option but to have

> you forcibly evicted from Hurlstone or other properties where he and his family members may be situated, and to use all other available legal means to restrain you.
>
> Further, he wishes to inform you that as of this day he has altered his final will and testimony to remove you and any of your present or future dependents as beneficiaries.
>
> Mr Sloper wishes you to know that he regards your personal conduct as unconscionable. Put simply he wishes it to be known that he no longer regards you as his daughter.

Ben can't quite believe what he's just read. He blinks theatrically a couple of times to emphasise this disbelief. He hands the letter back to Dorinda with a questioning look.

Her mouth twists into the beginning of a mischievous grin. She shrugs.

'But why?' he says. 'Why would Sloper do that?'

'All I know is what's on that piece of paper there. I typed it, right. And that's my writing in the corner. I posted it to both Charlene and her psycho arsehole of a dad.'

She pauses. 'Interesting mention of present or future dependents, eh?'

'You mean she had a kid?'

'Like I said, I just done what Uncle Howie ordered me to do. And everything I know is what's typed in that letter there.' She hands it back to Ben. 'Keep it. It's a copy, as you can see. It might be handy. Who knows, one of those newspaper people might like to see it some time.'

He knows it's gold. He pockets it with corresponding care. 'Thank you. I really mean that. This could help greatly. But why give it to me?'

'Cos I'm sick of all of the men round here and all of their bullshit.' She looks about the bar furtively. Lights a cigarette.

'Buy you a drink?' He figures it's the least he can do.

'No,' she says. 'I'm leaving right now – 'fore he comes looking.'

Her phone pings.

'And there he is. Never far behind. Bye-bye, Ben,' she says, gathering her cigarettes and phone.

'I'll see you,' he says.

'I very much doubt it. Good luck.'

Dorinda doesn't look back as she leaves the bar, but the frackers at the nearby table suddenly stop talking and follow her with their hungry eyes all the way through the door.

Ben goes to the bar for the one beer he's allowed himself. It will perhaps help assuage his anger. That lying prick Sloper and his horseshit ugly charade. Ben, along with everyone else involved in trying to save the women, has definitely been played. All that diplomatic nicety, the civilised negotiation and appeal to human goodness, was always going to be pointless.

But his anger is tempered by an emerging devil-may-care lightness, a dissipation of anxiety, that might just empower him to meet such ugliness in kind. He stands at the bar while the cop watches him in silence. Blunt is nowhere to be seen.

Waiting, Ben loses himself in thoughts about the letter. About Sloper's wanton cruelty, his general malevolence and motivations. It's clear the man likes money, and could certainly use more of it to improve his degraded property. And who is ultimately going to say no to a million dollars, supposedly in compensation for the life of a child you are demonstrably estranged from at your own accord anyway? From the moment Ben first saw Sloper on TV, his grief as the father of poor dead Charlene had struck him as self-indulgent and performative. Marion Sloper's words, that her son craves control over everyone and everything, that he just loves 'playing God', return to him now. Sloper had, after all, rejected the very idea of *diyyeh* at their last meeting. Maybe he was simply planning to play God for a little longer before ultimately accepting the money?

Or was Ben reading this all wrong? Impossible, trying to get inside the motivations of a narcissistic sociopath, a man conditioned to approach the world with cruelty, whose responses simply could not be rationally anticipated or understood.

As for the letter, if made public it would immediately expose to the world Sloper's hypocrisy over his daughter's death. Ben instinctively pats his shirt pocket where the letter is secured. Knowledge is power. For the first time since arriving in The Leap he feels empowered – armed, finally, with the means to force a positive outcome for his two countrywomen in Riyadh. All he needs to do now is maintain self-control, stay on the rails, and ignore those potent thoughts of worthlessness and the siren-calls to self-sabotage.

He could simply slip the letter to one of the many journalists about town. They were all desperately seeking any new angle on the story. It would be a scoop. The condemnation of Sloper would be multinational and damning. The pressure on him to show mercy, regardless of whether or not he accepted blood money, would be irresistible. But Ben is also aware that the letter points directly at Dorinda. Saucy would know she'd taken it. Ben doesn't want her to be further harmed.

Suddenly Blunt rises up from nowhere, literally, a corpulent zombie emerging from the cellar. He's sweating and puffing and swearing.

He nods at Ben. 'Just changing the bastard Reschs keg,' he says.

Ben orders a schooner and a pie.

'Pie warmer's still on the blink. Microwave okay?'

'Like the internet? Suppose it'll have to be.'

Blunt gives him a sharp look. 'You remain free to go elsewhere.'

'You know, the thing I value most about the Buena Vista is its absolute commitment to customer satisfaction. I can't wait to review it on Tripadvisor.'

'We don't take any notice of that around here. We don't believe in it. Latte-sipping, woke city nonsense.'

The microwave pings. Blunt removes the pie, juggles the searing, sagging, sorry thing in its steamed-up cellophane bag onto a paper plate with a sachet of sauce. He places the beer in front of Ben.

The cop, who's been sitting at the corner of the bar all the while, rises and steps over. He is a tall, bear-like man. His bulbous shoulders and thick neck strain the buttons of his blue shirt.

'Allcock,' he says. 'Sergeant Mitch Allcock. I run the station here. Have done for thirty-five years.'

He extends his hand. It's the size of a bread-and-butter-plate. Ben's own disappears into its crushing grip and he tries not to wince. He is cut off when he goes to introduce himself.

'Everyone knows who you are, Mr Fotheringham-Gaskill. You need no introduction. You've made quite the name for yourself in a few short days about The Leap.'

In an uncanny piece of timing, a composite of images of Ben in his various dishevelled states flashes onto the TV screen. UNDIPLOMATIC RESCUE MISSION the tagline reads.

'See what I mean?' the cop says. 'I mean, LOL, as the grand-kids might say.'

'Do you mind turning that down a tad?' Ben asks Blunt, who shrugs. He lowers the volume marginally.

'What's the matter? Got a problem with the news now too, mate? Ether doesn't lie. Ever.'

'Buy you a beer?' Allcock asks Ben.

'No thanks. I'm good. I'm just having the one.'

'Really? You can stop at one? No one stops at just the one. That just doesn't pass the pub test, mate. Not around here. Go on, have another. It's on me.'

'I can tell you again, if you like, in words of one syllable – no. I don't want another beer. Thank you very much.'

'Ben, has anyone told you about The Leap and our famous brand of genial hospitality?'

'Yes. Several times. And I don't care for it one bit.'

Allcock eyeballs him. 'Well, if they have told you, they certainly haven't explained it properly. So let me just fill you in. Listen up, son. A bloke can be broke and down on his luck. He can have no bed to sleep in. No food. No means of supporting himself. But if he comes to The Leap, the citizens of this egalitarian community will always buy him a beer. So, Ben, when a stranger offers to buy you a beer, you'd best say, Yes, please – thank you, I will have a cold one. Because shouting without expecting to be shouted back is the custom here. And, I'll have you know, it's also the Australian way. And I'd hate to think that you, a visitor to this, the very best town in the finest country on earth, not to mention the luckiest, were being deliberately un-Australian, Benedict. So now, you will let me buy you a beer. Or I'm afraid I'll have to arrest you and chuck you in the can with the drunks and the perverts and all the various other malcontents and misfits we keep off these streets in order to maintain such a decorous town.'

'Really? You'll arrest me if I won't accept your offer of a beer?'

'Correct-a-mundo.'

'You mean, you'd *actually* put me under arrest for declining your offer to shout me a beer?'

'At gunpoint,' the cop says, fingering his holster, looking Ben square in the eye. He nods emphatically as he says this. Then he smiles, a tobacco-stained toothy snarl.

Ben holds his gaze. 'Well, how very quaint your hospitality is, Sergeant Allcock, here in The Leap. I think I might now understand what it means to be fully embraced by this society. I get it. A man might ostensibly seem to encourage a visitor to sleep with his niece. That's just de rigueur. A scion of society can disown his daughter for God knows what reason and then claim to the world that she was the light of his life. He can declare his daughter a burgeoning actress when in fact she was some sort of damaged performer on lurid internet sites. That same man can bully his wife to death and oppress his son. A family can have all the Aboriginal people killed and take their land, and apparently keep the skull of one of those murdered on his mantlepiece. Indeed, the town itself can be named in honour of the place where those people were slaughtered.'

He pauses only long enough to wet his throat with his one beer. 'A man here can torture and kill wild animals while a child looks on. He can buy and take illicit drugs with impunity. He can have sex with a stripper in the main bar of the busiest hostelry in town while everybody watches on. It's a society, meanwhile, where everyone *must* call each other mate. Where that word is a term of both endearment and hatred, used for a friend but just as readily weaponised to mean: Listen, I just might decide to kill you. That is The Leap and its hospitality, as I understand and have experienced it these past few days. But heaven forbid a man should refuse the offer of a damn drink. He might just get arrested at gunpoint by the town's most senior policeman for such a social transgression.'

The cop is regarding Ben as he might a talking horse.

'I'm not sure I understand what you're getting at here, mate. So what's your poison?'

Ben relents. 'I'll have a pint of Reschs.'

'Please. Say please. Good manners are also very important around The Leap.'

'Please.'

Before Ben knows it he is shouting the cop back and Allcock is buying him another. And the beer does seem especially good this Monday afternoon. Icier than usual. Fresher. Within an hour or so of solid drinking and listening to the sergeant speak utterly forgettable shit (best Australian beers and cricketers; the world going woke; the last seven Crufts dog show winners; The Leap's unparalleled lifestyle and capacity for amity; why Ether is correct about most things) it's as if Ben doesn't have a care in the world. He's stopped worrying about whether Lucy and the kids will be joining him, or about the need to get back to Canberra to properly set up the Hamptons beach house. It. Should. All. Be. Okay. Ms Adair and Ms Kilfoyle, banged up in a Saudi prison and facing imminent execution, are, like the quandary about how precisely to use the letter Dorinda has given him, suddenly far from front of mind.

Ben is about to start on his next beer when somebody grabs him by the shoulder.

The pharmacist.

'Ben,' he says, 'I swear you've aged ten years since I saw you last. But then you did look very young when you arrived – like you were barely out of short pants.'

Ben is swaying. He regards the untouched pie on the paper plate next to his empty schooner and realises he's neglected to eat. Again.

The pub is busying with evening trade now. More frackers. He sees one of the pig shooters. Can't recall which.

The pharmacist is in his face now. 'Can I help you, Ben, with a little pick-me-up?'

And Ben thinks, Yes, why not? He nods, glancing at Allcock.

Ben's phone pings with a text from Saucy:

> My client, Cecil Sloper, will see you at Hurlstone, 11.30 sharp tomorrow morning.

Ben texts back saying he'll be there, before quickly reverting his attention to the pharmacist.

'I'm making like the three monkeys,' the cop says as he heads towards the men's. 'Hear, see and do no evil.'

The rest of that evening, as with his previous ones in the Buena Vista, is close to a blank.

Nelson says, 'Yeah, I packed your bags. Got all of your shit from the room and checked you out of that shitty place. That fella at reception, that greasy fat dickhead, he gives me what-for, says my type'll never be welcome under his roof. I tell the cunt I wouldn't be seen dead drinking there – I'm only there for you. He tells me you already paid for the room in advance. But I paid your bar bill. So you owe me a lot of money. For that bar bill. And all the driving around. Not to mention my general forbearance, mate.'

They are sitting at the kitchen table of Nelson's house at The Rookery this Tuesday morning, and Ben is wondering if he's somehow offended him. He's imposed on him. He understands that. He has a splintered recollection of calling Nelson last night and Nelson coming to extract him from the Buena Vista. Did he do something offensive during that process . . .?

Nelson pours tea from the ceramic pot into a handmade cup in front of Ben. He adds milk and three sugars without asking.

Ben's hand shakes as he lifts the cup. The sweet tea is good. 'Thanks for doing all that. I've little recollection,' he says.

'You really don't remember?'

'Scarcely a thing.'

'Mate, for fuck's sake, don't you reckon it's time you started to take control? You're here to do a job. But it's like you're sabotaging yourself at every turn. I mean, I don't hardly know you at all but it looks like you're trying to wreck things for yourself. From where I stand you're like a friggin' turkey voting for Christmas. I want to know why, I suppose. Why are you doing this to yourself?'

'Nelson, this has happened to me before —'

'Sorry to interrupt but you're making out like this is something that's all being done to you, when the truth is that everything you've experienced here in The Leap in the past few days is a direct result of a series of very bad decisions that you've made. The mad drinking. The drugs. The hanging out with those dangerous fuckwits. Staying on at the Buena even after I warned against it. I told you what a rank shithole it is. All crap decisions by you, my friend. No one but you. You alone.'

Ben wants to explain all that Nelson doesn't know about him. Everything he's been through. The injury indelibly tattooed on his soul. Nelson also needs to know just how useless, how totally ashtray-on-a-motorcycle worthless Ben really is when it comes to helping anyone in danger or trouble or need. Every counsellor he's seen – the good, the bad and the downright negligently incompetent – has said to him: you, Ben, are in charge of your life, even though you think you aren't. But how to explain to Nelson that when he sees danger in a place like The Leap, so much of his past instructs the injured Ben. Prompts him to ignore his flight impulse and to charge straight at the peril. Embrace it. To swallow the little blue pills. To drown himself in drinks with people he abhors, just to see what happens next. To go out to Paradise Downs with a blood-lusting bunch of malevolent morons with guns and vicious dogs. To cut the throat of such a sentient being while it looks you in the face so you might watch the life leach from its eyes. To do all of that, and more, so as not to sit alone with the experiences and memories that haunt him.

'Nelson, you're right. Shit decisions. But it's more than that. The stuff that has happened to me in the past so that —'

'Whoa, Ben, I know trauma backwards and inside out. I don't need a psych 101 lecture on it. Please, spare me. But on decisions – bad decision number one was you coming here, and two was staying.'

'I know that. I know. But I had no choice, I was sent here by my boss. But Nelson, I'm keen to know, why did you decide to help me?'

'When I saw you standing there at the airport like a shag on a rock, you were nothing but an opportunity for me. I told you, that's how I make money sometimes. It was a simple transaction. I gotta work my arse off to live, mate. People like you don't always understand that. So yeah, manual work. Driving people around sometimes. I didn't get to go to uni and then spend a lifetime sitting around thinking about how I might change the world. I've gotta work and make a quid and you just became part of that. Like that other poor English bookish type who drank himself to death in the hut the other side of the Babylon I used to help out sometimes, who I told you about. I'm not a fucken charity, mate. Don't overestimate me.'

'Yes, but last night – getting me out of the Buena and looking after me. Bringing me to your home. I mean, you didn't have to. Just like you didn't have to tell me about Marion Sloper or get her to see me.'

'What I saw after the airport was someone who's lost and trying to do a good thing. Someone who's away from his family and from love and home, and all at sea because of it. Not many people round here do good things. And you're not too bad a bloke. And Mrs Sloper . . . well, if something she said to you can help save two lives, then that's gotta be a good thing. And now, not to put too fine a point on it, today I want you to pay me back for your ridiculous bar bill.'

'Hmm. Naturally I'll pay you. Today. And yeah, you're right about me and the family. Home.'

'Where's your family right now?'

'Putney. London.'

'Well, if they're not gonna come to you, then you should go right back to them.'

'Perhaps. I'm leaving here tomorrow regardless. But today I've got to meet Cecil Sloper again.'

'What time?'

Ben looks at his phone, goes to the previous evening's text from Saucy. 'At 11.30,' he says.

'I suppose you want me to drive you?'

'Please. If you can.'

'It'll cost you another two hundred bucks.'

'Okay.'

'So, you planning to go see the silly old prick while you're looking like something the cat upchucked? Or you wanna clean yourself up, have a shower? Iron yourself a shirt?'

The landline interrupts. Nelson leaves the kitchen to answer it. He soon returns.

'It's for you,' he says. 'Phone's in the hall.'

'Who is it?' Who even knew he was here?

'Marion Sloper.'

Ben is cleanshaven. His bloodshot eyes would, however, give his game away if there remained a single soul in The Leap still unwise to the way he's been playing it. They've all been watching.

He has a freshly ironed sky-blue shirt tucked into suit trousers. His boots, despite his attempts to clean them, are still flecked with resistant little scabs of dried pig's blood that have congealed with dust and viscera. But at least the M.R.s are now fully worn in and comfortable. Authentically Australian-looking.

They drive out to Hurlstone mostly in silence. Something has been rising in Ben's stomach. And now it's like a great lump in his chest. It's not his old debilitating enemy, anxiety. It is another feeling altogether.

Fury.

'What'd she want? Mrs Sloper, on the phone?'

'She had something else to share about Charlene.'

'Gonna tell me?'

'Just let me get through this thing with Sloper first, then I'll tell you everything. Is that okay?'

'Whatever. It's all the same to me so long as I get paid. But Ben, you're shaking. DTs?'

'Not DTs. I just feel this outrage – like I've not known.'

'Who was it reckoned anger is an energy? Use it, Ben. Fucken give it to the old bastard. What's he gonna do, kick you off the property again?'

'If that's the worst he can do, I can cop it. This is my last shot to save those women.'

'What are you going to say?'

'I'll relay an offer. A million pounds – nearly two million dollars – divided between him and some sort of benevolent trust in Charlene's name. All he has to do is agree to take the money. The women would be spared. Simple. It doesn't mean he's forgiven them.'

'What makes you think he'll agree?'

'Because I know he didn't love his daughter. I believe he actually loathed her. Because he has a corrupted soul and a heart like a prune. He is venal, conceited and ugly. I reckon he'll take the money.'

The huddle of journalists rouses at the sight of Nelson's Valiant nearing Hurlstone's gates.

'Remember,' Nelson says, 'I don't take you all the way up to the house.'

'Yep. I know.'

Nelson sprays gravel and dust as he turns too quickly into Hurlstone's once majestic driveway. A cameramen and a stills photographer manage to get their lenses inches from Ben's window, capturing him slumped forward, face in hands. The staccato *rat-a-tat-tat* of the cattle grid vibrates through his body. The car skids to a halt when it shortly meets the red ute coming the other way, an apparition in the smoke and dust.

Its headlights flash as its engine idles.

'What the hell,' Nelson says.

Saucy scrambles out of the car. He ambles slowly with that dead leg, swatting blowflies from about his head with a hand as he approaches Ben's window. He gestures to him to wind it down.

'Good afternoon, Mr Fotheringham-Gaskill. Please come over into my vehicle and I'll take you to Mr Sloper.'

As Ben gets out, Saucy peers through the open door at Nelson.

'You can wait here . . . what's your name, boy?'

Nelson mutters, 'Motherfucker.' He neither looks at nor answers Saucy. To Ben he says, 'Call me when you're done. Or if you need me.'

Ben gets into the lawyer's car and Saucy does a seven- or eight-point turn on the eroded, potholed drive, narrowly avoiding the deep culverts on either side.

'Mr Fotheringham-Gaskill, I've a question for you.'

'What?'

'My niece – Dorinda.'

'What about her?'

'I understand she met with you yesterday afternoon. And now it seems she's gone.'

'What do you mean, gone?'

'Departed. Flown. Fled. Left town. Overnight, leaving everything behind. Her wardrobe. Her phone. Her job. Her dear uncle. Her whole life! Her vanishment corresponds neatly with irregularities in the Worcestershire and Associates legal trust account. You wouldn't happen to know —'

Ben's laughter stops him. The lawyer is piqued.

'This is no laughing matter. I'll have you know Sergeant Allcock is on the case. Tracking her and my clients' money.'

As they approach the house, Ben can see Kenneth standing in front of it. He is bare-chested in football shorts and thongs. Hands on hips, heavily muscled, he waves at the car. Saucy ignores him. He veers away from the house and drives instead into an open field of grass stubble. On Ben's left they pass a small cemetery enclosed by a rusted wrought-iron fence. Weathered and lopsided marble gravestones stand like crooked teeth amid the overgrown grass and bramble. A farm labourer in a blue singlet, arms covered in tattoos, curses while hacking a shovel at the parched earth. The making of Charlene's grave, Ben assumes.

'Where are we heading?' he asks.

'I thought you were too busy chortling to notice,' Saucy snaps. 'You'll see soon enough.'

A few sheep, heavy with dags, their fleece discoloured with dirt and burrs, wander listlessly about the desiccated field. In the distance is a red windsock, high on a pole. It stutters limply in the weak breeze.

There's a clearing in the stubble that Ben now recognises as a runway. At the end of it, sitting outside an expansive metal shed, is a small, red, single-propeller aeroplane.

Cecil Sloper stands beside it. Dressed formally in moleskin trousers, white shirt and a tie that precisely matches his aircraft.

'What's this about?' Ben asks.

'You'll be fine. He's never had an accident and he's been flying for fifty years. Not that I've ever gone up. I'm not much for such little planes. Yes, the aircraft is quite old. But don't worry – my client services it quite carefully himself. Doesn't like to pay an aircraft mechanic, see? He watches his pennies does Cec. Anyways, every Tuesday he goes up, just to have a look about Hurlstone from above. To survey his fiefdom. He insists you accompany him.'

'I've no intention of doing that.'

'Then I'm afraid you're out of luck. The case is closed after today. There'll be no more discussion with him about the witches who killed his darling girl. No more correspondence entered into about blood money and the like. It's your last chance.'

Ben sighs. He alights and walks over to Sloper. He's a bad colour. More florid. The burst capillaries on his nose more pronounced. Sloper ignores Ben's offered hand and instead uses one of his to squeeze the bicep of his opposing arm. He winces slightly as he squeezes, sighs with evident discomfort. He then wriggles the sore arm as if to shift blood into its extremities.

'Have it your way,' Ben says.

'I always do. Now, by way of explanation, you may come with me. And while we are about the heavens you may say your final piece. I don't want it ever said that I never listened to the case for compassion. I do this weekly, this flight, to remind myself of the land that belongs to the Slopers and to which we belong. All that my darling Charlene would have inherited and brought my heirs onto.'

It's a choppy ascent on a bed of updrafts as the plane grinds and bumps its way through the smoke, which is just thin enough that the Babylon River may be seen snaking its way around the border of Hurlstone, along with the sharp, thinly wooded ravine from which The Leap draws its name.

Sloper loosely holds the yoke as it bounces and wobbles in his left hand. Ben would prefer he had both hands on it for the ascent. But Sloper uses his free hand to sweep across the front of the cockpit as he says, 'My kingdom below. Take it all in.'

'Your kingdom? Is that how you see it?'

'O Lord, God of our fathers, are you not God in heaven? You rule over all the kingdoms of the nations. In your hand are power and might, so that none is able to withstand you. Chronicles 20:6.'

'Not this again.'

'What do you mean? God strike you down for your insolence, man.'

'What I mean, precisely, is this bloody nonsense about you being such a godly person. Such a moral man! Going around quoting the Old Testament like some fire-and-brimstone prophet to justify your vanity. Two can play at that. I know my scripture too. Bear with each other and forgive one another if any of you has a grievance against someone. Forgive as the Lord forgave you. Colossians 3:13.'

'Damn you, son! No discipline seems pleasant at the time, but painful. Later on, however, it produces a harvest of righteousness and peace for those who have been trained by it. Hebrews 12:11.'

Ben is done with Sloper's perfidy. 'Jesus, Sloper, you've already well and truly harvested your righteousness and indignation. I'm ready to tell the world what a fraud you are.'

Sloper's face turns puce with rage. He jerks the yoke forward and the little plane lurches sharply earthwards.

'What the hell do you mean?' he demands. 'I've just lost my daughter, man. I've got a mind to smash us into the ground, to pulverise the both of us, just to demonstrate how moral and godly I am. People know how unstable you are, mister. Everyone in this place has borne witness to your erratic behaviour. I'm quite willing to kill us both now. And everyone will think you're responsible.'

'I doubt you will. For at heart you're a coward. I'm confident you'll put us back on the ground safely.'

Ben is quite calm. He's pretty sure Sloper has no real intention of deliberately crashing the plane. But he can't help goading him.

And as Ben expected, Sloper levels the plane out again. They are climbing once more now, and the ground is obscured by the smoke and cloud. The sky takes on an eerie orange hue. Sloper must fly by instrument. It's no longer possible to distinguish any landmarks by eye.

'So, you didn't get me up here for nothing,' Ben says. 'What do you want to say?'

Sloper is clutching at his arm again. Wincing.

'My son and I have spoken. Kenneth believes, after discussions with my dear mother, that we ought spare the women.'

When Ben doesn't respond, he goes on: 'How much money, *precisely*, would my family receive in return for their lives?'

'Two million dollars will be paid. Though half of that must be put into some kind of memorial trust in your daughter's name.'

Sloper is silent.

We are nearing the moment of truth, Ben thinks. Sloper will toy around with the offer now, for sure. Contort it in some way. Pretend to accept and then throw it back at me, perhaps. Try to play with me. That's all he knows. Or perhaps he'll feign disinterest for a while. I'll bide my time up here. Choose my moment carefully. I'll play my own cards when I'm ready. I almost have him.

'You should understand that Kenneth has proven quite persuasive,' Sloper is saying. 'He's not good for much. Bit of a dunce. Afraid of everything and everyone. Like his mother. Muddle-headed and soft. But the money might help him stay on the farm once I've passed on. My mother has been in Kenneth's ear, you see. Of course, it's not my mother's decision. Saudi law, thankfully, has little regard for the views of women, I'm told. And Kenneth is not the senior male of the Sloper tribe. I make the decisions. And it's mine alone as to whether the witches die. So, after due consideration, Mr Fotheringham-Gaskill, my view is that two million dollars is not nearly enough money. It will take twice that amount to save both women.'

'Well, that's the only offer.'

'In that case, I'll take the two million and spare one woman. I don't much care who dies. And here's a little caveat: given that you're so critical of my morality, I will allow you to make the decision. So, tell me, who lives and who dies? I'm going to descend in a few minutes. I want your decision by the time we land.'

Ben sighs with a theatrical weariness. He turns to look at Sloper and says, 'Cecil, you can stop playing games now. Because I know exactly what sort of a man you are. I know everything, actually. How cruelly you treated Charlene. I spoke to your mother this morning. Would you like to hear what she told me about Charlene and Aaron Tyson – the young man from The Rookery?'

There is the merest, charged pause before Sloper explodes. 'It's not true. *That's a lie.*'

'It *is* true, Sloper. As you bloody well know. Their hidden love for one another. Their plan to head to the city together, it being too dangerous for them to stay on here because of what Charlene knew would be your disapproval. Your interference. And she was right, wasn't she? She knew you too well.'

'Lies!' thunders Sloper again.

'No. All true, *mate*. All of it. You rarely let her out of your sight when she was growing up, did you? Tried to possess her. Control everything she did.'

'Bunkum and bullshit. You're insane, and everyone here knows it.'

'Because you always had to know everything about her, and were so possessive and suspicious of who she was spending time with, you had her followed. Confirmed she and Aaron were together. But your mother always knew, didn't she? Though she'd never tell you. She only wanted Charlene's happiness, tried to protect her.'

'My mother! You don't want to listen to the ramblings of that demented old woman.'

'And then, odd coincidence this, Aaron was found dead with his head smashed to a pulp. After being knocked off his bike. The police never found out who did it, of course. Know anything about that, Cecil?'

A cold, hate-filled silence fills the cabin now.

'Course you do,' Ben goes on. 'But I'll just remind you anyway, shall I? After Aaron's death, you confined your heart-broken daughter to Hurlstone, virtually imprisoned her. And then when it was obvious she was pregnant you banished her, sent her away to have the child, promising she could return with the baby. But when the baby boy arrived – a boy who'd have been another heir, by the way, the heir you claim you've been so terribly denied – you formally exiled Charlene and her son from your family. Vindictively extracted them from your will. Why? Simply because that boy was of mixed race. And you just couldn't abide having that in the Sloper lineage, could you?'

Ben pauses. He wants his words to strike Sloper hard. Wants him to suffer. And he can see that he is now. But he sees, too, that it's the pain of exposure, not emotional anguish for a lost daughter and grandson.

Ben takes aim again. 'I know your daughter hated you, Sloper,' he continues, his voice level and calm. 'Despised you. And feared you terribly. Just like her mother, who you bullied to death. No, no – don't bother protesting. You carry on about how Charlene's death has denied you another heir, when she already gave you one! A child she had no choice but to adopt out. More heartbreak for her! You are poison, Cecil Sloper. And now, I'm wondering whether you'd like the world to know what you did to your family? I'm quite willing to say all this publicly. I've nothing to lose. And you have everything to forfeit. Unless you take the blood money. So, you *will* show mercy to the two women and I'll shut up about what I know.'

Sloper scoffs. 'Nobody here believes any of that old gossip. Anyway, you've no proof.'

Ben takes Dorinda's letter from his pocket and begins to read from it.

'Nonsense. A fucking forgery. Give it to me —'

Ben leans away as Sloper tries to snatch the letter. The plane begins to dive again, until Sloper puts his hand back on the controls, steadies the craft.

'Those damned rumours have been around for years. Nobody listens to them. I'm Cecil Sloper. My family discovered this place. Carved The Leap out of the wild. Changed the course of the river to give the parched lands water. Developed the town.'

'That may be so with the rumours. The whole town might be in your pocket. Willing to turn a blind eye, a deaf ear, to what you did – just as it has to everything else about this place, from the moment it was mapped. But the difference now is that the whole world is watching.'

'And the world is awaiting my verdict!' Sloper yells, spittle flying from his lips. 'So tell me: who gets to live and who dies? Tell me now!'

The man is actually insane, Ben realises. Acting as if he has the upper hand when he has no chips left to bargain with. For the first time on the flight Ben is fearful: Sloper has lost control of absolutely everything but the aircraft, and perhaps he really will deliberately crash it and kill them both.

Ben closes his eyes momentarily to steady himself. The fear is caressing him with its spidery fingers. The last thing he needs is a full-blown panic attack. He perspires as he repeats two words to himself. Control. Power. Control and power. I am in control and I have the power here. That is who I am right now. The good person. The strong person. The person who has always done his job no matter the circumstances. The person who has never left his post, who has always rallied and who has been injured badly for no other reason than that. And I am doing my job again right here.

All he wants now is for the plane to land safely.

Sloper is still ranting when he suddenly starts wheezing heavily and coughing hard, fighting for breath. He takes his trembling hand from the yoke and clutches his throat, fumbling to loosen his tie and undo his top buttons. The plane veers wildly to the left then banks sharply upwards, the centrifugal pressure forcing their heads to snap back violently into the headrests. He turns and looks Ben directly, urgently, in the eye.

Now it's clear that something is seriously wrong. When Sloper turns to the front and coughs again, a fine patina of ruby-red spritzes the cabin. He slumps forward, making a gurgling sound, and the plane jerks forward with him. A red light on the dash blinks madly as they spiral earthwards, a digital voice repeating a studiously calm warning: CAUTION, CAUTION.

Time concertinas and contorts. Split seconds seem like minutes. Ben thinks the tangerine sky so very beautiful. It feels like there is only sky. That the earth is no more.

Right now it would be so simple, a perfect solution to everything, to just keep falling until the abyss swallowed all the pain and anguish. All the disappointments and let-downs. All those thongs. The stinking bodies. The dogs. The poor screaming school dad with his drowned wife and kids. All gone for good.

But there is Lucy. Jerome, Suze and Amy. And Nancy.

And, yes, there are the two Ulsterwomen.

He uses all his strength to push the dead weight of Sloper back into the corner of his seat and away from the controls. The mantra from his therapeutic flying lessons post-Cambodia kicks in: assume control, aviate, navigate, communicate.

He clutches the yoke and gently pulls it towards him. The plane jolts about then slowly stabilises as Ben checks airspeed. Too fast. He responds quickly, slowing and trimming the aircraft. He sets the return course and turns the plane for Hurlstone's landing strip.

He issues a mayday call. Says he is a qualified pilot and can land the plane. But there is a medical emergency on board. The pilot appears to have had a coronary.

Through the murky air as they approach the runway, Ben sees the blue siren of a police car careening to the gates of Hurlstone, streams of red dust billowing from its tail. An ambulance follows in its wake. Nelson's Valiant, Ben sees as he guides the plane in low, is parked at the hangar, and Kenneth is there on his trailbike.

It's bumpy coming in. Ben brings it in too hard and bounces off the runway. He pulls back on the throttle and takes the plane up and around again, over the hangar and the heads of the solicitor and Nelson.

Minutes later he lands safely, just as a light rain starts to fall. He taxis to the hangar, cuts the engine.

When the paramedics declare there's nothing more to be done for Sloper, Ben puts a consoling hand on Kenneth's shoulder. Squeezes gently. 'I'm so very sorry . . .'

'Daddy,' Kenneth says with little emotion. 'Daddy. Really?'

'Yes, I'm . . .'

'So . . . does that mean Grandma can come home to be with me?'

'I'm sure, Kenneth. Yes.'

'And those two ladies. They can be alright now?'

'Yes. If that's what you want.'

'Yes. It is. I don't want anything to die.'

Nelson grabs Ben by the arm and steers him towards the Valiant. 'Let's get going, eh?'

'No, I want to feel the rain. To smell it. Let it wash over me. I feel dirty.'

'Okay. But tell me what the hell actually happened up there? What'd you do to him?'

'I didn't do anything to him. Nothing at all. I merely told him the truth about himself. And that I knew he'd cut his daughter off and written her out of the will. I've got proof of that – a letter that Saucy over there wrote to Charlene after she got pregnant. And I suppose nobody's ever confronted Cecil Sloper like that before.' Ben is speaking way too fast and he's tapping his shirt pocket as he does. 'I've got the letter right here. It doesn't directly say she was pregnant. But that's what the letter is about.'

'A baby? The letter? You've lost me. Rewind, mate.'

'Nelson, this is something you and your family should know about. It's what Marion told me this morning when she rang. She was desperate to tell me what she couldn't the other day at the nursing home. She was worried that people would somehow think less of Charlene because of it. Family skeletons and all that. Anyway, she changed her mind, she wanted me to use what she told me. She rang the Buena Vista asking for me and the receptionist told her that some bloody impudent young Black fella had come and checked me out. She figured it was you.'

'Don't give me *War and Peace*, Ben. What'd she tell you that's so important for us to know?'

'That Charlene and Aaron were a couple, and that . . .' He tells Nelson the story, including the detail about Sloper warning Aaron off.

'Well, he warned him off alright, didn't he,' Nelson says, his voice rising in anger.

'Yes, I'd say he did. Marion heard him ranting around the house. About teaching Aaron a lesson for messing with his daughter. She heard him confront Charlene about it, who pushed back hard. Told her father she'd make her own choices and that she and Aaron were going to Sydney together, and he couldn't prevent them. But . . .'

'You telling me that cunt actually killed our Aaron?'

'That's not entirely clear, though a lot of things would point to that. But whatever did happen to Aaron, it had the desired result for Cecil Sloper.'

Nelson goes silent for a while. Then he says, 'Jesus, she had the kid? Did Charlene have the child? Or did she get rid of it?'

'Sloper sent her to the city to have it. Said he'd support her and that she'd be welcome back with her baby, which didn't happen of course. But Charlene did have the child and she adopted it out.'

Nelson is shaking his head. He rubs his eyes. 'Jesus, this is a lot. What'd she have, did Marion say? Boy or girl?'

'A boy.'

'So he'd be, what, eighteen or nineteen now or something.'

'Yes. And the good news is that he got in touch with Charlene not too long ago. He wanted to know who he was. She'd met him in Sydney, Nelson. They were developing a relationship. And Marion was hoping to meet him too. Her great-grandson. That'll be easier with Sloper gone, I imagine.'

Nelson is grinning now. 'So there's a Sloper heir who's actually one of ours, connected in another way to that land they stole from us. Maybe in the white man's court he'd have another right to this property, along with Kenny, if that will was contested? This is too good! It's just poetry, Ben!' He throws his head back and laughs. He hugs Ben.

'Maybe the boy will come home,' Ben says.

'Man. He's a man now. And I hope. It's where he belongs. Though it's not a story that some around The Leap will be celebrating.'

A trail of sedans, SUVs and a satellite van – the journalists, enticed by all the action around the plane – is moving steadily up the long homestead driveway. Allcock and his constable head down to corral them away from the plane and Sloper's body.

'Let's get out of here,' Nelson says. 'Aside from Kenny, these people give me the creeps.'

'I need to make some calls first. Let my people know what's going on. I have to get Kenneth to pass on his verdict for our ladies in Riyadh. Maybe say something, while he's standing next to me, to all the journos.'

'You're going to talk to them?'

'Of course. I've got nothing to hide. Everything about me is already out there. They'll never know what happened up in that plane, though. Only that Sloper carked it. And that I landed it. And that Kenneth, now the oldest male in the Sloper family, wants to show mercy to the condemned women.'

'What about after that?'

'After that, I'm getting on that plane. Tomorrow.'

'So come back to my home on the way,' Nelson says. 'I'll chuck something on the barbie. I've got a six-pack in the fridge. Then I'll see you onto the plane in the morning.'

'Sounds great. But only if I'm not imposing?'

'You, impose? Never. Just so long as you pay me what you owe me, mind.'

It is a mild, sunny day in March. The air is pristine, and through the reddish-brown canopy of the dogwood tree there's a single white brushstroke of cloud on the cerulean canvas of sky.

He is sitting on a banana lounge in board shorts and an unbuttoned short-sleeved shirt, his legs, face and torso tanned. On his knees is propped a journal.

Write it all down, his latest psych had advised. Every part of it. And he has, even though everything about The Leap seems like a long, bad dream from which he's now awoken. His open-ended leave from work and his day-to-day sobriety, at least for the time being, make it feel even more surreal, as if it all happened in another universe and sometimes even to another person.

He looks from the sky back to the journal, lowers his sunglasses, and in his neat cursive writes a few more paragraphs:

I don't know quite what impelled me to answer the unidentified number just now – it's something I rarely do. But when I picked up I recognised Dorinda's voice immediately. I asked where she was calling from but she wouldn't say. Said it didn't matter. She said all I needed to know was that she had left The Leap for good and was doing okay.

She said thank you to me, which was a surprise: 'Thank you for saying to me, "You don't need a man to leave. Just go." So I did. And I took enough of that pig's ill-gotten money to set myself up safely, somewhere he'll never find me.'

Nobody had ever looked out for her in the way I had without trying to take advantage of her, she told me. This struck me as inordinately sad, given I'd felt unable to help her at all.

Dorinda had read all about what happened, including Sloper croaking midair. How I'd landed the plane. She'd seen my 'heroics' all over the TV and in the papers, and me explaining that just before he'd died Sloper had agreed to show mercy to Adair and Kilfoyle. She wondered if I'd had to work hard to convince Kenneth to confirm that compassion.

But Dorinda also had a few questions. Like, why hadn't I made public the letter she'd given me, and illustrated for the world what a true arsehole Cecil Sloper really was? Why hadn't I told the journalists about Charlene Sloper and Aaron Tyson? The truth about

Aaron's killing? Charlene's banishment? The baby? After all, this was the whispered story that pretty much every one of the white pioneering stock in The Leap had long been aware of but never delved into.

Good questions, I replied. Good questions, I thought, about a multigenerational disremembering, as Nelson termed it, of a whole series of none-too-secret secrets.

I told Dorinda that the truth would emerge in due course, as it tends to. But that even though I'd become central to it, it wasn't solely my story to tell. It was far bigger than me. And the reckoning was a matter for the Slopers and the Tyson families together. And not least for Charlene and Aaron's son, should he return to the place of his conception.

'I'm writing it all down,' I said. 'The truth. All of it. From the first settlers to that plane flight with Sloper. A lot of it is already in my report that I've cabled back to London.

'All confidential, of course. But who knows, one day I might blurt it all out if nobody else does. It would make a good non-fiction book, or maybe a documentary.' Dorinda said, 'Yeah, well, I'm not sure who'd believe it or accept it all, but. Not too many round The Leap anyways. And that's the thing, isn't it? People just go on believing what they want, most of the time. And that's got nothing to do with the truth.'

Which made me wonder if The Leap is terribly different to so much of the rest of the country.

Lucy comes out of the house.

He puts the journal and the pen down and watches her walk towards him. She is barefoot and wearing swimmers, stepping gingerly across the pavers. She's carrying a tray with two cups, a teapot, a small jug of milk. And a cupcake on a plate. It has a single lit candle in it.

She puts the tray down next to him, sits cross-legged on the other lounge, reaches over and takes his hand.

In a few hours the kids will be coming home from school. Until then, they will lounge in the sun and swim on one of the last temperate Canberra autumn days when that is possible. They might nap. Or make love. They'll walk Nancy up the hill, with an eye out for any late brown snakes. Then decide what to cook, or where to go, for his birthday dinner.

They have some big decisions yet to make. Whether Ben will go back to work. Here or in London. Whether to stay or to leave. They may have no choice but to stay for the time being. The national, state and territory borders are about to close due to the pandemic. And that, in itself, imposes the welcome certainty of where they must remain for now.

Bigger decisions are for later. For now, for today, all they must do is be together.

He lifts her hand to kiss it. There is silence but for the distant squawking of cockatoos and a gentle, rustling breeze. It carries just a breath of the changing season and a swirling medley of russet dogwood leaves. They flutter onto the pool's surface. The flame of the candle on his little cake flutters.

'Happy birthday, darling,' Lucy says. 'What a life you're having.'

Acknowledgements

It takes a village to turn an idea for a novel into a book and *The Leap* is no exception. So many people were involved in making it a reality, beginning with my wonderful agent, Gaby Naher, a tireless advocate for and supporter of my writing. Thank you.

I am incredibly fortunate that Jane Palfreyman at Summit is my publisher. Jane's enthusiasm for this novel from concept to fruition, her sage advice, celebrated editorial touch, outrageously fun work lunches, and endless faith again made this one a joy. Thanks, Jane.

Thanks also to the wonderful, detailed feedback and hands-on work on the manuscript by Ali Levau and Meredith Rose, who both embraced my characters (the good, the bad and the very ugly) and helped me to fully realise them with their remarkable eyes for detail. You both made it so smooth – and enjoyable – for me.

Thanks also to everyone at Summit Books (Simon & Schuster) for all the care and support at every level. I'm delighted to be associated with such an esteemed publishing house and honoured to be on Summit's list.

Thanks to my ever-reliable early readers, Peter Fray and Michael Brissenden. Sometimes you need a mate to say, 'Yes – keep writing.' They did. And I did.

Special thanks also to novelist Julie Janson, a friend who read early and late drafts, and offered me such salient advice on plot and characters. *The Leap* would be a far lesser novel without her very wise creative suggestions and encouragement.

My appreciation also to Mike Bowers for the author photographs of me, and to Ian McPhedran for advice on how to fly a light aircraft.

Fiction grows from many places, including sometimes partly from the works of others. A novel I read as a teenager and have returned to often is Kenneth Cook's haunting, deeply unsettling *Wake in Fright*, first published in 1961. The book made a seminal, twentieth-century contribution to Australian letters and culture. Its legacies remain profound. It triggered an explosion in my teenage consciousness about Australian society – a detonation of reality that was compounded when I eventually saw the movie directed by Ted Kotcheff. The book and the movie vividly evoke a landscape of physical and social malevolence, with their acute critiques of Australian class and the divide between urbane coastal life and the interior's dark heart. Early in my life they helped inspire in me a contemplation of another, less appealing, more troubling and troubled Australia.

While The Leap is, however, primarily a place and a book of my imagining, it intentionally acknowledges another Australian novel that I admire enormously – paying tribute to its influence on me as a writer of non-fiction books, novels and journalism.

There is no one crime to solve in The Leap. No single big secret to unearth. For the whole place is an overwhelming colonial and contemporary crime scene involving countless offences against race, gender and social function. I mentioned 'ugly characters'. They live in The Leap, a place that is also drawn from some very familiar locations across this country. I quote them as they speak – offensively, obscenely and derogatively – about other people in the town. It is a town marred by unresolved history – a past of frontier violence and massacres that have been airbrushed out of the dominant cultural narrative that the place has curated for itself. The Leap is nowhere on our actual map. But it is also all over this continent.

I wrote *The Leap* in the countdown to the 2023 referendum on the proposed Indigenous Voice to Parliament, a time when the worst excesses of Australian racism towards First Nations peoples were shamelessly paraded in the name of civil political discourse. That is mainly where The Leap – the place and the novel – grew from.

As with all my work these days, *The Leap* was written on the Gadigal lands of the Eora nation, where I'm fortunate to live. Here and elsewhere – where I've been generously welcomed and invited to listen and learn by First Nations peoples – I'm impelled to try to understand and convey the experiences and enduring legacies of violent dispossession and colonialism.

Finally, but not least, thanks to Lenore (always my first and most important reader) and my children, Claudia, Joe, Jahni and Nick, who understand and support what I do even when I can be grumpy or preoccupied (yes) after a bad day at it. I'm endlessly fortunate to have such love and encouragement at my back.

Mike Bowers

Paul Daley is an author, journalist and essayist. His books have been finalists in major Australian literary awards, including the Prime Minister's History Prize, The Nib, the Indie Book Awards, the Manning Clark House Cultural Awards, and the ACT Book of the Year Awards. He has won numerous journalism prizes, including two Walkley Awards – for Investigative Journalism and also for Indigenous Journalism – for his coverage of Australian cultural amnesia on frontier violence, and the historic theft of Aboriginal ancestral remains. He is the collaborative winner of the NSW Premier's History Award for *The Guardian*'s 'The Killing Times' series on frontier massacres. He writes a regular column and features for *The Guardian*. His novel *Jesustown* was published to great acclaim in 2022.

pauldaleywrites.com
Instagram @pauldaleywrites